SEP 1998

ALSO BY T. M. MCNALLY

Until Your Heart Stops
Low Flying Aircraft

ALMOST HOME

T. M. McNally

SCRIBNER

SCRIBNER
1230 Avenue of the Americas
New York, NY 10020

DESIGNED BY ERICH HOBBING

Set in Adobe Garamond

Manufactured in the United States of America

1   2   3   4   5   6   7   8   9   10

Library of Congress Cataloging-in-Publication Data

McNally, T. M.
Almost home/T. M. McNally
p.   cm.
I. Title.
PS3563.C38816A79   1998   97–52707
813'.54—dc21   CIP

ISBN 0-684-84469-9

Grateful acknowledgment is made to Alfred A. Knopf, Inc., for permission to use a line from *Plainwater: Essays and Poetry* by Anne Carson. Copyright © 1995 by Anne Carson.

To Sally

ALMOST HOME

Water is something you cannot hold.
—ANNE CARSON

1

He was the boy with a dog. Standing in the first row, singing, she'd turn sometimes when she heard his voice: first tenor, clear and bright. For days he'd wear the same baggy sweater—burgundy, worn at the elbows, covered always with lint. Once, before her family moved to Paradise Valley, her father had promised she could have a dog.

He wasn't from here either. In 1978, nobody was. He was new a transfer, midsemester, from Illinois. He was quiet, and shy, and strangely confident of his own voice, as if just waiting to be discovered. Standing there, with him behind her in the choir, his sweater all full of fur, she would listen to him pierce a high C. She knew a lot about scales, would spend ten minutes a day, the start of each practice, warming up on her flute. In the afternoons, after arriving home, having departed the bus, having walked the three long blocks in the sunshine home, there she would wait for her father to call from his office and ask if she'd practiced yet. In Paradise Valley, the streets were newly paved, and there were no sidewalks, or telephone poles. Her father, excited about the possibilities of fiber optics, explained that here communication traveled underground. He explained that here everything was new. The valley, he explained, was fed by a series of rivers, the Salt and the Verde, the Gila, tributaries of the Colorado now linked by a growing system of canals and locks which had brought their family, as well as everybody else, here to live. At home, meanwhile, she spent a lot of time practicing, even if she knew it would be hopeless. She was good enough to know why she would never be really good—exceptional, her father would say, hopefully. She was smart enough to know the world didn't need another girl who could play the flute.

Once a guy learned she could play the flute, she knew precisely what he thought about. When she played, she'd lift the piece to her mouth, set her lip, her wrist now in full display. She kept her sleeves uncuffed, each rolled twice, but never more. The scars from a childhood accident began at her fingertips and ran past her elbow, toward her shoulder. When people asked what had happened, usually girls, because guys were too ashamed to admit they had noticed . . . whenever a girl asked what had happened, she always wanted to know just how.

A pot of boiling water? You were eleven?

Elizabeth doesn't remember any of it clearly. She doesn't recall the trip to the hospital, the sirens lit up like a parade, bright as day. Her mother once confessed the police had called to check up on her. They worried, her mother explained, it might have been done on purpose—the water, scalding, and the flesh it had destroyed there on her arm. Now her mother says that true pain is always merciful. It hurts only by way of memory, long after the fact, and by then it has become bittersweet: like a kiss, provided by a shy boy you will not grow up to marry; or a slap delivered sharply by somebody you have been instructed by your life to love. Somehow, her mother says, tenderly, you have been made . . . *not necessarily better, but stronger . . .* for it.

Do you see?

It's not the pain which matters, she has come to realize, but the way you carry the memory of it with you afterward. Each day she would rise, and dress, and then roll up the cuffs of her sleeves. When she was tan it was easier not to notice. In Paradise Valley, you could spend a lot of time working on your tan. In the pool, swimming, *like a fish,* her father says . . . in the pool, swimming, you could let the water lead you to reflection. The sun also provided a fine excuse to put lotion on your body. On one arm, the skin was gnarled, twisted with burnt tendons and ligaments, its design complicated further by repeated skin grafts lifted from her hip and thigh. But on the other . . . *the other* . . . and her shoulders, her belly, and those places surrounding those territories plundered for grafts . . . there the skin was smooth as water. Eager as light. There she felt it possible to slip away inside herself, often, as if she were a dream.

Nights she found herself dreaming about the boy with the dog. He was short, almost scrawny, with black curly hair, and he could hit a high C. His name was Irish, like a song, the way you could cause the name to lilt, lingering a while in the back of your mind, or throat. Sometimes a boyfriend would call her up, usually after eleven, while she lay in bed dreaming about the boy with a dog.

"Hello?"

"It's me."

"Hi."

"What are you thinking about?"

And then one night she realized it was best never to ask a question unless you really wanted to hear the answer.

McConnell . . . that was his name. *Patrick McConnell.* The boy with a dog. The boy who could hit a high C and make your flesh goosepimple—the skin, rising of its own accord, as if to meet with someone warm. The boy who sat by himself during fourth period while she walked by every day with Bittner, or others, and who always pretended not to notice, never looking up even to catch her eye. Still, she noticed things. She noticed he wrote with his left hand, that he read from a different paperback each week, often tucking one into the back pocket of his jeans; she noticed his eyes, blue, and the nails bitten to the quick, and the old leather shoes with bright red laces. He had skin like a baby, too—opalescent, and sweet. Once she even stood behind him in a line. Then she pressed her body into him, like a kiss, and held it there.

"Oh," he said, turning.

"I'm sorry," she said, pleased with the excuse.

He smelled like fresh laundry and wet wool and bread. His sweater was dark as blood, nearly threadbare, and then he receded, farther into the line, into the throng, until he disappeared entirely from view.

That night she had a dream he came to her.

2

My dog, his name was Germs. He was an English setter with orange points, which is a big kind of dog. The kind that stands right up to your hip. I'd never had a girlfriend.

Of course I'd thought about it, often, and then for a while I thought I wasn't exactly the type that was supposed to have one. I thought, Well, you get what you deserve. You get what you never wish for. My father used to say strength was the gift of humility. He'd say only the humble can be truly strong. Then when I asked him once how I might become humble, he told me not to worry. The world will take care of that, he said. *Soon enough.* I remember because we were in the garage, and he was smoking a cigarette, the smoke curling up alongside his arm, and it was winter then, and cold. I remember he was building a set of jumps, regulation size for my dog—a project to clear his head—and he asked me to pass him the hammer. Then he taught me how to use a plumb line.

A year later, after he had died, and after we had moved to Arizona, in February, I was standing in line in my new school, waiting to purchase lunch. I was standing alone at school, just standing there, because of course I didn't know anybody yet, and I was paying attention to the floor so nobody was going to bother and notice me. Being new at school generally means you're going to get picked on, as opposed to *up,* and I was standing there, looking at the cement floor when these legs came walking by, just these legs in these nice faded jeans walking by, and of course I lifted my eyes, lifting them slowly, you know, to have a look at some girl . . . and then, well, it turns out to be a girl dating a guy who lifts a lot of weights. What struck me about the girl were her eyes, green, which locked onto mine, as if they had been just waiting to, and then the sheer fact of her hair: long, wavy—dark as walnut—reaching past her waist, dressed with a bit of purple ribbon skimming the surface of her hair.

"What you looking at, asshole?" said her boyfriend, stepping forward.

"Nothing," I said.

He put his arm around the girl, who blushed sharply, and said, "You looking at my girlfriend?"

"Nope," I said, because by now I was looking at him, preparing to be pummeled.

"You looking at me then? You a faggot or something?"

It made me nervous, then angry. It's not that I had anything against gay people—in Illinois, where I had gone to school, I knew a guy who always starred in the school plays, and then there was my voice teacher, in the city, and he lived with a man who had a red beard. For special recitals, at my teacher's home, the man with the beard was always nice to me and congratulated me often. Also the assistant curate at my church, who had overseen my confirmation, was conspicuously single and took up liberal causes. And I remember feeling especially befriended by these men. At the same time, I was also pretty certain I wasn't going to be gay, which is to say I knew even then I was destined to prefer the company of women, even if I did sing in the church choir, and two of the choirs at my high school in Illinois, before I transferred, and even if I'd never been able to hit a decent line drive, or play hockey, or golf. In a choir, a really good choir, it is possible to hear truly a woman's voice; listening, I believe, can be just as fine as looking. On the cusp of sixteen, I spent a lot of my life looking at girls and dreaming about them wanting to be with me, which of course when you are in high school, and recently transferred, you spend a lot of time standing by yourself doing. But I also knew this guy who lifted weights wanted to pick a fight. So instead I shrugged my shoulders. I stepped out of line, thinking I'd go off to the library, maybe to the art books, where I'd be safe.

"Sorry," I said, stepping out of line, making my way.

I could hear people laughing behind me, calling me names, and suddenly I missed my father, who had been a strong man and would have told me what to do. At the funeral, for which the casket was decidedly closed, I had been advised by various counselors that my father was in fact dead. Apparently it was an important thing to make clear—especially in cases of suicide. They meant well, I knew; they also felt sorry for me, which made me feel sad and tolerated. Meanwhile at church I had taught myself to pray for my father, because he was dead, and then I would pray as well—and still do—for myself to become a good person.

Teach me to be humble, I would pray. *And strong. Teach me not to sin.*

Since we'd left the Midwest, I no longer went to church, because my mother had lapsed, she said, but still I prayed often. At the time I was also deeply afraid of becoming a pervert. Regarding sin, my priest would always say, winking, one hand feeds the other: it's the very nature of the beast, this self-abuse. And even though my priest was now over a thousand miles away, and my family was officially lapsed, every night I'd always resolve to become a decent man. Every night I'd say, *Okay, this is absolutely the last time I commit a sin,* and then I knew absolutely I had to be a pervert because it was impossible for me to stop even that: the evidence involved doing a lot of laundry—mornings, before anyone in our dark house was yet awake, except for me and my dog. And then one day, doing the laundry, balancing my feet on the cool tile in front of the dryer, I became inexpressibly sad. I became sad because I knew I was damning my soul, repeatedly, to eternal and everlasting fire. That was why we'd moved to Arizona,

I thought, exploring the idea: because here we were intended to be closer to the fire? In English I once read the nakedness of woman was the glory of God, which seemed right to me. Sometimes I got so sore it was hard to walk.

And then I really did stop. My father would have, I realized; so, too, would my Uncle Punch. Also one of my father's secretaries was barely twenty. At the funeral, while she was weeping, I could see part of her bra, and her pale skin, while she stood weeping at the grave site. She put her arms around me twice, once when my mother was particularly cold to her; the woman smelled like a vase full of flowers, like a garden, and I could feel her ribs beneath the fabric of her dress. Holding her, I wanted to be brave. I wanted to be still, and comforting, and always in the right; I also wanted her to love me instantly. Turning away, I pictured my father, someplace overhead, perhaps with a fine telescope, peeking down this girl's very blouse. My father, you see, understood perfectly the way a man was designed by God to behave.

So I stopped, aching loins and all, in order to prove to myself I didn't have to, as the saying goes, burn in hell. I simply stopped and thought about the twenty-year-old girl my father had seduced: lying awake, pretending, we'd have conversations, and sometimes I would rescue the girl from lions, or bullies. Once I even saved her by swinging on a rope from a burning three-flat and carrying her away in my arms. Each night, while falling asleep, this girl deep in my mind, I'd hope for one of those dreams which would let me wake up feeling all refreshed like a soap commercial. The thing about those dreams, which are wonderful, entirely amazing . . . the thing about a good dream like that is you never get one when you really want it. Instead you get one while you're camping with your friends, if you have friends, or when you've fallen asleep on the couch, and then there you are all sticky and damp and your dog Germs is digging away at your jeans— beats me—and your older sister's stepping out of the kitchen . . . your sister who just never happens to wear a bra, stepping into the family room, looking at you just that way and saying, *Hey, have a nice nap?*

My sister, Caroline—because she was a woman, and older, when you looked into my sister's eyes, it was clear she knew more than most people. Among other things, she was soon to graduate and fluent in French and smoked cigarettes late at night. Sometimes she drank red wine. She was smarter than me, also lonely, and rail thin. And while it was she who once explained to me the biological function of those dreams—*nocturnal emissions*—I knew as well some things foreign to Caroline's experience. I knew, for example, that sometimes when you have one of those dreams, the good kind, you never even see the person to which your body longs to be intended. Dreaming, you can be in a car, or a tree fort; you're dreaming about a blackbird, or a brand new saddle, the monsoons in your hair and then maybe you see a lock of hair belonging to a woman you might someday meet up with in a cafe, or on a sailboat, a twenty-two-foot sloop with an ocean nearby, a worn shoe washing up with the tide, and then that's it—you wake up, all alone, perfectly refreshed and all a mess. In your dreams, at least, it is possible for a man to make love to more than just a human body: it is possible to love the essence, the very fact of these lives to which we hope someday to be introduced. And what drives you, always, is the idea of it—longing, and the physical consequences of its release—into the very heart of desire.

I didn't understand this then, only felt it; I didn't understand the miscibility of angels, and maybe saints, and ghosts. At school, two days later, still my first week after having transferred, I was walking to my morning class when some guy stopped his beat-up Camaro. I was late, of course, and seeing me, he called out in front of the school and pulled a U-turn, right there, the tires squealing. He stepped out, saying something to two guys in the backseat, and then he said to me, belligerent and clear, "Hey, ain't you the new faggot?"

At the time I didn't really recognize him. I could see his girlfriend, though, sitting in the front seat of the car. With his friends in the back, most likely he wanted to provide a good example. I said, calculating my options, dropping my voice into its deepest register, "Fuck you, sweetheart."

I was hoping for a tinge of Humphrey Bogart, who was also a fairly small guy. But now, of course, somebody had to defend some honor, regardless of whose, which also meant I was going to be humbled smartly, right here and on the way to school. And she's pretty, I remember thinking. She's pretty, this girl with the ribbons in her hair, sitting in his car . . . *Pinski. Elizabeth Pinski* . . . and she's sitting there, saying, *Mark. Mark, I've got to practice. Come on, Mark* . . . and there's ol' Mark, being a gentleman, saying, *Hey, hey, it'll only take a sec, hon* . . . and the next thing I know there I am sitting on the curb, my face in my hands and all full of blood, because, you know, if I weren't the new faggot at Gold Dust High School I'd know how to fight better. I wouldn't be getting the shit kicked out of me by some guy with a lower than C average old enough to buy beer. I'd have more testosterone, et cetera, and huge arms, and I'd pick a guy like that up by the neck and really thrash the son of a bitch. I wouldn't kill him or anything. I wouldn't want to have to feel guilty over that, too, later on, certainly not for eternity, and I wouldn't want to make his mom and dad feel bad, either, not just because some guy had thrashed their son who thought he was going to kick the shit out of some wimp who turned out, actually, to be a really tough son of a bitch who maybe even knew karate. Mostly I'd just scare him a lot, especially there in front of his girlfriend.

I'd say, "You should be nice to people who are smaller than you."

Of course, if Germs were there, my dog, he'd rip out the guy's entire throat.

3

Her father has a thin book written by a man with a Polish name. In the book a man is lying in bed with his lover telling stories. One of the stories, the one she always returns to, is the story of a man in line. He is in a foreign country where lines are popular—or maybe it is just a crowd, an absolute throng of human flesh, where people there wait differently. Either way, the man steps up behind a woman; he closes in, and then he presses his body up against her. He is already hard, and the woman, realizing he is hard, begins to lift her skirt. And what thrills Elizabeth about the story isn't necessarily what happens next, which is obvious to all, even those standing nearby. What thrills Elizabeth is the specific context: this man, lying in bed with his lover, and the fact of his telling her. In fact, when she stood behind the boy with a dog, in line, she was thinking of that very story and someday telling somebody herself—a potential act of disclosure, thrilling to the core. And she remembers pressing her breasts into his back and breathing in the smell of his neck, which reminded her of bread. If it hadn't been for all the people, all the people standing in line, each waiting to be next, she never would have dreamed this possible.

She wonders who's next, and for what? Tonight when Bittner picks her up for their date, he waits outside across the street. He doesn't go to her door ever for fear of witnesses, which might in turn allow for commitment. The sky is quiet and empty, the air full of woodsmoke, because it's still winter: she's wearing a sweater and her favorite pair of jeans. Bittner's car is severely dented, missing a fender, and partially blue; before he moved here from California, a Puerto Rican wrecked it by running a light. Bittner was driving faster than he should have been, he explained, given the conditions.

Once she steps into the car, Bittner puts the car into gear, testing the clutch, and says, "Here we go, hon."

She's not necessarily sure just where she's going. He drives fast, taking the turns too quickly, the tight car skidding around the curves of her subdivision. Eventually he reaches to turn down the radio, and then he says, "There's a party in Tempe. Off Mill and Apache. Lotta drugs."

She's been to Tempe, once, but she doesn't really know any of the streets. She imagines it must be near the university, which is where most people go to college, Arizona State University, because the tuition is inexpensive and people there drink a lot of beer. When she graduates, next year, she imagines she will be going somewhere else, maybe California, which is fine by her, though she doesn't want to study music. In Choir today, they were singing a piece by Brahms, badly, because the music program here is pathetically bad. The man who directs the choir is a short, bald man who also leads the marching band: at football games, the band plays the theme song from *High Chaparral,* which was a television show in the sixties, like *Big Valley,* and *Bonanza.* It's a hard song to play, especially for all those trumpets. The man is tone deaf, too, and so when he sings out the parts, his voice always fails to agree. In Choir he will point to the boy with the dog, Patrick McConnell, and ask him to sing out the part . . . *by way of illustration* . . . and when the boy does so, almost shyly, the rest of the choir stands still. What's amazing about the human voice, she thinks, is the way it simply lifts itself up into the air. And today, when the marching band director called on Patrick McConnell, in Choir, and when he sang the three phrases, each rolling off the other, she understood that she was going to have to break up with her present boyfriend, Bittner. Before, she dated somebody else, for about three months, who went to a community college, and then somebody else before that. Then she started dating Bittner, who seemed older for his age, and because he seemed to know a lot of people: most people think he is a drug dealer, which he may be, though she's never seen him make a deal, per se. Certainly together they do a lot of coke, which is good enough—one line, then another—and the way it feels like sex . . . *a little blow* . . . and then the way after, after the coke falls away, like a song, and you are drifting down from the sky . . . the way once the coke fades and you're coming down and there's your boyfriend, maybe Bittner, buckling up his belt, tucking in his shirt, putting his car into gear.

To give a man head is merely a way to feed his ego; she knows this now. And the ego is part of the mind, invented by Freud, who believed that all human behavior was entirely motivated by sex and aggression—as if the two were in fact the same, which in Psychology her teacher says they are. Though she's not absolutely certain. In fact Elizabeth often does lots of things which do not seem obviously related—like tying her shoes, or doing her math. Where's the sex in that? As for Bittner, her boyfriend, he doesn't seem to have an opinion on the matter. Last month he was allegedly arrested for beating up a fraternity boy, though she's never asked him about it. What he and his friends do is cruise bars in the city and look for fights. After, they come back to school, Monday morning, bragging about their swollen eyes, their raw knuckles. Bittner used to be on a football team, in California, before the coach had him removed: excessive force, Bittner explained, proudly. Bittner is also the biggest man she's ever known. Not that he's so tall, which he is, but that he is so tall and strong. He lifts weights. The shirts he wears, usually blue, are extra large. He likes to make the muscles in his chest move independently when he thinks nobody is looking. One summer he said he worked for his uncle's cement business in Los Angeles, and while she's never seen his house, or met his parents, Elizabeth knows a lot of girls in her school would love to be his girlfriend— at least until they came to know him. Still it makes you feel good, standing beside so tall a man; it makes you feel safe, and important, like the guy she used to date, earlier, before he went to the community college and died while drunk driving a Bobcat: it rolled right over and snapped his neck. In half, people said. Standing next to a tall man, one who's alive, makes you feel as if you've got nothing left to lose, and mostly, right now, sitting beside her boyfriend while he drives his beat-up Camaro to Tempe, Arizona . . . mostly what she doesn't want to lose is the way she feels, right now: so full of longing and desire for God knows what. Desire is what makes you hot—not like a flame, but the space around it. Desire is a place you sidle up to and wrap your arms around your chest while you wait and hold yourself in place.

When she thinks of the way she saw that, the way Bittner beat the boy with a dog—his eye blistering, and blue—while she sat waiting in the car, waiting while Bittner said *Just a sec, hon* and then began beating the boy . . . she feels lonely and afraid and cold. She feels the way she does when she wakes up after she's done too much coke. As if she has fallen into a cold lake overflowing with ice. The ice is sharp as glass, and cold; the ice is going to slice into your chest and turn your heart to stone. When you throw a stone into a lake, it casts a ripple, and then it sinks.

What's popular in Phoenix is California rock, which is nearby, and which has a lot of country influences: Linda Ronstadt, the Eagles and the like. What's popular even if it's not from California is Dan Fogelberg and Billy Joel and Neil Young, and everybody hates John Denver and Barry Manilow and those bands excessively influenced by geography: Kansas, and Boston, or Chicago. Foreigner is particularly whiny. Donna Summer is good sometimes, depending.

And Earth, Wind and Fire is a different matter entirely: Elizabeth knows it is because of the way the men use their voices. The music may be electronic, but the voices are always true.

At the party, which belongs someplace inside a house, a huge house with two stories, which in the Valley of the Sun is rare as a lake, or a hardwood tree . . . at the party she wanders around people she hardly recognizes, sipping a tequila sunrise—her third or fourth, she's stopped counting. She decides she likes Al Stewart, too, mostly because of his reliance on the piano—"The Year of the Cat." She likes that phrase, the woman like a watercolor, wearing a silk dress, running in the rain; sometimes, when she tires of practicing, she puts records on the stereo and then plays along. To play along is also to pretend, after all. In the backyard, people are milling around the pool and Jacuzzi. Steam is rising off the surface of the water, which must mean that it's heated, and all across the lawn people are talking over the music. Apparently, the house belongs to a guy from California; a stepparent bought the house so the guy could live in it while he went to college. It's an investment, Bittner said. It's also a great place to score.

If the opportunity arises, ideally before the night is through, she intends to break up with him for good. Usually she just starts seeing other guys and the guy she was with starts seeing other girls and everything goes its course, the way water will, on to the path of least resistance. It's not sensible to try and stop it, anyway, because once it's flowing, the water, once it's flowing, it's going to go its own way—like the Colorado River, which eventually turned into the Grand Canyon; or the banks of the Delaware when it starts to rain; or the tide, in California, where she's still never been. Still, once the tide starts to rise, the water is going to follow, and to break up, she thinks, is merely a simple way to avoid resistance. It's a way to keep yourself on the surface. Because once there, on the surface, you still maintain the possibility to lift yourself above it.

What's important, she's telling herself, what's important now is timing. And seeking out an appropriate level. She's doing a couple of lines with two guys who say they are Accounting majors. The coke has been cut, one says, with crystal meth. That's going to make for a headache, she thinks, but still she isn't sure. It's not as if she wants to be a chemist.

"Hey," says one of the Accounting majors. "Hey, what's your name?"

She thinks it's time for a little invention. She thinks it's time to spice things up with crystal meth. But then she says, shaking her head, feeling the rush, "Jesus. Oh, Jesus."

"It's the meth," says one of the guys. "Hey, you need a beer?"

What she needs is a man, which is odd, because she's never put it just that way before. She's never said this to herself . . . *I need a man* . . . but she knows precisely what she means and she knows precisely where she wants to place him. She says, rubbing her fingers over her gums, "Hey. Hey, what's your name, anyway?"

"God," says the Accounting major. "God, this is good shit."

He looks like the guy she used to date, before Bittner, who died after he went to a community college. A rising tide lifts all boats, her father says. She wanders away now, away from the pool, and steps inside the house where it is warm. Somehow hours have passed since she first arrived. Hours have passed and she has never felt so inexpressibly light . . . *buoyant,* she thinks, as in clouds; or orange blossoms on the surface of a pool. In the kitchen she talks about monogamy with a girl whose shirt has been partially unbuttoned. Apparently, the girl's parents are reconciling in San Francisco, so her little sister won't have to pick any sides; the little sister is going to be able to stay in the same school . . . *in San Francisco, you know.* Until three minutes ago, Elizabeth didn't know a thing at all about this girl. The girl stands there, beer in her hand, talking; once in a while, the point of her breast becomes self-evident. A man leads with his chin, Elizabeth once read. A man leads with his chin, but a woman with the point of her breast. Elizabeth says, standing there, nodding, "You have a very good point."

Elizabeth is thinking about something remarkably important,

though briefly it escapes her. She says, "Mostly what we need is just somebody."

"Love," says the girl. "You know what I mean?"

"Mm hmm."

"Not me," says the girl. "I mean, what *is* love? I mean what does love *mean?*"

"Need," Elizabeth says. "If you ask me, love is what you need."

"I need another beer," the girl says. "I need to find myself a ride home."

Some guy, a short, evidential dork, who's also probably majoring in Accounting, steps inside the kitchen. He takes a beer and says, pouring it over the girl's head, "You need to take the train. Take the A train."

The girl's eyes widen; clearly, she's about to understand she's been humiliated. Instead she decides against that understanding, and she pushes the new Accounting major in the chest, playful-like; she rests her hand on the guy's chest and says, tweaking his nipple, "You want to give me a ride?"

"Nah," says the guy, blushing, because men are mostly cowards. "Night's young."

The girl says, removing her hand, wiping the beer from her eyes, "There are no trains. Only buses."

"Some chick," says the guy, humiliated. "Honest. Some chick's upstairs right now pulling a train."

"Oh."

"Yeah," says the guy, nodding. "You know."

Elizabeth doesn't know, but she has the general idea. She's heard about such forms of locomotion before . . . *a train* . . . and now she's heading for the stairs . . . *kinda like the bunny hop.* The stairs are empty, except for some guy who's passed out at the bottom, lying back on the stairs, a bottle of sap-colored whiskey tucked away between his legs. She reaches for the whiskey and takes a pull, which burns her mouth, she's certain, but also she's pretty certain she is numb—a tooth, preparing to be drilled. At the top of the stairs lies a hall, and in the hall there are certain doors just waiting to be opened. In one room, a girl is peeing; there's also a tub full of beer and ice. In another, the room just off the stairs, two men are having an argument about Keynesian economics. One of the men has his shirt off. She says, peering inside the room, "Is that in Africa?"

"What?"

"I'm looking for the train," she says. "The bunny hop? The mambo jambo?"

"Down the hall."

"Oh."

And then one of the guys says, "Hey. Be careful."

"Uh huh."

At the end of the hall the door is partially open, and through it she can hear the voices of men, most of whom are drunk; they aren't particularly loud, just sloppy and shrill. There also doesn't appear to be any special music here to dance to. Now somebody breaks out into a loud, nervous laugh, and stepping through the door, she enters a vast room full of light and soft carpet. In the center sits a bed . . . *king size* . . . with mirrors behind it, and on the bed a girl with long red hair is taking a man by the mouth. She's on her back, and the girl is naked as the day is long, though now it's night, and there's a pool of semen on the bedspread, another on her belly.

"Outside," says somebody. "It's getting crowded."

And now another recognizes her. He's a short guy who hasn't shaved in three weeks, though still he hasn't managed to grow a beard. He says, jacking off, "Hey, you want to give her a break?"

Bittner calls to her, stepping down the hall, approaching from behind. He takes Elizabeth's shoulder, turning her from the doorway. "Hey," he says, "you should be downstairs. Go downstairs."

The guy who spoke to her, his dick in his hand, going nowhere, looks at her vaguely. "What?" he says. "What the fuck?"

Bittner says to him, stepping into the room, "Shut the fuck up."

The girl lies stranded now, by herself, wiping her mouth. She's crying, silently, and now Elizabeth knows exactly who she is—a woman in the company of men. She understands she is the only person in the world who can make them disappear.

"Cops," Elizabeth says, pointing at the door. "Cops are here!"

The room empties all around her, men pushing by her roughly, racing for the door—Bittner playing guard, as if on point. Now she tells Bittner to wait for her downstairs.

"No," he says. "Goddamnit. You—"

"No," she says, pushing him out the door. "Just call the police. Please?"

She shuts the door, locking it. Downstairs she can hear people screaming, then laughter, their voices rising through the ceiling. She locates the bathroom, and a towel, and she's pouring warm water over the towel. She's locating another . . . blue . . . and now she's sitting beside the girl. She's washing the girl's face. The girl's eyes are rolling up into the back of her head, and Elizabeth is covering her up with the big towel. Now the bedspread, inside out, which she manages to drape partially over the girl. The girl is shivering, driven entirely by a lack of warmth. Elizabeth wraps her arms around the girl and says, "You're going to be all right. Honest."

"Oh God," says the girl, not quite hysterically. "Oh God!"

"Water," Elizabeth says, nodding. "You need some water?"

She finds a glass, fills it up. Outside the bedroom door men are gathering, their voices rising and expectant. Now she calls the police, certain Bittner will be too afraid, and provides directions . . . Off Mill and Apache. Fire, she says into the phone. A house is on fire! She returns to the girl and helps her sit up and says, "I'm going to start a shower, okay? For you. You'll feel better."

The girl says, nodding, "Better. I want to feel better."

"You will," Elizabeth says. "Promise."

Though she knows it is a lie. She knows the girl needs to find a source of genuine heat and that, most likely, it's going to be a long time coming. She wraps her arms around the girl and helps her into the bathroom; once there, the girl begins to vomit, and then she's in the shower, and Elizabeth is at the sink, washing her own face, trying to wash the tequila and beer out of her system—drinking water by the handfuls, she's so thirsty. Now she's sitting on the toilet, her head in her hands, weeping. She is weeping because she knows there is no other possible alternative. She is weeping, her hands in her face, and now she rises to wash her face all over again. The girl's still in the shower, and for some reason, some reason she never intends to know for sure, she feels the need for reassurance. She feels the need to check, and as she adjusts her focus—first her eyes, there in the mirror, and then the glass door behind her—she sees the girl stepping out from the shower. She sees the girl holding a broken razor in her hand.

And then the blood, running from the veins of her wrist.

"I'm cold," the girl says, shivering. "I'm really, really cold."

4

Then I fell in love with a girl with a burned arm. When she was eleven, her mother spilled on her a pot of boiling water. Sometimes, having now lived a decent life, at least I hope a decent life, though there have been times when I have failed in my attempt toward that decency . . . sometimes I think that I was saved. Her name was Elizabeth, and she was beautiful.

Our family wasn't in particularly good shape when we moved to Arizona. My father, an investment broker, had been caught by the SEC embezzling close to three-hundred thousand dollars, which in the wake of the 1973 oil crisis was even then a considerable amount of money. Apparently he'd lift the funds from his own accounts and then, during lunch, walk down to the commodities exchange—pork bellies, bushels of grain, barrels of light-sweet crude—to place his bets. He needed a quick fix, he said, in order to cover up his losses, those losses brought about by the great bear market of '73, and by which he meant his clients' losses: over a period of eighteen months, the stock market would fall some 44 percent, not to recover until 1980, long after my father's death. I remember my father explaining to me, though I was too young to understand, that a bear market was a bad thing, and that it was no accident the Soviet Union was also called *The Great Bear:* together, our way of life might just someday implode. He meant nuclear war, of course, should the international community begin to hemorrhage.

This was my father: the kind of Republican who will sometimes vote Democratic; the kind who is asked for his opinion, and who is also free to give it. I remember he was close with a number of politicians: senators and congressmen, and he also served on the boards for several nonprofit institutions, administering various endowments—a couple for small colleges, each barely making it, he often said. One year he personally bought our church a new roof—anonymously, the priest explained to me, years later. *He always gave anonymously.* As for myself, a kid growing up, I never thought we were either rich or poor, though I do recall spending most of my childhood with a sense of surfeit. There were riches everywhere in our household, like new clothes each fall and spring for school; like dancing and diving lessons for my sister, who competed well; and private voice lessons in the city for me; and a cupboard full of soda pop and cookies and an entire freezer in the garage dedicated to a side of beef, delivered personally twice a year by the butcher in town. We lived in North Barrington, which wasn't supposed to be flashy, but comfortable; we had a stable, and horses to teach us discipline and confidence; we had a pond almost the size of a commercial acre in our backyard, and a canoe; and of course we always had immense treasures waiting each year for us beneath the Christmas tree. And I know now my father wasn't trying to get rich, simply because he already was, and I know certainly he had set aside significant trusts for me and my sister, and I also know that he was merely trying to give his own clients the same degree of good fortune which he had also enjoyed. Because when you are a broker, it doesn't matter if you win or lose, because what matters is the fact of the trade itself. A broker by nature is always paid. And my father was a broker who believed this was fundamentally unfair, and in the end he was caught tampering with the system, and then one November day he shot himself in the mouth with a shotgun—a twelve-gauge pump, never before used. He had left the price tag on the stock. Two weeks before the trial was officially to begin, early one morning, I found him in the stable. He had forgotten to close the gate. I remember the water tank had frozen over with ice, and that we needed a new salt lick. I remember thinking it was time to order in some hay for winter.

As for the trial, there wasn't much need to follow through: the entire world seemed to know already that he was guilty of violating the law, and one congressman even claimed my father had become corrupted by the Mafia, which simply wasn't true. What was true, I realized, was just how quickly the world could turn on you. For several months afterward I lived in Colorado, with an Episcopal priest, a friend of my father's, and Caroline was sent to Uncle Punch, another friend of the family, in order to permit my mother to recuperate in private. Because my father had taken great pains to protect what assets he could, my mother eventually decided to cut her losses and make a fresh start for us all. She held a big estate sale, and sold the horses, and the horse trailer, and two of her cars; she sold a lot of statues and paintings and hand-painted china. And my mother, who had never had a job in her entire life, though in high school she had once written a column which appeared in a newspaper, decided she would like to live in Scottsdale and become a poet or a screenwriter. At the time, I was almost sixteen; my older sister was doing a lot of drugs and learning to drive. In Scottsdale, Arizona, we bought a smaller house than we were used to: it had one story, and the yard was covered with yellow granite, instead of grass, and we had a couple tall saguaros by the driveway. In the backyard, of course, we had a pool, which became my job to clean, and to fill, and then my mom decided we could no longer afford my private voice lessons. I wrote to my old teachers for two or three months, because I missed them, especially Mr. Mark, who was still nice to me in Illinois after my father shot himself, and because the choir in my new school was so incomprehensibly bad. I mean, even the band leader was tone deaf. In Arizona we didn't have a choir director. We had a band leader.

The Cactus Curtain, my sister called it. *The Wild West.*

One two three, one two three . . . eventually, the bald band leader gave up on Brahms, though not without a lot of pouting, and then we started singing Barbra Streisand songs about people who need people. In Arizona I no longer needed my parents' permission to select my classes, so one day I quit Choir and signed up instead for Driver's Ed. My mother, after making a brave start, disappeared into her bedroom, months at a time, and I started showing Germs in obedience trials all over the state. My sister would drive me to the shows; we'd sit on the grass, waiting for our turn, and afterward she would give me pointers. We met a man named Windham, who owned a kennel and was encouraging, sometimes taking us out for lunch, and who reminded me of my father: if, that is, my father had spent his life working in a kennel. And of course I played my guitar, late at night, and dreamed of showing up someday, years later, handsome and famous with really long hair and three beautiful women standing right behind me, singing. Then my sister Caroline cracked up and went away to college in New England.

I was conceived on a train. My father had flown down from New York to meet my mother at a funeral—my maternal grandmother, who had died of stomach cancer. The next day my father picked out a modest coffin: then, as the story goes, on the train ride back, the Kansas City line, that's when I came about. I was conceived on a train. And for years I never knew just what that meant. When I began to get an idea, it was still just an idea: I thought, *They decided to have me, you know, while riding on a train.* Eventually, of course, in junior high Biology, I understood what *conceive* in this particular context meant, and so I pictured my father— doing it, right there, thumping away—on the train with my mother. My mother would always tell the story on my birthday, and other holidays, usually after a lot of wine, and by the time I was in high school, it had become mostly uncomfortable: this history of my conception, and her insistence that I know my father had to do it, right there in the aisle, that he simply couldn't wait . . . this insistence, like her opinion of his secretary, seemed calculated to lower my opinion of him. Then one day, in American History, I learned about Mr. Pullman, and the sleeper car, something which I had never before heard of. People had places to go back then, I realized, and at last it seemed a fairly decent thing to do. *A sleeper car?* It seemed possible at least that people didn't have to step over my parents, sloshing their drinks, while the train went on around the bend.

As for my mother, once we settled in Arizona, she simply began to disappear. And I know now what it's like to disappear, for months, sometimes years at a time—to crawl inside yourself because it's the only way to keep yourself feeling safe. Having been there since, I'm more inclined to forgive her, but at the time I was looking outward: I was sixteen, going on seventeen, which meant I was simply going on the best I knew how. My mother, bless her broken heart, was beginning to decide she no longer could.

I know, for example, it's harder to make friends when you are older, if only because there's so much raw material you first have to introduce: there's more to know, like the fact of your suicide husband, and there's so much more you're going to be inclined to deny. My mother, living in Arizona, sitting each evening beneath a saguaro, whipping off her screenplays . . . my mother was an uncommon sight. First off, nobody in our neighborhood ever set foot on his or her front yard. The yard was something to be groomed, preferably by a Chicano, perhaps decorated at Christmas with lights and candy canes, but never, never to be used, let alone enjoyed. One had a backyard, surrounded by a six-foot cinder block fence, for that. My mother would sit out there in the front yard, her pink sunhat floating in the hot breeze, and people would drive by and stare. They didn't wave. They didn't stop to introduce themselves . . . *So, you're the new movie writer?* Instead, they stared, and then they went home to lock their doors and tell their children to stay away from the drunk, weird lady in the pink hat. Clearly, she was divorced—which she had been, right before my father killed himself, in order to protect her—and clearly she was a little dangerous, sitting outside in the sun, writing movies, sipping at a tumbler full of scotch, as if she were Raymond Chandler. Faulkner, she explained, drank bourbon. F. Scott, gin. First there was the whiskey, and then the Valium and Thorazine, and then there were all the bloody arguments with my sister, Caroline. Like my mother, Caroline didn't have any friends, either.

Once, on a lark, my mom decided to introduce herself to Erma Bombeck—also a fellow writer, she explained. My mom had looked up Ms. Bombeck's address, and we climbed into her car and drove for three hours, because none of us knew any of the streets yet. My mom was fairly tipsy with all the wine from dinner, and Caroline was sullen and impatient. Personally, I kind of wanted to meet Erma Bombeck, and I remember feeling hopeful. Because my mom had big plans. She wanted to meet Og Mandino, too. And she had planned to develop a special center for the families of disaster— by which she meant *suicide.* She had been working on a proposal with our lawyer in Chicago to send to an important Arizona senator whose family owned department stores. And I know, too, that, in addition to these plans, the sky overhead could make us feel electric. In Arizona, when the light was right, in Arizona you could see for days; you could see right through the clouds and into the eye of the sun. It was blinding, looking at the sky like that, enough to make you feel dizzy and realize precisely where you were: in the center of the desert all by your very self. At the same time, there you were, which could be thrilling.

That day Bittner introduced himself to me, stopping his beat-up old Camaro, stepping outside to thrash me some, afterward I sat on the curb with my head in my hands. I watched the car drive off, sitting there, the blood from my nose and lips running into my hands. I was supposed to be on my way to school, but instead I was sitting there, listening to all the other cars driving by—the parents, and those kids who had their own cars to drive. I sat there and eventually got up my nerve. I stood, wiped my nose with my sleeve, and walked back home.

At home, eight-thirty in the morning, my mother was still awake, sitting at the kitchen table. She hadn't been to bed yet simply because she didn't like to sleep. She was sitting there, a tumbler full of scotch, and then she said, "Is that you?"

"Germs," I said, greeting my dog at the door. "Let's disappear."

We knew lots of tricks. My dad had given me Germs, for my birthday, the last one before he died. I'd seen a movie about a blind kid and decided I wanted to have a dog like that. The kind that carries your books to school and knows which bus to take and knows how to dodge speeding cars and warn you before you trip. I went to the library and found several books on obedience, and what it means to obey, especially if you're a dog, and then I followed the instructions. Sometimes we'd walk with the mailman in our neighborhood, for practice—stopping at each house, learning to be polite. We joined a club in Illinois, and then in Arizona I kept showing for the first year. And I taught Germs not only how to show, but also how to live amid traffic, and curbs, and how to leap into a car through an open window. Mostly what I wanted was for my dog to be able to go anywhere with me without a leash, and what I taught myself, of course, is that with discipline comes also enormous freedom. Because my dog always behaved, he was often able to be with me. Germs finished his CD before he was a year old in Illinois; his CDX came a year later, in Tucson—these are degrees, awarded by the American Kennel Club. The final degree, UD, for utility dog, we never finished.

When you train a dog, when you're really getting ready to show it, that is, you always, always use a lead: the reasons get fairly complicated, but the general thrust involves the idea of correction. A dog working without a leash gets sloppy because he's harder to correct; he starts sitting a little crooked, lagging half a step behind, sticking his nose into the grass . . . most people have no idea, as well they shouldn't: it's an anal way to treat a dog. And with me and Germs, it wasn't as if I wanted him to be some kennel superdog. By the time we arrived in Arizona, I just wanted an excuse to leave the house, repeatedly, and I wanted to do something I was able to be good at.

So we'd take our walks. We'd find playgrounds filled with kids, where I'd put Germs on a sit-stay and ask the kids to throw their tennis balls in front of him—temptation. We'd practice on jumps by using a fence, or garbage cans, as well as the regulation-size jumps my father had built for us. After working, then we'd play fetch, and chase, for hours. And Germs wasn't like my broken-hearted mom or my dead dad or my very sad sister, even. The thing about Germs is that he was the very first thing I ever chose to love. Later, I would choose my music, also, because I was good at it; but I didn't know then growing up meant also choosing to love your parents, if only because each was bound to fail you. Back then I was still learning about discipline. I was fourteen at the time of my father's funeral and eventually Germs turned into one fine, handsome dog which, when you come to think of it, didn't have a thing to do with me at all.

To disappear, that was the easiest. All you had to do was want to. It was the reappearing part which could become complicated, especially on command. Later that summer, during the monsoons, the wind would rise up over California and come knocking on our door: the wind would fill the swimming pool with dust, and it would tear down the bougainvillea growing along the oleanders; it would knock down two of our very own saguaros and blow the patio furniture into the pool. According to the insurance company, this was a deliberate act of God. My sister, Caroline, would call it instead an act of faith—not the wind, but the cleaning up after it.

•   •   •

When my sister came home from the hospital, she had special bandages wrapped around her wrists: tennis bracelets, the kind designed to soak up excess fluids. My sister said she didn't like to play tennis. "Too bourgeois," she said, which at the time I thought had something to do with a woman's bedroom. Apparently, she had been bombed out of her mind, she didn't understand what she was doing, she was not crazy.

"Confused," said her shrink. "Confusion complicated by excessive cocaine use."

He ordered her to a detox unit. Because we were no longer rich, but now middle class, my mother explained, Caroline was sent to the Superstition Mountain Care Facility, just beneath the mountains where a lot of people with middle-class problems could get themselves fixed up. The program lasted six weeks, during which Caroline received school credit, so she could graduate on schedule, and where she spent a lot of time on self-esteem, which even back in the seventies was important: self-esteem and the adjustable rate mortgage, which led, of course, to the balloon payment. My mother had bought the house with a balloon payment and then spent close to forty thousand dollars fixing up the front yard—a fountain, and some cacti, and mounds which were designed to reflect the mountains in the distance. With Caroline in the hospital, I didn't understand why my mom was suddenly complaining about money.

There were no balloons when Caroline came home. My mother was resting, had been for the past week; nights she came out to refill her supply. Mornings, before I went to school, I'd check the bottles of scotch and Chablis beneath the sink: the wine, I understood, was used to chase away the spirits. She'd usually lay in a supply good for two weeks, and when I checked the declining levels, I could confirm that things were continuing on as normal: she wasn't dead; she hadn't left us for Minnesota or Colorado or the Bahamas. Caroline, meanwhile, paid the cab and stepped inside the house and went directly to her room. She shut the door. Germs went to the door, waiting to be let in, to welcome her home properly.

I knocked, of course, to show I understood her privacy.

"Caroline," I said. "Caroline?"

Eventually she opened up, first just a sliver. She peered out the door and said, "Yes."

"Do you want a sandwich or anything? I could make sandwiches."

"No," she said, standing back, letting us in. She sat on her bed with kelly green sheets and Germs leapt up and took over her pillow. She lay back, her head on Germs's rib cage. "They give you lots of pills that make you sleepy," she said. "Not very hungry."

"Uh huh."

"They're supposed to make you happy, too. You know, so you don't feel too bad about who you are and try and kill yourself."

"Oh, yeah. Those kind," I said, nodding. "I'm glad you didn't kill yourself."

She held up her wrists and looked at the bandages. "I don't need them anymore. I mean, the cuts are all fixed in place. You can hardly see them. But they remind me, you know? I can always try again if it gets that bad."

"What?" I said.

"What?"

"The part that gets bad," I said.

"Oh," she said. "Everything, I guess. It's not like I really thought I was going to do it or anything. You taking any drugs?"

At first I thought she was going to yell at me, like a parent; then I realized she just wanted to know. "No," I said. "I don't do that stuff. Not that it's bad, I mean. I don't really know how, actually. Once I had some scotch, before school."

"You shouldn't do that, Patty Mick."

Sometimes she made me feel as if I hadn't grown up at all. Still, only Caroline ever called me that. "It burns," I said to her. "Makes me tired."

"Come here," she said, patting the bed.

I sat on the bed beside her. The bedspread was made of white cotton and smelled like her. It reminded me of flowers and the soap she used and the oil from her long, red hair. She made me lie down beside her and then she put her arms around me and held me to her chest. I could feel her breath, on the back of my neck, and then she said, "I missed you."

"Are you going to be okay? Do you want something to eat?"

"I'm sleepy," she said. "Let's sleep."

"Okay," I said, but of course I wasn't about to let myself sleep, not with my sister holding on to me like that. I had to keep myself alert. I had to teach myself to be watchful and awake. The sun was setting, you could see it falling through the blinds, and the shadows they made on the wall of my sister's bedroom. They were long, the shadows, and eventually they disappeared completely and the room became completely dark.

Safe, I think. I felt safe then and worried it would go away.

Nights I would wait for my sister to wake. Lying in bed, first I'd wait for my mother, the shuffling down the hall. She'd return, the ice cubes tinkling, and shut her door. Then my mother would simply vanish and I'd wait and then I'd hear my sister's door. I'd listen to her in the bathroom, the moment for the flush; I'd wait for the slide of the glass door leading into our own private yard.

The pool was heated; in the winter, steam rose off the surface into the sky. My sister, standing on the diving board, the moon filling up the pool—I'd watch her from behind the sliding door and wait for her to dive. She'd taken years of lessons, had been trained to do just this: first, she'd take off her T-shirt, then her underwear. She'd fold everything neatly and set it on the back of the board. Then she'd stand on the edge of the board until it became too cold for her to stay. She'd cross her arms and shiver and then she'd shake them loose and balance on her toes, one step, another, and then she'd be sailing into the pool. She never even made a splash, she was that sure of herself.

One night, late June, after she was home from the hospital, I stepped outside. It was hot now, even at night. My sister was in the water, and I stepped outside and sat on the diving board in my underwear. She rose to the surface, wiped her eyes, and looked at me.

"I was lonely," I said.

She smiled sadly and said, "Me, too."

She said, looking for the moon, "I'm going to go to college in Massachusetts and you're never going to see me again."

"Why?"

"It's her fault," Caroline said. "He didn't have to kill himself, Patrick. He could have given all the money back—hell, he *made* them money; he didn't *lose* any. He could have opened up a restaurant or shopping mall or started teaching. He didn't have to kill himself and she made him do it. That's why she hates me. Because I know. You can't let her know you know because then she'll hate you, too. If she hates you, Patrick, she'll try and kill you the same way—"

"She's not trying to kill anybody, Caroline. She just likes to sleep because she feels bad, and then she has bad dreams, so that's why, you know . . . that's why she does all that."

"Drinks."

"Okay," I said. "Drinks."

"The living dead," she said, sputtering. She took a mouthful of water and spit it into the air, like a stream. Caroline had taught me to do that when we used to swim in the pond in our backyard, in Illinois, and she would practice her dives off the raft, and I'd call out numbers, like a judge. I could spit out water better now, better than her, because of the space between my two front teeth.

"He was in love with somebody else," Caroline said. "I saw them."

"Dad?"

"Dad. He was in love with somebody at church. Mrs. Langly,

the lady who wanted to be a priest. He was in love with her and Mom called the SEC and told them to do something. You know, pretending to be concerned."

"How do you know?"

"I was there, Patty Mick. I watched Mom make the call. She called the SEC from the kitchen while I was making supper. She said Dad was in trouble and needed help and that she was going to help him."

"What about us?"

"We are what's left, Patrick."

I sat on the board and shivered. The grit was digging into my skin. I couldn't really imagine my father in love with anybody, not even my mother. People were supposed to love *him*. Caroline skimmed the surface of the water with her hand and said, "You watch me. Every night?"

I looked at the water, and her hair, floating on it.

"Sometimes I see you," she said. "It's okay. You're not a pervert or anything, if that's what you're wondering."

"Sometimes," I said, shrugging. "Sometimes I think I am."

"Come on in. You're not a pervert."

"Nah."

"You can keep your underwear on. It's okay."

"It'll still . . . you know. It just does it by itself."

"Perfectly normal," she said, laughing. "It feels like a bath."

I slipped into the water, feet first, and it was warm. I hung from the diving board to keep myself from having to move, and I was hanging in the water, just keeping warm, trying not to move when we each turned and looked at the window in my mother's bedroom. She was standing there at the window, holding her drink. The light glanced off the window, complicating her presence, as if she had become a hologram, increasingly transparent, and I understood now everything had changed. I understood the power of a secret. I understood I had become capable of doing enormous damage.

"She's watching," Caroline said. "She's going to keep watching."

"I know."

"She counted his condoms, Patrick. That's how she found out."

Then the moon passed behind some clouds and it was dark. I could feel Caroline, treading water in the pool, and the waves she sent brushing against my body, and then I let myself go. I let myself sink into the center of the pool where it was impossible to breathe. When I surfaced, after my breath ran out, she was gone.

5

Her father says a coincidence is that which merely becomes known. If it's meaningless, you call it trivia; if it's important, you call it something else—*fate,* or maybe even *accident.* And faith, Elizabeth knows, is the hope for things yet unseen— like coincidence, or better yet, providence, and the possibility always for recognition; like voices on the telephone, calling out your name. She didn't recognize Caroline, but she would eventually recognize the name, McConnell.

A week later, after the fact—a naked girl with red hair, stepping out of a shower, her wrists slashed to the core. That night when the fire trucks arrived, and then the paramedics, she led a team upstairs into the bedroom. She answered questions and later she was taken to a station where she called her father for a ride. Bittner, along with most of the others, had been long gone.

Her father sells a quarter-million dollars' worth of real estate through his brokerage once a month. He is a short, bald man and slightly overweight, because of course he drives around town a lot, showing people property. Now he drives an expensive foreign car with a CB radio and encourages Elizabeth to visit with her mother, Lydia, who is building her own house on top of Mingus Mountain in Jerome. According to her father, Elizabeth's parents divorced *amicably,* which means they still liked each other, and since Elizabeth was already in the best school in the region, and because her mother intended to travel a while, before settling back down . . . *a period of transition, dear* . . . everybody agreed Elizabeth should stay with her father until she graduated, anyway. Recently her mother had returned from South America; after giving Elizabeth and her father a lot of nice presents, Lydia moved to Jerome, which used to be a mining town until the mines played out. Her father explained there was no longer sufficient demand to pay the men to keep on digging. If it weren't so pretty, set up on top of a mountain in the middle of the sky, the town would have long since turned into a ghost. And now it has become an arts community—pottery, and jewelry made from silver and beads—and Elizabeth visits often to please her parents, because things are so much better for everyone when they are amicable.

In the car, that night he picked her up at the police station, her father asked her if she was hurt.

"No," she said, brushing back her hair, which smelled like smoke.

"Are you all right?"

"I'm okay, yeah."

"You're sure?" he said. He turned up the heat in the car and turned to face her. The car smelled like a den full of leather furniture and pipe tobacco.

"Dad, I'm okay."

"Okay," he said, putting the car into gear. "You did the right thing, calling me."

"I know."

"You know? You know you did the right thing? You know?"

"Dad, I'm sorry, okay? I didn't know where we were going."

"So . . . so . . . ?"

"Okay," she said. "So I'm grounded. Is that it? You're going to take away my allowance?"

Her mother would say *campused. You're campused,* which was supposed to be a more sophisticated way of being grounded, like electricity, and the way it travels through you. When you are campused, it's more akin to being a college student, on a campus: in junior high, shortly after her parents moved here, where her father had started up a brokerage with his friend, Flip, and before her parents became divorced, her mother would say, "Elizabeth, you're campused." Afterward, her mother would sigh and say, "For your own good," but then her mother had an affair with her father's accountant and stopped campusing her daughter. Eventually Elizabeth realized this new permissiveness had something to do with throwing stones, and glass houses—a sudden opportunity to turn the other cheek and look the other way and never having a specific reason to tell your father what had become so clear . . . *Dad, Dad . . . did you know Mom's having an affair? With your accountant?*

There never was any real proof of it. She just suspected. Her mom, putting on a bottle of perfume, swimming in the stuff. The laundry was suddenly being done with uncommon frequency and there were a lot more trips to the dry cleaners, usually after Elizabeth's flute lessons, for which her mother was always late to pick her up. Her mother would apologize for being late; they'd drive to the dry cleaners, and Elizabeth would run the clothes inside, and take the claim check, and on the way home her mother would ask her questions about school or her favorite novels—*Jane Eyre, Wuthering Heights, A Tale of Two Cities.* Once in high school, Elizabeth began catching a ride from her math teacher to Phoenix for her lessons. On the way the math teacher, who talked often about sports, being an assistant football coach . . . on the way the math teacher would make passes at her, as if she were a part of the team; he was young, handsome, and married. Once, at a particularly long traffic light, he touched her breast, sighing, and then she unzipped his slacks—jacked him off, just so, and said, "No more. Okay?" She remembered wiping off her hands on his sweater, to indicate his responsibility for the very mess, and later the math teacher left his wife and moved to Bahrain. Elizabeth later discovered several other girls who had also done him a good turn, here and there. One girl on his desk, in his classroom, just beneath the clock. Meanwhile her flute teacher, a German lady with short hair, would always set the metronome, and Elizabeth would play out her lessons, standing in the living room, swaying slightly. The living room was always full of flowers, and afterward, Elizabeth would wait outside, on the sidewalk, for her mother to come pick her up. By spring her mother often failed to show at all, and Elizabeth would watch her teacher's students coming in for their forty-five-minute lessons, and leaving, and then she would wander over to a coffee shop, and drink coffee, and eventually call her father's office to explain. When her mother sometimes did show up, glowing and happy, she would actually start talking about the birds and the bees, beating her hand to the music on the radio, swaying her shoulders, keeping time. Her mother would sigh and adjust the volume and explain the way pollen attracted certain impulses; the way a flower would open itself just so . . . *just like a woman's heart, Lizzie.* "Poetry," her mother would say, giggling. "Pure poetry." In AP English, during the poetry section, Elizabeth's class had read a lot of Shakespeare's sonnets, and she knew a summer day was supposed to be beyond compare, and she knew that the couplet, which came at the end, was always supposed to rhyme. And then one day, glancing at the kitchen clock, she understood her mother was having an affair.

That night in the car, her father driving, two hands on the wheel, because he was always careful, she said, "Dad, I didn't know it was going to be this way."

"So what? So you go out with some thug who doesn't even knock at the door? Some prick who can't drive you home?"

"I'm grounded," she said. "It's okay. I deserve it."

"You want to be, is what you mean."

"I was bad."

"What am I going to say that you don't already know? How is punishing you going to make you any better? Any safer? What, I want to feel good and cause you pain? I'm your father. You called me in the middle of the night because you needed me. You did the right thing. You want, you can be grounded later, after we get home. It's up to you."

"There was a girl," she said. "At the party."

"I know."

"It could have been me," Elizabeth said. "It could have been anybody."

Now her father reached across the seat; he put his hand on her shoulder and squeezed, gently. "But it wasn't, Lizzie. It wasn't you."

She hadn't planned on crying. She hadn't planned on needing one of her parents and being picked up by the police. The night was dark and she was sitting in her father's well-upholstered car, following the lights they made into the dark: the headlights, leading the way, up Tatum, which would soon begin to curve. She curled herself up into a ball and let her head rest against the window. The window was cold and after a while her father said, sighing, "Almost. We're almost there."

It could have been anybody but it wasn't. It was a girl she'd never laid eyes on. At school, the following week, Elizabeth went to her classes and avoided awkward conversation. There were thousands of people at school and each day it was almost possible to get through an entire day without having to say a word. Singing, the way she did in Choir, didn't count. In Choir she'd stand by a sleepy girl with brown eyes and pay attention to the band leader. One day the boy with the dog stopped coming to Choir: he simply did not show up, and the band leader, who was a nice man, even though he was also tone deaf, looked sad. He said, "I guess Patrick's sick, eh?" He said that every day for a week and then, finally, he decided no longer to bring him up. She recognized the decision as it crossed his face, this need to let it go. That day she had even put a new ribbon in her hair, to attract notice from behind, and Mr. Dyers tapped the music stand and said, shifting his weight, "Well now. Let's sing. Everybody." And thus the days passed. In the mornings she went to Choir, and then in the afternoon, after lunch, during Band and Orchestra, and with her flute in the air, poised, she'd begin to play. Sometimes she passed the boy in the hallways. Sometimes when she knew the piece by heart, playing, it was possible to close her eyes.

It was inevitable she talk to Bittner. She'd already seen him with other girls in the hallways, and she knew she was being cast aside, not just by him but by the circles in which he traveled. After a week he came by her house, in the afternoon, the sun out; he came around back, knocking on the sliding glass door which led to her father's study. She drew the curtain and took a breath.

"Yes?" she said.

"Hey," he said. There was a scab on one of his knuckles. He wore a blue T-shirt and jeans and thick black boots. "I got a job."

She stepped outside, folding her arms across her chest. She caught his eyes looking at her chest. Community Chest, she thought, as in Monopoly. "I was practicing," she said.

"Yeah. Sounded nice. You should join a rock band or something. Like Jethro Tull."

"Uh huh."

"I got a job. You know? Shell station—on Shea. If I work overtime they don't take any taxes out—get that? Under the table. When I graduate, I can become manager, assuming things work out."

"That's great, Mark. I didn't know you wanted a job."

"Thinking of the future. High school doesn't last forever. Good way to keep friends, though: working at a station." He said, balancing, "Hey. You know that girl . . . you know she's going to be okay."

"You were going in there," she said, earlier than she expected. "You didn't know where I was at all!"

"No," he said. "Not quite."

In Monopoly, she realized, the idea was to build houses and hotels. The idea was to take over everybody's property and charge a lot of rent. She said, realizing what she meant, "There are other girls, Mark. Plenty."

"What do you mean?"

"You don't need me," she said, unfolding her arms. She set her hands on her hips. "You can get that anywhere."

"Yeah. Well, everybody knows . . . thing is, maybe this is best," he said, shrugging. "Maybe it's right."

"Knows what?"

He stepped back. He looked her up and down and said, "I guess I thought you were different, that's all. Different from the way you are."

She put her hand to her chest, where she felt her heartbeat. Standing there, his arms stretching at the seams of his shirt, and his shoulders, she realized he was simply the kind of man it would be impossible to bruise. Meanwhile her heart was working hard. She wiped her eyes, beginning to tear, and said, "You know, I wanted to like you. I thought people just didn't know you, Mark. I thought people, they just don't understand what a strong, sensitive kind of guy you are."

He began smiling now, showing his teeth. "They sure as hell don't," he said, shrugging. "Who knows anybody?"

Then he suddenly withdrew, shifting his feet. Talking with him was like playing Pong, the paddles sliding up and down against a black screen. "But the thing is," she said, "you're not. You're mean. You hurt other people. You were going to fuck a girl half out of her mind."

"I wasn't going there to fuck her, Elizabeth. Some things— You should be careful what you say."

"No," she said. "You would have, just like everybody else there."

"McConnell is a coke whore, Elizabeth. She's got a thousand-dollar-a-month habit. She blows guys for a line."

"McConnell?"

"Yeah. Little brother we've met before. I didn't hurt him that bad. But you're right," he said, withdrawing. "Least about some things. We should, you know . . . go our ways. I just wish you thought a little better about me, is all. I'm not always an asshole."

"You shouldn't have been there," she said.

"Look," he said, getting angry. "A girl like that, she's fucked up. She's not like you. But all she had to do was keep her Goddamn clothes on. I checked, Elizabeth. I checked. She's the one that stripped. She's the one that wanted to fuck the entire room."

"According to who?! I mean, Jesus. You think they're going to tell the truth? That could have been me," she said, "if I were drunk. Drunker. I mean—"

"No. It wouldn't have been you," he said. "Men can be danger-ous—you know. There's a lot of assholes, and yeah, sometimes I'm an asshole. You're right. You're right. But not always, Eliza-beth. Not always."

Before, when they weren't arguing, sometimes he'd reach for her, lay a finger on a button on her blouse. He'd draw his finger across her breast, toward a lock of hair. He liked her hair, she knew; men always liked your hair so long as you kept it free of tangles: so long as you brushed it every night, stroke after stroke. Suddenly, too, she realized it was done. They had become entirely irrevocable, and she realized she wasn't sure if this was what she meant.

Though it was—doing it just made things harder. "I have to practice," she said, crossing her arms. "You have to leave." She was crying now: if she could disappear she might slip into the pool, below the surface, just out of sight.

"It's okay," he said. "Your wanting to break up."

"No," she said. "I am not breaking up. I am not!"

"Best this way," he said, offering his hand, to shake. "Okay?"

She said, stepping into her room, "Please. I'd like you to leave."

She slid the door shut and stood there, watching him stand alone, on the other side of the glass, waiting for him to decide and leave. He opened his mouth once, as if he had something left to say, and then he picked up a yucca plant, still in its pot, and threw it into the pool. He kicked a pile of stones with his big black boots.

She turned her back, briefly, and then he was gone. *Solve for X,* her math teacher used to say, before he left his wife for Bahrain. Just because you do not know the answer doesn't mean you cannot find it. *Work it out,* he'd say. *Try harder . . .* and moments later, she heard Bittner drive away, his exhaust roaring. Standing before the window, looking out at the pool, the blue sky overhead, she looked for evidence of the plant—some grain of dirt, perhaps, dissolving into the surface. Now she leaned her head against the glass. The glass was hard as stone, like her heart. The glass felt hard enough to break, but not quite.

In her dream, the dream in which he comes to her, he is wearing the same burgundy sweater. He has recently shaved, because she can smell the soap, and it breaks her heart, the fact of this shaving, because there clearly isn't any need for it. Once the heart breaks, you have no longer the ability to stay alive: she decides, in her dream, that she is merely bruised, and it hurts. *At least I am alive,* she tells herself, and then him, this boy in the blood red sweater with his face smooth as glass, smooth as your reflection in a pool. Then he leans over her bed and she remembers not for the first time that he is the boy with a dog, and that somewhere he must have one. She reaches for his sweater and plucks a thin, white hair.

You have a dog?

In the dream she is sleeping naked. In the dream he lifts the covers from her bed and stares at her naked body. Then she takes his hand, and draws it to the center of her chest, there where it hurts. He draws his finger down the center of her chest, across the sternum, the bone which ties itself up with the ribs, from whence she came, eons ago. He looks at her body and she doesn't feel cold at all. Now he takes her arm, the arm which has been burned, and holds it in his hand.

It didn't hurt, she says. *I don't even remember.*

The arm is warm and part of her, same as any other, full of

blood and sinew and bone, and now he lays her arm across her chest, as if to pledge allegiance, and never says a word. He draws his finger across the scarred tendons of her arm and as she begins to wake, because this is not precisely what she thought her dream had in mind, she watches him disappear into a pool of light. Waking, she realizes she is all alone. She is entirely alone in her dark room with the blinds pulled shut, the sun fading in beneath the fabric, and she is holding her breast with her damaged hand. Her hand is beneath her nightshirt holding her breast. And then she begins to rise, sitting up in her bed, opening the blinds, if only because there must be a perfectly good reason, and because it's time to dress. She is alone in her room on a Sunday morning with her body and the dark and the meaning of the day gathering just outside her window: break of day, which is coming, she knows, because it follows night. Because she knows it has to.

6

Most people know only what they want to believe: it's the first rule which governs over all others. As for my father, he knew he had done something wrong, even when he didn't want to believe it. Had he been a normal man, he would have denied his wrongdoing, properly, like a congressman or televangelist. Instead my father broke the rules and, as a matter of course, the world killed him for it. The fine long arm of the law.

Summer has come and gone, insufferably. I have found a special harness for my dog, Germs, which fits him to a T. Caroline lives in Massachusetts where in the fall she will begin college, and where she will also begin an affair with a bisexual former priest deeply committed to human rights in Central America. I have passed Driver's Ed and am now legally permitted to drive to school and elsewhere. And I have also secured employment at a full-service gas station—*filling station,* my mom calls it—and I have become good friends with Mark Bittner who has taught me, among other things, to avoid repairing split rims so as not to go decapitating myself. Bittner has spent two entire weeks training me, teaching me how to dip the tanks and use the racks. The gas station is fraught with dangers, particularly in summer, and working there causes me to feel self-sufficient and important. I can replace a fan belt in ten minutes, sometimes less, and I know how to balance a set of rims. I can change the oil in your car. Sell you a coolant treatment for seven-fifty your car most certainly does not need. But in Phoenix, in August, the heat is always constant, and that's a good selling point: for two months, the temperature falls into the nineties, but only after midnight. Days, wearing my jeans and boots, I feel myself adapt to the climate and look forward, always forward, to the nights I spend with my girlfriend, Elizabeth.

My arms are hard and full of muscles. My body is lean, constantly worked at by the fact of the sun and those things I am doing right beneath it. Sometimes, while working in the sun, changing a tire, I wear gloves to protect my hands from the heat. Bittner has taught me to wrap a rag around my hand to keep myself from burning my knuckles on an overheated manifold. He says to me one day, "She's a nice girl. She putting out much?"

We are standing in the doorway, looking out over the islands. My shirt says *Harold* on it because the shirt man brought us the wrong batch last week. I spend fifteen dollars a week on my laundry bill. Across town, specifically at Jimmy Mulenbach's Shell station, I imagine *Harold,* whoever he is, wearing my shirt with my own name, *Mac.*

I say to Bittner, nodding, looking out over the islands, "Uh huh."

He is curious, I think. So am I. Elizabeth and I date frequently but I have yet to see her put anything out. I'm wondering what, specifically, this is meant to be slang for. It seems more appropriate to apply to a male—the act of putting out. I'm wondering where that came from, that particular idea, when Bittner says, "Hey, she's not like other girls. She's different, I mean. Cool hair. And smart!"

"Yeah," I say. "Want a Coke?"

It's my turn to buy. Usually, we go through six dollars a day, sometimes seven. Filling the Coke machine is one of the best duties there is: you get to stand in front of it for a while, the refrigerator blasting out at you, while you stack cans slowly as you can and count the change. Fuller, the owner's son, keeps beer at the bottom, to stay cool, and also because you have to get the key from him directly.

"She's gonna be a brain surgeon or something," Bittner says. "She ever join a rock band?"

"Nope."

"Too bad," Bittner says, smoking. He stands in the doorway and smokes, because this is a suggestion: *No Smoking Beyond the Door.*

The fourth or fifth day I showed up, in my best casual clothes, to show I could be *neat,* and because I really wanted a job, Bittner said something to the owner—Mr. Brush. Mr. Brush has cancer and coughs for hours and has given the station to his son, Brush Jr., whom everybody calls Fuller: it's a nickname, I'm told. Fuller used to be a college swimmer before his dad was diagnosed with inoperable cancer just as Fuller was expelled, anyway, for failing to show up for either practice or class. That day, I was standing in the bay, beneath a gutted Ford up on the rack, explaining to Fuller, not for the first time, that I wanted a job I could really roll up my sleeves for. I liked cars an awful lot. I learned real fast, et cetera.

Fuller carried a chrome derringer on his belt, just by the buckle, so you'd be sure to see it. Then I saw Bittner, which scared me: now that he had graduated from high school, I'd been thinking I was safe. I raised my hand and waved, because of course he'd recognized me; he had a rag hanging out of his hip pocket, professionallike.

"Hi," I said, waving.

"We have one rule here," Fuller said. "Just one rule."

"Uh huh."

"No fighting."

"No fighting," I said. "That's a good rule. I don't let my dog fight, either."

Fuller lit a cigarette and looked at me, awkwardly. He had one eye which didn't work quite right. He said, pointing to the sign over the bay, "No fighting. You can be late. You can be sick. You can come up short in the drawer. But you cannot fight."

"Okay."

"Bittner here says you're a good guy. He says he kicked the shit out of you. That true?"

I shifted my feet. "More or less, I guess."

"Bittner," Fuller called. "Come here."

Bittner stepped across the bay; he stood on his toes, rocking. He looked at me and smiled. "You go out with Elizabeth Pinski," he said to me.

"Well. Yeah."

He held out his hand. "I thought you were somebody else," he said. "That day. No hard feelings?"

Fuller coughed. Then Bittner coughed. I shook Bittner's hand, which was hard and full of knots, and said, "Yeah. Sure. I mean, yeah."

"Elizabeth," Bittner said. "She's a smart girl."

A minute later I left the station employed for the very first time in my life. As I was walking through the door, the door leading out into the front lot, Fuller called, "There's a few suggestions we have, Mac."

Nobody had ever called me *Mac* before. Secretly, it thrilled me. My father had been called Mac all his life. I stopped in the doorway, turning.

"No smoking beyond the door," Fuller said. "The front is always first. No stealing. Don't be late. Don't cuss. Most important, no smoking beyond the door. This is a gas station, you know. Things blow up."

Driving home, on the way, I stopped at another gas station for my very first pack of cigarettes. At first, I didn't know what flavor to pick. I spent a week teaching myself to smoke in the backyard, while playing my guitar, with nobody looking: most serious musicians smoked, too, so this job would provide good experience. It takes a while to handle a cigarette without looking like you do not know how to handle it. Now, standing in the door, with Bittner, having fetched the Cokes, I am resting my haunch against the brick. Inside the flowerbed is where the butts go.

"Thanks," Bittner says, taking the soda, popping the tab.

I light a cigarette, toss the match inside the flowerbed. An old guy is gassing up a truck out on self-serve. Bittner says, pointing across the street, "Look at that."

The street has four lanes and is generally crowded. Across it a man is walking with the traffic; there is no sidewalk. Now a car honks at the man, and then he pivots, flipping somebody the bird. The man is walking slowly now, shifting his feet; he's wearing no shirt, and his jeans are tight, really tight, with the waistline pulled up to his navel. He has wavy yellow hair, like Fuller, only more yellow, as if dyed, and longer. Now he begins to cross the street, wandering amid the traffic, and even from a hundred yards I can see his ribs. His ribs are sticking through his flesh, like victims of the Holocaust, or drought, and he's coming right for us.

"Jesus," Bittner says.

Fuller calls my name from inside. I go to him, where he's finishing off a tire on the machine, and he says, handing me the tire wrench, pointing, "Patch this."

"I'm not very good at it," I say.

"You're telling me," he says. "Learn."

He points again to the deflated tire, leaning against the wall, and now I go to it, and lift. The tire is warm, from being driven on for thousands of miles, especially in the sun. I lift and set it in the tank. I am looking for the leak, and locating the hole, the air bubbling out, I circle it with the yellow grease pencil. Now I'm breaking down the tire on the machine, which is the easy part, breaking it down. Even getting the tire off is fairly easy, torquing the wrench, stomping on the pedal which activates the hydraulic seal, which in turn kicks on the compressor from behind the closet, the same as when you hit the hoist: once you activate the seal, the machine then propels the wrench, dug in beneath the tire, to lift the tire and peel it off the wheel. But it's hot, gruesome work, especially when you're not very good at it. Eventually, I'm sweating hard, putting on the glue, blowing on it to dry. When I look up, for approval, I understand Fuller is no longer paying any attention whatsoever.

He's standing out at the flowerbed with Bittner. Because the glue has to dry, I mosey on up, see what's happening. And I see Fuller is talking with the gaunt man from across the street: up close, the man's ribs are even more discrete. His eyes are sharp and full of hollows. His skin, I see, is not tan, but orange. It's actually orange, and with his pants pulled up so tight, you can see his cock, which looks huge, all tangled up inside his designer blue jeans.

"Hi," I say, waving.

Fuller turns sharply. "Aren't you doing a task?"

"Oh. Yeah."

"Get to it."

Tears sting my eyes. I look at the man, who's swaying, and then he smiles gently as if he understands. When he speaks, I understand he has a lisp, and that he is describing California; I understand he is explaining that he's sick, but not contagious, and that he has no experience and is asking Fuller for a job, anyway.

I figure if I had experience, maybe Fuller would like me better. Back at the tire machine, I'm still smarting at the slight, and I feel unexpectedly sad. Still, the patch looks as if it might hold, but of course it's so much easier just to plug a tire than it is to patch one, anyway, even if it is a radial. Now I'm trying to get the tire to mount, without denting the wheel, and I can hear Bittner, laughing, and when I turn I see Bittner, running out to the front, and Fuller stepping toward me.

"How's that tire going?"

"I'm learning," I say, bitterly, because he has hurt my feelings.

Fuller reaches, puts his weight on the tire, to help me put it back onto the rim. "Push," he says, "here."

"Here?"

"Yes, Goddamnit. Don't fight it. Balance."

I step on the pedal, the machine hisses, and now the tire wrench jams up and then it pops and leaps up, hitting me just under the eye. For a moment, I'm not sure where I am.

"You okay?"

"Uh huh."

"Put some ice on that."

"I'm okay."

He goes to the cooler, rips opens the lid, reaches his greasy hand into the water, and pulls out a fistful of ice. He wraps the ice in a utility rag and says, "Here, Goddamnit." He takes a breath, and says, gently, "Put it on your eye."

"I'm okay."

"Put it on your eye, Mac. Then try again."

That part about Elizabeth—I guess I took it as a compliment. Of course I wanted it to be a compliment. Going out with a smart girl, specifically Elizabeth Pinski, helped me feel as if I might be smart, too. My grades had never been particularly good. I'd never had any real friends. And I was still young enough to hope that each bit of this world might bear some direct influence upon my character, which of course it did, and still does, if only because I was born in the United States during the 1960s.

My father, before he killed himself, said I was part of the Baby Boom—part of that population explosion which took place because we hadn't lost the war. At the time, Vietnam was taking place, and I had no idea what he was talking about. But by the 1970s, and after one gas crisis, and with another in the works, and with people talking about the B-1 Bomber, versus the MX Missile . . . mostly I understood the world to be increasingly combustible. When I arrived home, that day after popping myself in the eye with a tire wrench, there was an old, beat-up station wagon in the drive out front, and a new Mercedes parked behind that.

I stepped inside the house and realized Germs wasn't nearby; otherwise he would have greeted me. "Patrick," my mother called from the dining room. "Patrick!"

Inside sat a tall, old man with thick, black glasses, in dungarees and a threadbare sweater, the same color as the one I had lifted from my father's closet, *Plum*. Beside him sat another, a fat man, losing his hair, dressed in a fluorescent three-piece suit. The old man stood, wearily, as if dusting himself off, and reached to shake my hand.

"Senator," my mother said, proudly. "This is my son, Patrick McConnell."

"Hi," I said. "Sorry I'm dirty."

"Good hard work," said the senator. "Been chopping wood myself."

My mother, of course, stood primly in her very best pantsuit. She said, giggling, "And this is Mr. Jim Walenka . . . who's been helping me with some of these sticky investments?"

"Jim," said Mr. Walenka, rising, shaking my hand. "Bottom line? Call me Jim."

"Okay, Jim."

"Big Jim Walenka," said the senator, vaguely. He had returned to his seat and was pretending to glance over a several-inch-thick report, one which had been prepared by an independent secretary. He nibbled at some hors d'oeuvres, recently delivered by a catering service: special occasion, my mother would say, given that she simply could not cook. I understood they were all sipping coffee from the good china. Apparently untouched, a decanter full of spirits sat discreetly on a sideboard. The report, entitled *Challenge Life,* had been drafted several times by my mother, hoping to draw attention to the various *challenges* life presented the surviving victims of the suicide, she had explained, often, especially those *challenges* relating to matters of self-esteem and self-identity and self-worth. The idea was to secure federal funding to build a facility in the mountains, preferably by a nice lake, dedicated toward the rehabilitation of shattered lives, which of course my mother would direct, while concurrently advancing her career in cinema.

"So, Patrick," said Jim Walenka. "I see you got a shiner there!"

I pointed toward my eye and said, proudly, "Tire iron. At the station."

"Work," said the senator. "I love hard work."

"We're thinking . . ." said Mr. Walenka, with a wink, "we're thinking of looking at some copper mines, your mother and me. Specially up around Heber."

"Oh."

"It's part of that new Jefferson Trust," my mother said, almost giddily. "And since Jim here thought the senator might be interested, we thought we'd discuss Challenge Life, too."

"Yeah," I said. "That's a good idea."

"Indeed," said the senator. "I used to chop wood as a boy, you know."

"I have a show," I said, stepping back. "I need to get cleaned up. Will you excuse me?"

"Patrick trains dogs," said my mother. She said, turning to me, "He's in your room."

"You're a fine young man, Patrick," said Mr. Walenka. "I'm pleased to have met you. We can count on you in eighty?"

I looked at my mother, who mouthed, behind Mr. Walenka's back, lest I say the wrong thing, *Republican!*

"Certainly," I said. "Of course."

I went to my room, and changed, and took a fast shower, and called Elizabeth to tell her I'd be late. We had a date, and I wanted to be clean, and presentable, in case we spent a lot of time kissing, and she said on the phone, *Okay,* and then I said, *Okay,* and she said, *Okay,* and then one of us finally hung up first. By the time I stepped into the living room, all spruced up, my mother was sitting alone with Jim Walenka, holding his hand, engaged in meaningful conversation, and the senator was long gone.

The next morning, and after very little sleep, I left to show Germs for the very last time, though I did not know it then. I was going to Las Vegas, where my mother said I should have a good time so long as I drove there safely. I woke before sunrise, and she sat in the kitchen, smoking, drinking the last from a water glass full of wine.

"Morning," she said, shaking her head. "Morning."

"I'm off to Vegas," I said, which was also the name of a popular television show. "How'd the senator like your plan?"

"He's thinking about it. He's going to give it every consideration."

"That's great."

"Are you going to gamble? In Las Vegas?"

"I'm not old enough, Mom. They don't let you into those places unless you are accompanied by an adult."

"Hand me my purse," she said, from which she removed a twenty-dollar bill. "For your lunch," she said, passing it to me. "Be sure to eat something nutritious."

I called Germs, reached for his leash, which I kept hanging behind the dryer, along with his choke chain, and dumbbell, and we hurried out to the truck, eager to be gone. The truck was a big Chevy my father had bought to plow snow from our driveway in Illinois. He liked playing with it in the winter, he explained, because it was warmer than a tractor, and because my mother used to keep getting her cars stuck into the woods. Beneath the hood was a 454 V-8, which meant a four-barrel carburetor and close to eight miles a gallon, as well as duel tanks, the kind for which GM would later be sued, on account of traffic accidents and fire hazards, but which nonetheless could hold together some forty gallons of gas. My truck was four-wheel drive, and brown, and sitting in it, smoking my cigarettes, driving through the desert with my dog, Germs, I felt important as Columbus—always on the brink of discovery, even if his just so happened to take place on the wrong continent. The drive to Las Vegas took hours, up through the mountains, over the Hoover Dam, and I was sixteen, driving across the desert with my dog to Las Vegas where people made a television show. There was a long train, running hard toward California, and I remember waving to the conductor, who blew his horn and waved back. Driving, I was becoming my own man, and eventually I stopped worrying about the cops and increased my speed to prove it.

An important distinction: we didn't show breed; we showed obedience. That weekend we placed fourth. To earn the final ranking—the UD—Germs would have to place in the nineties for three separate shows. Someday I thought we might show for a championship, just to see if we could do it. In the ring the exercises required work off-leash and a scent trial and an exercise based on visual commands. To say a word was to flunk the exercise, and to fail an exercise was to fail the trial. Even a sloppy dog in the ring can look glorious. What's important is that the dog enjoys what he is doing, and Germs always liked to show off. On the send-out, he spun a little three-sixty, and you could hear the people standing around the ring going *ohhh* and *ahhh*. On the recall, he cleared the bar jump by a foot and nearly sailed into me, his tail a propeller, fanning the breeze, but he came in so fast he forgot to straighten himself out. That is, he sat crooked, which knocked off three and a half points, and so we lost third place to a golden named after Bruce Babbitt. It was Mr. Windham's dog, a professional trainer who did a lot of guard dogs on the side. He was thin and smoked too much and drove a yellow pickup with a three-speed column. When he'd take me out to eat, usually at a Bob's Big Boy, he'd tell me about his daughter, or the auto body shop he used to own, and then he'd ask me questions about what I wanted to do with my life. He'd had a son who died in a traffic accident, he said. Rear-ended by a drunk driver. *Gone,* he said, snapping his fingers, *just like that.* That weekend he was in Las Vegas, Mr. Windham had four goldens he was showing for other people, along with a young black Lab for himself.

It's a small world, the dog show. You get to know those you show against. You can tell who beats his dog and who doesn't and who bribes his dog with treats. Sometimes a dog shows well because of his owner; sometimes the dog is just plain goofy or epileptic. Germs was a good dog, especially for a setter, which are not known for their consistency and sound judgment, and it didn't bother me that he placed fourth. I didn't even care if he lost. Mostly I just liked it that people respected me: in the ring, watching me with my dog, people could tell I loved my dog, and that my dog loved me, and that I knew precisely what I was doing.

After the awards, while we were standing in the ring, receiving our purple trophies and listening to all the people clap, grudgingly, Mr. Windham offered me congratulations.

"Congratulations, Patrick," he said to me, smiling. "Germs did right fine today."

"Thanks," I said. "So did Bruce."

"Ol' Bruce," Mr. Windham said. "Ol' Bruce thinks he's going to be governor forever."

"Not Germs," I said.

"No," Mr. Windham said, winking. "Germs has more important things on his mind."

It was a real wink, person to person, and I wished immediately he were my father. My father, he was a criminal. My father blew his brains out, literally, with a shotgun: in the stable, there were parts of his body on the tack, and in the hay, and all over the stalls. Before he died my father gave me a dog and told me never, never to hit it with my hand. Standing in Nevada with my trophy, I felt lonely and small, because I hadn't come here for a trophy, and on the way out of the parking lot I heaved it into a Dumpster. Then I drove through downtown Las Vegas, searching for the strip, whatever that was, and looking at all the lights and prostitutes and overweight men in cowboy boots fiddling with loose change. For a while I thought about stopping, just to have a look, but I could tell Germs was impatient to run, so we drove to the edge of the city, and there you could see Nevada the way God intended: in the growing dark, all of it, the city lights behind us and the sky descending overhead. I set Germs out, removed his collar, and let him go—running, all lungs and legs, as if his life depended on it, which I suppose it did. I had a girlfriend now, and sometimes we would sit in the back of my truck and kiss for hours. Sometimes she would let me hold her breast. Her name was Elizabeth, and if you allow it to, the sky can also change the way you feel about your life. Elizabeth practiced with the symphony, she was that sure of herself, and eventually I was going to have to go far away: I think even then, watching my dog run across the state, I knew I wasn't meant to stay because, for some reason—it sounds vain to say, narcissistic, even—but I knew God wasn't going to let me stay, because I also knew that I loved God, and when you love, you also become obligated to something other than yourself. You become obligated to your girlfriend, or the world, or both, and I knew even then I was going to have to find my own place, which had now become finally possible. Because when Elizabeth said my name, especially at night, I believed at least for a while it was possible. And standing there on the edge of the desert, watching my dog, I began to pray. I began to pray for my mother, who clearly was in danger; and my sister, who was headed someplace equally dangerous, if not unexpected; and then I prayed for my father, because I wanted him to be in heaven, if only so we could meet up someday in the future, after I had done him proud. Next I prayed for Elizabeth and thanked God for permitting her to like me. And then I whistled in my dog, and watered him down, and then I found a gas station and filled up both tanks and headed home.

7

At seventeen, approaching eighteen, and having been instructed by a decade worth of Catholic school, and having been taught to read music, and to play volleyball with an overhand serve and to drive fairly safely, and having been fitted properly for a diaphragm as well as advised to study in depth at least one foreign language . . . after all of this what she longs for most is simply meaning. She longs for an explanation which will truly satisfy.

Meanwhile, and insufferably, the summer passes. It's a word her mother uses, *insufferably,* because it's hot—this sun, lighting up the desert. This particular weekend, on top of Mingus Mountain, in Jerome, Arizona, she's with her mother, working on the roof of her mother's house, laying shingles. She's wearing gloves, and she is teaching herself to swing a hammer smartly. Her mother says often, laying out the shingles, pausing to wipe her brow, "This is insufferable."

Elizabeth can feel the blisters raising inside her hand. When she swings the hammer, she lets herself follow its lead. Her mother describes the process as being very Zen-like, on account of the large size of the roof, and the need for patience. "You're not supposed to suffer, Lizzie," she says. "You're supposed to go with the flow."

"You mean the heat?" says Elizabeth.

"Yes," says Lydia. "The heat."

"It's not that bad, Mom. It's in the teens at home."

"Home?"

"You know, Dad's. Our house. Paradise Valley?"

"Ahhh. Home," says Lydia. "Home, dear, is where you hang your hat. Home is where you pound your hammer."

"Of course," Elizabeth says. She reaches to loosen the knot in her hair, which is heavy and hot. If she lets it loose completely, her hair will be entirely in the way. She looks at the mountains in the distance, the San Francisco Peaks, and the valley far below.

"Home is where the heart is, Lizzie dear. And you are my home."

"That's a Billy Joel song, Mom."

"Of course," Lydia says, setting down her hammer. "Shall we drink some iced tea?" Lydia scoots her bottom along the shingles, toward the ladder. Once there she pivots, slides into the ladder, her big white sunhat flapping into the breeze. Halfway down, Lydia pokes her head over the ledge of the roof and says, "Billy Joel?"

"He plays piano. He's pretty good."

"He stole that. That's what. He stole that from this very conversation!"

Inside, sitting in the cool part of the main room, which her mother calls the *vortex,* they drink iced tea, with lemon, and watch the hummingbirds gather sugarwater from the feeder. There are several, darting in and out of view. Lydia's house is only half-finished, but that is because she is making it by herself; she hired an unemployed miner to dig out the foundation with a rented bulldozer: the rest she has done by herself, and with friends, slowly, one month at a time. After the house is finished, Elizabeth knows her mother merely intends to start another. "I'm a homemaker," Lydia says. "It's what I was raised to do." Because Lydia also believes in Nature, and Ecology, the house is designed not to need electricity, and it is full of bookshelves which she spent last winter building with a painter named Fernando. Fernando is also her lover, and Elizabeth thinks he is nice enough—in one room, which serves as his studio, he works on canvases the size of windows. When she visits, Fernando always insists Elizabeth play something after dinner. This summer Elizabeth is practicing with the Phoenix Symphony, which is doing Bach's Mass in B Minor: it's a long, beautiful piece and makes her feel as if she is part of something complicated. Her chair is near the tail end of the row, but she also is the youngest, and the conductor, a Czechoslovakian with white hair, Dr. Merick, always makes a point to say something nice to her at each practice. He is a visiting conductor from a university in Connecticut. Sometimes, Elizabeth imagines living in Connecticut, or Massachusetts, which is a place she's only seen pictures of, mostly in her history textbooks—Lexington and Concord, Boston before the Tea Party. She imagines living in a place with snow and all that history. Her boyfriend, Patrick McConnell, says he's going to be a rock star, and that college will be less important because of that. Because of rock music.

In general her mother agrees, though she is also eager to meet Patrick. Today, looking at the hummingbirds, she asks Elizabeth if there is anything she needs to tell her.

"What?"

"Do you have any specific questions?"

"No," says Elizabeth. "Do you?"

"Touché, dear. Touché, touché. That's French, for sword fighting. These books you read about your teenagers—we're supposed to be open and available."

"You live on top of a mountain, Mom."

"Yes. And you visit me often because I want you to and because my heart is in your home. Billy Joel."

"Mom. I'm fine. I've read books. No questions."

"It's different for a boy. It's different than you think."

"How's that?"

"There's so much tangled up with who he thinks he is. Be gentle, that's my advice. Don't expect so much. Remember to talk afterward. You have to have a conversation, otherwise it's just like having dinner. It's about conversation, you know. You're supposed to rise above the quality of the food. You're not supposed to pay attention to the weather. It's about saying what you really mean and think about. About what you really feel."

"Okay."

"I want to meet him. Does he really have a dog? I love English setters. So big and fluffy. Strong, and pretty. A good dog. Your father never liked dogs."

"He likes Germs. He says Germs is the best dog he's ever met."

Lydia smiles now, gently. "That's a good sign. Your father," she says, lifting her chin, sipping her tea, "has exquisite taste, you know."

"Uh huh."

"Yes. Perfectly exquisite. That's how we came up with you, dear."

It's a moment like this which reminds her to pay attention to the light outside, which is falling. Eventually the day is going to cool off. Elizabeth says, sleepily, because she loves her mother, even if her mother is sometimes careless, "Can I stay over?"

"Of course."

"School starts next week. I'm going to be a senior."

"Yes," says her mother sadly. "Now go call your father. Not to worry."

Her parents agree: don't be in such a hurry to grow up. Specifically, this is what she knows about her boyfriend, Patrick McConnell. He plays guitar, often for several hours each day, often outside in his backyard with his dog, Germs. He believes the best guitar players are Eric Clapton, Jorma Kaukonen, and Mark Knopfler. Leo Kotke is also important, he says, and Dan Fogelberg, who lives in Durango, Colorado, is going to become very famous. Patrick says James Taylor is underrated as a musician just because he's popular on the radio and lives with Carly Simon. Patrick is also taller than he used to be, and stronger, and shaves twice a week; his shaving cream smells like almonds and aloe. He is also remarkably inexperienced.

Last spring, in the school parking lot, she recognized his truck, the big brown Chevy with four-wheel drive—the kind boys liked to drive so much, going through the mud, or dust, or the river bottom. She saw the truck and stepped in between some cars and into the lane so that he would have to stop. It was lunch hour, and she knew he was driving away during lunch hour so he would have something to do; she knew he didn't want to be sitting by himself, and eating, during lunch. She called, waving to him.

He hit the brakes hard and skidded—a loud, wrenching sound. He put the truck into reverse, skidded again. Now he rolled down the window, nervously, and said, "Hey."

"Yeah," she said. "Hey."

"What'cha doing?"

"Oh, you know. I'm waiting for my friend. We're going out for lunch."

"Oh. Yeah. Want to come with me?" he said. "I mean, if your friends don't mind."

She thought about it briefly, for his sake. Then she crossed in front of the big truck, and he opened the passenger door, and she swung her books onto the seat and climbed inside. It was a big truck and she kicked up her leg on the wide seat, interrupted by a huge storage compartment—for a cooler of beer, or soda, and maybe sandwiches—and turned to him, saying, "Okay. Where to?"

It was something she never did: go out for lunch. Usually she went to the store with some friends and bought a diet soda. Patrick, meanwhile, pulled out and drove across a dusty field, tearing across the landscape, heading for a fast food restaurant in McCormick Ranch: there was a big new road, Hayden, with four lanes, recently extended all the way to Cactus. Going there, Patrick drove the truck fast, pounding his hand with the radio, thinking. She looked out the window and thought about some conversation. It was hard, though, thinking of things to talk about—out the window, hundreds of new houses were going up, all across the desert. According to her father, so long as the state could keep siphoning water away from California, the boom was on. The development, McCormick Ranch, had been named after a man who invented better ways to farm.

She said, eventually, "You're not in Choir anymore."

"Nah. I mean, I had to take some other courses."

"Uh huh. We're not very good. The choir, I mean. Mr. Dyers is just supposed to lead the band."

"He's nice, Mr. Dyers. In Illinois we had a bunch of choirs and went to competition and stuff. I mean, Mr. Dyers is nice. It's not the same."

"I'm trying out for the symphony," she said. "This summer."

"You play real nice," Patrick said. "I've heard you. On the lawn."

He meant the lawns out behind the gymnasium, where she practiced sometimes during lunch, before she had friends with whom she could go to the store and buy a Tab. After she broke up with Bittner, because he never said anything, especially about himself, and because he just wanted to fuck her, and know everything she knew about everyone she ever talked to, as if she weren't company enough . . . after and now that she had broken up with Bittner, certain girls had slowly begun to speak with her in the hallway. She had imagined her name would be spray-painted on the walls . . . *Elizabeth Pinski sucks big cock* . . . and she imagined she'd never have another friend ever again, but it hadn't worked that way. To her surprise, Bittner was always nice to her, passing her in the hallways, nodding, saying *hey;* he'd even asked her once if she was going to be at his graduation. Usually he had his arm around Val Henry or Erin Drew, or other girls, cheerleaders: tall girls with beautiful skin and athletic legs in patriotic outfits. And Val Henry and Erin Drew were nice enough, once they were no longer hanging onto Bittner's side, and sometimes in the bathroom, or in line at the bookstore, waiting to buy a pencil or a compass, sometimes one of these girls might engage her in a

moment of tender conversation. By way of their common associ-
ation with Mark Bittner, of course, Elizabeth knew far too much
about these girls—and they, her—to ever become intimate, and
so Elizabeth began, eventually, to make friends with those who
weren't quite as popular—those who, on account of their looks,
or lack of social status, never would have had occasion to let Mark
Bittner feel them up beside the lockers. Instead Elizabeth made
friends with those who spent most of lunch hanging out behind
the music building, on the lawn, practicing their instruments.

She said to Patrick, while he was driving, "Do you have a girlfriend?"

"Me?" He blushed instantly and steered a little. "Well, in Illinois. I mean, I had this friend. She's in college now. We write letters sometimes. I guess not."

"Me too."

"You're from Illinois?"

"Michigan. I don't have a boyfriend, either." She said it to
make her position clear, like an announcement of a paper topic.

"I thought, Bittner . . ."

"Nope," she said, shaking her head. "Nope."

Then she smiled, and she leaned over and punched him in the
arm, because she didn't know him well enough to kiss him, not
even on the cheek, and she said, "So, Patrick McConnell. Where
are we going?"

He blushed again, his face and throat. He took one hand off the
wheel and shrugged. "Lunch," he said, driving. "I guess I'm hungry."

For dates they often went driving. Sometimes they went to a car
wash, where they'd wash Patrick's truck, and then maybe they
might wax it. Once or twice they even cleaned the engine with
special chemicals. Sometimes they went to movies, but it could be
embarrassing, being carded. When they went to see *Saturday
Night Fever*, with John Travolta, the ticket lady wouldn't let

Patrick in. *Star Wars* was still playing, at the Cine Capri, each night for well over a year, down at Camelback and Twenty-fourth Street, but they never went to see it because of the lines. Sometimes they drove to South Mountain, down Central, past all the high school kids and their low riders. Sometimes they bought Germs an ice cream at the Dairy Queen and headed east, toward Fountain Hills to watch the fountain, the largest in the world, shooting hundreds of feet up into the air—lit up from below with floodlights. Seven Springs, north of Carefree, was a good hour and a half out of town, but from Seven Springs you could get out of your car and count the stars. The sky there was full of stars, enough to paint with, enough to light up your heart, inside-out. "It's like a Lite-Brite," she said. "Remember those?"

Once summer came, once Patrick started working at the Shell station, he would pick her up after Symphony practice, downtown, and they would explore the city streets, driving down Indian School, and then maybe passing by the new mall right off the freeway where it was always cool inside. The streets would be bright, and the sun would be blazing through the windshield, cooking away, as if they were in a microwave, and Elizabeth would tell Patrick about her practice. Germs would be sitting in between them, panting, drooling on the seats. Once they were driving down Van Buren, past a pawn shop, and Elizabeth decided they should stop and go inside.

"I've never been in one," she said.

"They sell guns," Patrick said. "And guitars."

In the parking lot they could see a prostitute, across the street, stopping traffic, and a man with one arm was yelling at a streetlight. Patrick put Germs on his leash, regretfully, and they walked across the lot. In the window, up for display, sat a stereo, a rifle, and a wheelchair. There were also a couple dusty guitars and a trumpet.

Patrick said, pointing to a guitar, "Not very good. Martin copy, made in Japan. Cheap."

"You sell things here?"

"You loan them. You give the guy your guitar and he gives you money and then if you come back, and pay, you get it back. Sometimes people buy the stuff, before you get back. Then you're out of luck."

She looked at the wheelchair in the window. It was the kind driven by a motor. It made her sad, a wheelchair in a pawn shop—which had nothing to do with chess, unless you understood that the function of a pawn was simply to advance the safety of the king. Her father liked to play chess. She said, taking Patrick's hand, "Let's go."

The door leading inside had iron bars and a bell which jingled. Patrick stepped inside and said to a man behind the counter, "Can my dog come in?"

The man had a huge gut and wore glasses and a fat gun on his hip in a decorated holster. He looked startled, then angry, "What," he said to Patrick, "you blind or something?"

"Nope."

"Then no fucking dog, buddy."

Patrick looked at Elizabeth, quickly. Then Patrick said, turning to the man, "It's hot outside. In the car. My dog's real good."

The man considered, drew his thumb across a countertop, measuring the dust. "He do tricks?"

"Lots. I'll make him lie down, right here. He won't bother anybody. Promise."

"I like a dog that does tricks. Like them right across the street," said the man, jerking his elbow toward the window, laughing. "Bring in your dog," he said. "But you gotta buy something."

Patrick put Germs on a down-stay, out of the way of the door, beside an old dresser. Then Patrick and Elizabeth looked at the cabinets which held all the guns. There was an old Gibson Hummingbird hanging up behind the counter, and Patrick asked the man how much he wanted. There was also some jewelry—dozens of wedding rings, some turquoise belt buckles and bracelets. The store was covered with dust, and grime; flies were everywhere. Behind a sofa, Elizabeth paused to look at a stove.

"It's the kind we used to have," she said. "When I was a little kid. Gas."

"Oh," he said.

But she knew he didn't understand what she meant. It was the same *brand*. The same stove they had in her kitchen when she was a little girl and her mother had spilled a pot of boiling water. She took Patrick's arm, and held him tight, which was something she liked to do even if he didn't understand. Once, in the back of his truck, while they were parked on top of South Mountain, kissing, he had asked her what happened. *Hey, what happened to your arm?* he said, and then she told him. Since they had only done a lot of kissing, he hadn't yet seen the skin grafts from her hip and thighs. But she told him there had been a lot of operations, in Michigan, and that was over now. *Fini,* she said, and the scars, besides, didn't hurt, even if you noticed them. It's not as if it had happened on purpose. It was an accident, she said.

"Hey," called the man from behind the counter. "You, Dog Man."

Patrick turned, smiling. He said back, "What?"

Germs growled, baring his teeth. Patrick gave his dog a look, one Elizabeth had never seen—sharp, and fierce—and Germs relaxed. She realized Patrick had more confidence than she, that he wasn't frightened easily. She turned with him toward the counter, feeling brave, taking Patrick's hand. A green bottle fly stood hovering over the gun on the fat man's hip.

"This," said the man, hoisting a harness onto the counter. It was a special harness, the kind used for a Seeing Eye dog.

"For your dog," said the man. "One in a million!"

"I'm not blind," said Patrick.

"Yeah," said the man, stepping around the counter. "But sometimes you *want* to be, if you see what I mean. So's you can be with your dog. Me, if I was an asshole, I'd a said no fucking way, no fucking way you bring that dog inside my establishment, and so he'd be out there in some car baking his brains out. See what I mean? Fried dog brains."

Patrick said, "How much?"

"How much? You think these grow on trees? You gotta be blind to have one of these suckers. You gotta get it through a prescription and such and then you gotta go through an agency! Them dogs, they cost thousands, and then you gotta get on a waiting list—"

"How much?"

"A hundred. Even. No tax, even."

"What if he comes back?" Elizabeth said.

"What if who comes back, missy?"

"The man who left it?" she said. "The blind guy who left it here?"

"Dead as a doornail. Not everyday somebody needs a blind dog leash. Been here for years. That's why I'm giving it to you for just a hundred-fifty bucks."

She said, "You said a hundred, mister."

"Price goes up. Time is money. You think about it, honey. You think about it."

"I'll take it," Patrick said. "Fifty bucks."

"One in a million!"

"Twenty," said Elizabeth, reaching into her jeans. Her father insisted she always keep a twenty for cab fare, or lunch, or an emergency. The bill was folded up into the size of a quarter. Now she began to unfold it, properly. She pulled it from both ends, tightly, and began to rub in on the counter to get the kinks outs.

"Twenty," said Patrick, shrugging his shoulders. "Time is money. Before the guy comes back."

"I told you he was dead."

"Yeah," Patrick said. "Right."

•   •   •

Gratias agimus tibi propter magnam gloriam tuam . . .

The *Coro,* this is what she lives her summer for, that and Patrick McConnell's breath on her neck. By late August it is finally time to perform the Mass, all three hours' worth, and she invites her mother, Lydia, and Fernando, her mother's lover, and her father, and of course she invites Patrick. She arranges to have seats for them in the fifth row, dead center, and the night of the concert it takes only a few moments to find them in the audience: her mother in a sandstone summer dress; and Fernando, in a tux, smiling lazily; and her father in his bola tie, westernlike; and Patrick, wearing a blue blazer, sitting right in between her parents, his arms crossed, his eyes concealed by a pair of dark glasses—and Germs, dressed up in his special harness, sitting at Patrick's feet. Patrick has sung the piece before, she's learned, in Chicago, long before she even met him. He knows the key passages which move her most. He loves the *Coro,* its relentless progressions, steps, its constantly ascending thirds. He also believes in God, and this comforts her, knowing that she is not alone, while Dr. Merick, white hair flying, leads her and the orchestra. And the choir, leading the audience, until eventually they are all corresponding with the living and the dead, the hallowed and the grave, by way of Johann Sebastian Bach, who is buried, she has come to learn, in Leipzig, Germany. It's a place in Eastern Europe neither she nor Dr. Merick is permitted to visit, on account of the cold war and the threat of nuclear bombs, on account of the iron curtain. She is wearing a white silk blouse and a thin, gold chain upon her wrist, which Patrick has given to her for her eighteenth birthday, and it's like a dream, and she just happens to be living it with a bracelet from her boyfriend, on her arm, providing anchor.

Afterward, the applause, and then later backstage the farewell to Dr. Merick, who actually hugs her . . . *Come and visit me in Connecticut, Elizabeth. Come and visit us . . .* and she comes to understand that she has nothing left to hide. She has only herself and this glorious faith to live by. Because the secret to understanding music is this: it always, always rises. She wants to tell Patrick . . . *alone, tonight. Tonight* . . . because she knows he'll understand precisely what she means. Meanwhile, they go to a coffee shop and drink coffee and sodas. Her mother, and Fernando, and her father and Patrick, and Germs, his tail thumping against the table—everyone is beaming, talking about her future as a flautist, which strikes her as a peculiar word even now. Sipping her coffee, she wraps both ankles around Patrick's foot. He sits shyly in the corner, pretending to be blind, so as not to arouse suspicion by the waitress, answering questions only when he has to. Her mother likes him, she can tell, if only because he's beautiful and kind. Her father does not think her boyfriend is beautiful, but certainly he likes him, always inventing new names to call him, and often shaking Patrick's hand. "Your McDoodlewiz has a fine grip, Lizzie," he'll say. Now Fernando says to Patrick, lazily, because that is Fernando's way, especially while fondling her mother's hand, "And Patrick, you are a maker of music, too? No?"

They laugh, because of the innuendo, and the severe degree of Patrick's blush. Everybody orders another round of coffee from the waitress and now, finally, a full hour and forty-five minutes after the applause has concluded, Elizabeth and Patrick are permitted to make their escape. She takes his arm to help guide him out of the restaurant, properly, the girlfriend of a blind man: in the parking lot, looking for his truck, Patrick releases Germs from the harness. Then Elizabeth takes Patrick's hand and puts it to her breast. Her blouse, she says, is made of silk.

"Here," she says. "Feel."

Later that night, with the rhythms of the *Coro* still in her mind, as well as her heart, she makes love to Patrick for the very first time. First they drive in his truck across town, talking, and then not talking, and then they are driving up and over Mummy Mountain . . . *I know where we could go, Patrick. If you wanted to* . . . and they drive to a house currently on the market for over half a million dollars. For this very purpose she has secured a key to the lockbox: the key

belongs to her father's closet, in the den, beside the filing cabinets
and maps and all the keys.

"Here," she says, using the key. "Inside."

Inside the lockbox rests another key: it's like music, the way a
night will open up. The night is sweet and hot, dark, like a blanket or an invitation. Inside, the house is empty, and they walk
across a tile floor, and then they are on a carpet thick as cream. On
a counter, near the kitchen, there is a sheet of paper beside a
night-light: on the sheet is a picture of the house, describing its
features, and in the upper right-hand corner is a picture of her
father, wearing the same bola tie, with the name of his brokerage
just beneath. Germs wanders into the center of a vast room,
beneath a chandelier, and lies down, thumping his tail.

"The lights," she says. "We'll have to keep the lights off. In case
of security."

"Nobody lives here?"

"Nobody but us."

They step through the sliding glass doors, out onto a vast deck,
surrounded by gardens. Meanwhile the pool is deep enough to
drown in: they find the switch, light it up, because in a pool like
this the light comes from within—visible only by a helicopter, or
God. The light will not carry, and now they are sitting on the
ledge, looking at the water, and the light which intersects and
binds up all the waves—like electricity, when you can see the currents traveling. She's sitting on the ledge, and she can feel the
sweat dripping down the backs of her knees, beneath her black
skirt; and she can feel the sweat on the back of her neck, beneath
her long hair; and behind her arms, bleeding into the white silk of
her blouse.

"Do you want to go swimming?"

"Swimming?"

"Yeah. You know . . ."

"I don't have a suit," he says, loosening his tie. "Trunks, I
mean."

She says, unbuttoning her blouse, "Neither do I."

"But . . ."

"Patrick. It's just us. Nobody has to know."

"I know but . . ."

"We don't have to do anything," she says. "We can swim. I want to see you. I want you to see me."

When she kisses him, she puts her hand in his lap, the hand which is scarred by skin grafts, and she is measuring the distance: this distance between them, and this pool, and the water all around—impossible to ground, these currents, impossible as the sky. And now, standing, Patrick begins to undress. First he folds his tie, and then his slacks. But she leaves her clothes to lie where they fall—a slip, a camisole—scattered about the deck, and then she leaps into the pool. Patrick says, looking at her, nodding, "I'm going to take off my shorts now."

"Okay."

Naked, she is waiting to be described. And she knows this is a moment meant to last: the water, the heat, the white patch of light on Patrick's throat. He stands now on the ledge, awkwardly; a naked man is hard to ignore, especially when you know you love him, and rising, she stands up on her own two feet. She rises from the surface of the water and opens up her arms and says to him, "Hurry. Hurry."

Speed, she has come to realize, is no longer of the essence, but the fact. And to hurry is to rush what simply is inevitable—namely, the future. One needs simply to measure her pace according to her own score. When her father asks her what time she came home, not meaning to intrude, she says, "Early. It was really, really early, Dad."

"You know I trust you, Lizzie."

She nods, reaching for her orange juice, thinking about all this. Patrick's mother trusts Patrick to betray her; apparently, she says this to him often. He will betray her the same as his sister, Caroline. Caroline lives in Massachusetts now, and Patrick doesn't know they've met: Elizabeth and Caroline, a meeting which represents one of the many secrets Elizabeth has kept from him. Probably—Elizabeth hopes, and for her sake—Caroline also has no idea they have previously met. When Elizabeth asks questions about Patrick's family, he always becomes embarrassed and evasive. Recently Mrs. McConnell has begun sending Patrick to the liquor store before he goes out on a date: once she has been fully supplied for the evening, only then is he free to leave. This semester Patrick is going to work the night shift . . . *graveyard. It'll be cool . . .* at the Shell station. This way, he'll be able to sleep when she does . . . *during the day . . .* which will prevent the need for conversation. *This way, we won't have to talk so much . . .* And Elizabeth knows the fights are brutal. Sometimes, while talking on the phone, she can hear Mrs. McConnell screaming in the background. Often she is simply wailing, as if at the moon.

Elizabeth says, looking up at her father, "Trust what, Dad? I mean, what do you trust me to do? Or not? Or not to do?"

He says, looking at his empty glass of juice, "Is this going to be one of those conversations? The ones where you start talking about philosophers? I mean I have an early appointment, Lizzie."

"I just don't know what that means exactly. Trust. Do you trust me not to hurt you? Do you trust me not to get into trouble? Do you trust me to do what I am going to do because that's just who I am. I mean, what if I do exactly what I'm going to do—true to myself, and all—and I end up getting arrested by the police and on the front page of all the newspapers which in turn ruins your business and you have to move out of town to Los Angeles?"

"To thine own self be true," her father says, kissing her on the forehead, preparing to depart. "I have to sell a condo."

She wonders what Patrick's father did, before he died. Patrick says he died from a sudden blow to the brain, but everybody knows his father killed himself. She says, "What I mean, Dad.

What I mean is, Dad, I would never, never hurt you on purpose. I would never hurt anybody on purpose. I hope."

He leans toward her chair and ruffles her thick hair. "I know that. You're growing up, is all." He picks up his keys, stops in the doorway and says, as if suddenly struck, "You're not pregnant, are you?"

"No," she says, laughing.

"I mean, it's okay. I mean, we'd figure it out."

"Dad, I'm not pregnant."

"Will you talk to Lydia about this? Sometime soon? Pills and whatnot?"

"We already have. I'm perfectly safe."

"I doubt that. Nobody's ever safe. You have to be careful."

When the garage door rises, she stands to look out the kitchen window. Her father always drives with two hands on the wheel; when he goes backwards, he relies strictly on his mirrors. Her father, she realizes, is a careful man. He looks sad, she thinks, and suddenly older. His hair is graying quickly. She understands, too, that he is lonely, and watching him, watching her father negotiate the corner of his driveway, bumping into the neighbor's mailbox, just slightly, lurching the big car into gear, she's glad to be his daughter. She's glad that she belongs to him. Love, she thinks, has made her capable of even more, and eventually she returns to her chair in the kitchen, and there she props her feet up and wraps her arms around her knees and sits very, very still—breathing: first in, then out. It's important to respect the center.

In the pool, when she reached for him, pressing her breasts to his body, he came instantly. He came up against her belly, and she could feel it, his semen—hot even against the cool water of the pool. He blushed, even while it was happening, and pulled back, apologizing, utterly mortified. Then she took her hand, scooping up a cloud of milky water. She held her hand up against the light from the pool, lit up from below, and said, *Look. Look. It's okay. It's the stuff of life. Honest . . .* and then he smiled, almost reluctantly, and she kissed him, and he put his mouth on her breast. His tongue felt electric, pointing there, tracing the shape of her nipple, and then the other, while she felt him rising, all over again, and then she led him inside her properly. On the steps, her arms splayed out across the deck, her ankles clasped around his spine, she felt her body draw him in. She felt herself locking on, into the heat, so that it became impossible to move, and not to. *Slow,* she whispered. *Oh, slow . . .* and after he came again she took his hand, and placed it just so, to have her say. *Here,* she said, guiding him, fucking their two hands, breathing, until she finally came— his thumb lifting her hood, as if by accident, lighting her up: simply she was full of blood and fire, and this sudden release caught them both by surprise. Her voice terrified him, she was certain, and then she was holding him to her breast, breathing in the scent of his hair and the pool. She wanted to explain she'd never come with somebody else. *I mean, not alone . . .* but she felt ashamed, saying that, as if she were defective, or complicitous, and then she started crying, she did not know why, and so he held her, in the cool water, the waves growing still all around them, because it was important to respect the center. Because it's important, she's telling herself, breathing, again and again, to make each one count.

8

These are the places we have made love: in the cab of my truck, and on the bed; in Elizabeth's swimming pool, as well as several others; on a blanket laid across the desert floor; and on the roof of her mother's house in Jerome, Arizona, overlooking the Mogollon Rim, under the sun. The blanket I carry in my truck was made by my grandmother for my father. It's a quilt, blue and white, tattered evenly and wearing thin. Spreading it out, here and there, Elizabeth calls it beautiful.

Caroline comes home for a visit, during which she does some shopping and I go out on dates and establish for her evidence that I am in fact growing up. I show Caroline a picture of Elizabeth I carry in my wallet. In it, Elizabeth has long, wild hair, which I explain reaches down past her waist, and I explain also that in the picture, though you cannot see it, Elizabeth is wearing a thin, gold chain I have given to her for her birthday. For homecoming, I explain to Caroline, I bought her a corsage—an orchid.

But now it is Thanksgiving, which we intend to celebrate, as well as make, and Caroline is thinner than before: she has been wearing jeans and a new V-neck sweater, navy, without a bra. Lambswool, she says when she catches me looking. *Very fine.* It's a dangerous visit, despite the spirit of the holiday; my mother, for example, insists on sharing it with her newly separated investment advisor, Big Jim Walenka: the guy who knows the senator, whose office, the senator's, refuses to return her calls. Still my mother likes the fact of Jim Walenka's Mercedes, often sitting in the drive. Jim's wife, after being struck last spring by a car, requires 'round the clock care; apparently she can barely feed herself, and then only soup. Closer to home, Caroline is spending too much time in the kitchen, where my mother often sits, fighting. My mother, drinking heavily, is angry with Caroline about her grades, which Caroline has refused to allow sent home, though privately Caroline tells me her grades, mostly As, are her business alone, as are the courses she takes. Also my mother is angry about the rips in Caroline's jeans, at the knees, and especially those in the seat; and like Elizabeth, and women in Europe, Caroline doesn't shave. My mother also says Caroline's hair is a mess and that she looks like a tramp. She says Caroline is trying to betray her father's memory.

"He loved you so," wails my mother, late one night.

Outside smoke is filtering into the cool air from neighboring chimneys. You can smell the smoke, which reminds me of sex, especially when I happen to notice, which is always, and the smoke reminds me of Elizabeth who is personally responsible for introducing me to the very fact of it. Smoke reminds me of sex because it must always have a source of heat, and because of the smell of it—creosote, and oak, and pine, burning into the dry night air. When my hands smell like sex, I spend a lot of time with them near my face, breathing in, the way a man who smokes will raise his hand to his nose, and inhale, when he cannot easily have a cigarette. At home I smoke cigarettes now, which has the additional effect of providing my mother with an alternate supply to her own.

I am sitting outside on the diving board, with Germs, smoking. It's something I can do: have a smoke. I also work at a gas station thirty-two hours a week. And I also go to high school and talk with Elizabeth and three of my six teachers. Meanwhile I play my guitar and dream about taking Elizabeth someplace with me and becoming famous as a singer, a songwriter . . . coming in over the air, making the radio come alive. Jim Walenka used to have a lot of money tied up in radio stations. Now he runs a branch of Jefferson Thrift, to which my mother has moved our trusts, Caroline's and mine, a move which has recently caused Jim to befriend me, warmly, on account of my being a fellow investor. Of course I have no idea how much I have invested, given that my mother holds the figures close.

Enough, she says, when she is sober. *You have more than enough.*

When she is drunk she says, *Your father left it all to you. I have just a pittance.*

At the same time, she continues to buy a lot of jewelry. She has had installed a new Jacuzzi, beside the swimming pool, and she has construction workers in the backyard making plans to build a tennis court. We never play tennis, not a one of us, but my mother says tennis is nonetheless a good investment. Maybe she will even learn to play. She is worried, she says, knowingly. She is worried about capital gains.

Caroline steps outside, onto the porch, lighting a cigarette. She wanders over to the diving board, where she straddles the board, like a guy, and begins to explain to me that our mom has been liquidating her own stock. She's been selling off her shares of AT&T and GM and Union Pacific and Motorola and IBM and Sears. My father liked to invest in places you could stay awhile, but Jim has ideas, and because of the liquidation, my mother has grown terrified of paying taxes on her capital gains: not inconsiderable, given that these shares have been in her name, the dividends reinvested, for well over a decade. To keep the federal government away from her due, Jim has explained, my mother should reinvest in her house: hence, the tennis court, and the plan to add on an addition, a fifth bedroom, when only two of us are living here, and despite what the neighborhood market will bear. Jim, Caroline explains, is going to manage the rest for her. He's also going to manage our trusts. He's going to put a lot of it in copper, the rest in a half-dozen LPIs.

"What?" I say.

"Limited Partnerships," Caroline says.

"Like a marriage," I say.

"Jim says he's going to go bottom fishing," Caroline said. "Dad hated fishing. He has no right to do that."

"He drives a Mercedes. He introduced Mom to the senator?"

"Dad spent a lifetime building up that inheritance. He never touched it. Not even for taxes. Remember that crappy house we lived in? At first?"

She means the house on Wilmington Street, in Illinois, before my father became a partner in the brokerage firm he was working at and bought a seat on the New York Stock Exchange. He was twenty-eight. I remember we could have ice cream only on Fridays, and then never a double scoop. I remember he made our mom drive a car from the fifties, a Chevy, and I remember that he always walked to the train, and that he always wore the same suit and became angry whenever our mom tried to dress him up. He had two pairs of shoes, wing tips, which were constantly being resoled. Then he loosened up, around the same time he stopped coming home at six and started making a lot of money, and then we bought a big house, in the country, North Barrington, and my mother became expansive: she joined clubs and went to parties and my father bought me a new bicycle for the heck of it. He bought us ponies, against our mother's initial protests, and then a couple quarter horses and years of lessons—a minibike, he believed, was far too dangerous. And I remember too that he put himself through college. In those days, he explained, you had to be smart to get into college, but he was poor—*grime-poor*, he called it—because his parents both were dead, as well as grime-poor . . . *Seaboard grime,* he'd say, *the kind that won't wash off . . .* and I remember that the initial inheritance—some twenty thousand dollars—came from a grandparent he had never even met. It arrived one week after I was born to the day. A windfall, he called it. Out of the blue.

Caroline is looking at me crossly. I say to her, because I don't want to think about it, "What's the harm?"

"She's sleeping with him, Patrick."

"Well, maybe."

"Maybe?"

"I don't know. I work at night. It's not like she's committing adultery or anything. She *is* single."

"If he's so smart, what's he doing in Phoenix? Why isn't he in New York, or Boston, or St. Louis? Why isn't he in San Francisco? He's slimy and he has no right—"

"You don't live here anymore. He keeps her happy. Happier. That's good for me, Caroline."

"She needs to open up some windows. Let in a little air. She needs to get out and see some people. Like an accountant. A tax accountant. And a lawyer, maybe."

"Uh huh."

"It's a trust, Patrick. We have to keep it safe. Don't you see? It's not hers. It's not ours even. It's the family's. And we have to keep it in the family."

"The family is fucked," I say.

Caroline lets out a laugh. "This one, yeah," she says, growing serious. "But not the next. You know it doesn't have to happen to the next."

Easy come, easy go. When I was born, the story goes, my father was elated. He wanted a son. On hearing the news, he borrowed a car from work and drove to Ingalls Hospital, where I was born, and which has since been destroyed, in Harvey, Illinois. To get to Harvey, you take Dixie Highway: from the very start, it would seem, race relations weren't meant to be very promising there. On the way to the hospital, my father drove the '57 Chevy, stopping at a liquor store, where he bought a fifth of Canadian whiskey, and where he then asked the man for ten dollars' worth of change.

In dimes, my mother always explained. *It had to be in dimes.* And on the way out of the store, my father beaming like a headlight, he was stepping into his car when he was jumped by three men. In the sixties, they were still called Negroes, and the three men, whom my father would later simply call *grime-poor,* jumped him hard. They hit him in the face and broke his nose, tore his lip to pieces. They kicked in three of his ribs. When he was lying on the ground, beside the old, beat-up sedan, his arms over his face, one man took a knife and held it to his throat and said, *Tell me why I shouldn't kill you?* To which my father replied, *My son.* Then my father reached into his back pocket for his wallet and handed it to the man with the knife. *Please,* said my father. *Please.* And then the man, who may have had his own children, put away his knife—*a switchblade,* said my mother, repeatedly—and left my father lying on the ground with a fifth of Canadian whiskey and a paper sack full of dimes. The wallet, my mother would always point out, greedily, was by then empty, and at the hospital, my father refused to see a doctor. Instead he went directly to the nursery, where a nurse pointed me out, and he stood there, holding his ribs, trying not to breathe for all the pain. I was lying on my back—stubborn, having put my mother through ten hours' worth of labor. And now, having had a sufficient glance, my father went to my mother's room, where she would be permitted to rest for a week, because my father had insurance, and when he came into her room, he poured them each a drink in coffee cups. It was time to make a toast. In the version my mother tells—each and every Christmas, and birthday—the cups were porcelain, and badly chipped. Certainly the whiskey must have stung his lip. Then, she says, always . . . then my father reaches for the phone. He sits on the floor, cross-legged in his shabby suit. He pours out his sack of dimes onto the floor and proceeds to call everyone he has ever known.

It's a boy, he says into the phone, lighting up a cigarette, inhaling. *It's a boy!*

The story, of course, is problematic. Once I saw my father beat two men to a bloody pulp: the men each required an ambulance, to be rescued, and my father certainly had not begged for mercy then: the long scar above his nose was, in fact, a direct result of this encounter. Clearly my mother was fudging details. And with this particular story of my birth, something besides my father's cowardice, alleged or otherwise, felt askew, though it took me years to realize what it was that didn't jibe.

I was seventeen, sitting in the kitchen, with my mother's lover Jim Walenka. Having just come home from the gas station, where I had been working all night, I caught him on the ledge of sunrise. I was still in my work clothes, and my shirt was streaked with blue ink over the pocket from my pen going in and out, writing up work orders and credit slips. In the kitchen I caught Jim fixing himself a cup of instant coffee. He seemed shocked to see me and said, checking his belt, "I just dropped by some papers. For your mother. Thought I'd—"

"Hi," I said, stepping through the garage door, looking for Germs. "It's okay. You're an adult."

"Don't you have school today?"

"Yep. Two hours. Where's Germs?"

"In your room. Your mother said he'd be happier there."

"Uh huh."

Jim said, yawning, "When do you sleep?"

"Afternoons. Sometimes in class. Depends."

I went to the fridge and reached for the orange juice. I set it on the counter, where the phone cord was tangled up, covering a pile of papers. My name was on some of the papers, along with the name *Jefferson Thrift*. I spilled some juice, looking at the papers, and then I reached for a towel, but I was sleepy, and clumsy, and when I reached my hand caught the phone cord and brought the headset crashing down onto the floor. The force of the crash caused the bell inside to ring.

"Mr. Walenka," I said, wiping up the mess.

"Jim," he said, being friendly. "Friends call me Big Jim." He was big, but most likely not in the way that he imagined: his gut was expansive, and his hair was thinning briskly, made worse by a pathetic weave, sewed crookedly into the scalp. You could see clumps of his hair in a comb he'd left sitting on the counter. He also needed a shave.

"Jim," I said. "You know in hospitals?"

"Yes," he said, earnestly, meaning to be my friend, reaching for his comb. "I mean, I've been to some."

"In hospital rooms, you know the phone? They don't make you pay for it, do they? I mean, you don't have pay phones in the rooms, do you?"

"Usually they bill you. If you make too many calls."

"So, if, like, I broke my leg, and wanted to call home—I wouldn't need a dime or anything?"

"No," Jim said, laughing. "No. The only time you need a dime is when you are in jail. Otherwise they bill you."

I went to the kitchen table and sat down. I sat very still holding my orange juice. There was grease from the station on my hands, and I smelled like sweat, and gas, and my wet boots were making my feet itch. Then Jim sat down across from me, with his instant coffee, stirring it, and said, "You drink coffee, Big Pat?"

"No. Thanks."

"I was thinking I could fix a cup, is all."

"No," I said. "Thank you."

"Your mother," he said, solemnly. "She's planning a nice Thanksgiving."

For Thanksgiving supper, Caroline refuses to dress up. My mother has ordered turkey and mashed potatoes and cranberries from a catering service. She pours wine liberally into her glass and also into Jim's. When I ask for wine, she says I am too young, then pours me a thimbleful. Caroline scoffs, and listening to Jim tell stories about his adventures in the banking industry, I decide he is mostly harmless. He makes my mother think about other things, like how to hide the fact of their intimacy, which is touching.

After Jim leaves, early, and to my mother's disappointment, Caroline and I do the dishes. Then my mother instructs us to place the china in the breakfront. When I pass Caroline a glass, it slips from between my fingers, or hers, and crashes to the floor, and my mother flares instantly. She flares wildly, her eyes flaming, and says, "Your father gave me that glass, Caroline. Why must you always seek to destroy his memory? In my house!"

"No," Caroline says, shaking her head. "No. You are not going to do this."

"Do what? Speak the truth? The unutterable?"

"Certainly not that," says Caroline. "Not in your house. We do not permit the truth in your house. We permit silence. And wine."

I can see Caroline pouring herself a glass. I believe she, too, is maybe drunk. My mother, of course, has been drinking steadily since September. In between glasses, she is either with Jim or else she is asleep, and everybody's safe; it's the refueling process which is becoming dangerous. Twice since Caroline has left for college I have physically tried to prevent her from killing herself. Pills, usually. Once my mother came home and claimed to have tried driving off a cliff.

Later I realized she hadn't been gone long enough to find one. But Caroline now is drunk, and I am fearful of the unexpected, so I kneel to sweep up the last of the glass. I duck into the hallway, beside the closet, out of firing range.

"You," says my mother to me. "You are leaving now? Have you betrayed me, too?"

"Betrayed you? Mom, no."

"You two. You always gang up on me. Always. Patrick, your sister is rude to my guest. She will not dress decently. She is a whore, Patrick. She sucks men . . . there!" Now she says, turning to Caroline, "Deny it. Deny the truth!"

"You are drunk."

"I read your diary! I had to. Your shrink made me find it!" she says that word, *shrink,* with absolute disgust.

"No," Caroline says, shaking her head. "No."

"Patrick," says my mother, tacking in the wind, "is that what you want? A sister like that? A sister who fornicates with animals. With anybody!"

"It's okay, Patty Mick," says Caroline, weeping. "It's okay," and now Caroline is stepping out through the door, spilling her wine. It's red wine, like a symbol, or a stain. I decide, right then, that I'd like some wine, too.

I reach for a water glass, pour it in. I say, gently, "You shouldn't have read her diaries, Mom."

"You, too," says my mother, bitterly. "You, too?"

"It's Thanksgiving, Mom. We're supposed to eat pumpkin pie and tell happy stories."

"I didn't kill your father. I didn't make him pull the Goddamn trigger. And I certainly didn't ask him to buy me a pony!"

It's an attack toward me now. The reference to *trigger,* and the stable where he pulled it. If I hadn't wanted to ride a horse like a cowboy, it never would have happened. I say, cautiously, "Nobody ever said you did."

"She," screams my mother, pointing outside. "She—"

I see my sister, out the window, holding herself with one arm. She is too thin to be outside in the night air alone. She is sipping her wine, now wiping her eyes with the back of her hand. She is my sister and I love her. Not the way I love Elizabeth, which is from the belly, and the mouth, but the heart: the center of my chest: the place which causes all the blood to circulate. The chest, I'm learning, can be a sturdy place. A vault, if you want to make it one, and I can feel myself turning, not for the first time, away from my broken-hearted mother. In seven, eight months, I shall be free to leave her for eternity.

Like St. Louis, or Berlin, it's a place I have not yet been to.

• • •

Hours later Caroline and I are sitting by the pool, dressed in thick sweaters to protect us from the night chill, the bottle of wine between us. My mother's light is on, though we believe by now she is asleep. "Passed out," I say, a phrase that I am learning.

Caroline says, nearly a whisper, "You getting some? A lot?"

"Caroline," I say, shrugging. "It's Elizabeth."

"She's pretty," Caroline says. "She'll tear your heart."

"Break," I say.

"No. Tear. Yours is too strong to break. Beside, tearing hurts more."

"She makes me feel strong."

"Oh?"

"Not like that. I mean, she makes me feel like I can do things. Like Dad doesn't count. Like it's okay Mom's crazy."

"She's getting worse. Duane says that's what happens. To addicts. They slide and get worse unless confronted. He's a recovering addict, too."

Duane is her theology professor. He's married. He also wants to be a stockbroker. He wants to make some money for a change and stop being around undergraduates. Caroline is an undergraduate, but this she says doesn't count, because she is so experienced. *At living,* she says, meaning she's grown up. "Like you," she says to me. "Just like you."

I say, "I thought you weren't supposed to drink."

"Wine doesn't count. It's good for you, too," she says, finishing off the bottle, which is vast. "Here's to wine."

I realize I'm a little dizzy. I believe I am squinting one eye to help me focus.

"You know," Caroline says, "I just came home to say good-bye. To you, Patty Mick. I didn't want to tell you on the phone."

"Good-bye?"

"I'm not coming back. Not here. Not while she's alive."

"It's not a very nice house. It's always dark."

"It's an ugly house. It's empty. There's no light. Why is she building an addition?"

"Saves energy," I say. "I don't know."

"You can always buy that kind of energy. No, it's hers," Caroline says, looking at the porch light. "It's hers . . . she wants to kill me, you know. Not *really* kill. I'm not paranoid. I mean she will not be happy until I'm gone. And you know why? Why? Because I know. I knew it then and I still know it and now you do, too. I told you."

"Maybe she didn't mean to."

"I saw her look up the phone number. I heard her speak politely. You know, the charm? I listened to her explain and then she hung up the phone and said, It's for his own good, Caroline. This will make him a decent man."

"She was mad."

"She wanted to hurt him. To maim him. Ruin his career. Make him dependent on her. Just what she does to us. But you know, Patty Mick, we don't need her money. And once you're twenty-one you won't even need her signature. You can take out loans against your trust. That's what Uncle Punch says. It's up to us."

"No."

"I don't mean you should leave. I mean you should know you always can. Just knowing," she said, shaking her hair. "I'm leaving. I'm not coming back. But I am not deserting you. She's going to claim I left you. She's going to say how this is because I hate you and am jealous, et cetera. But that's not it. You have to know that. She can not divide us."

"Okay."

"No. You have to know that."

"I'm drunk," I say. "Is this what it feels like?"

"Swear it. You always have me. No matter what happens."

"I swear."

"Swear you'll always be nice to Elizabeth."

"What?"
"Swear you'll always be nice to her."
"Okay. I swear."
"No matter what. Even when she tears your heart."
"Swear."

The next day, early on, my mother starts another fight with Caroline. The fight lasts for hours and by eight my mother has called the police, to take Caroline away, because Caroline is trying to take over her house, whatever that means. Before the police can arrive, I drive Caroline to the airport, where she intends to wait for her flight. I give her sixty dollars, most of my last paycheck, for cab fare and meals. Because I have to work, I can't wait with her; also, and increasingly, I am eager to be alone. The airport is busy and crowded and bright, giving me a headache: being with my family makes me sad. Meanwhile, Caroline says, tiredly, her plane will not be leaving until seven the next morning. She'll sleep on the big chairs by the gate. At the airport, she hugs me, fiercely, and then she sends me on my way.

Later at work, in the middle of the night, ducking beneath two cars up on the racks, I am scrubbing down the bays. I wait to do this after the bar-closing rush. Tide, evenly distributed across the floors, the racks up, the hoses all wiped down with solvent and coiled away, the tire machine tidied up . . . at night I become a model of efficiency. Meanwhile my boots are soaked, my pants—gas station issue—are damp up to the knees, while the soap foams beneath the wide broom and makes the floor slick and almost clean. Germs is sleeping in the office, protecting me.

When Bittner steps in through the back door, the one we drive the tow truck through, he calls out to me. First, I am startled; I have been singing to myself, a song about stars and moons. I've borrowed the melody slightly from an old James Taylor song. I try and lilt my voice like Cat Stevens, but I sound more like Paul

Simon, actually . . . or a dork. Mostly I have been pretending once again I'm famous.

"Caught you jacking off," Bittner says, laughing. He's in street clothes with a fancy gold chain around his neck; in the distance, I can see his hopped-up blue Camaro, recently repaired, sitting in the back. He pries open a six-pack and tosses me a beer. To catch the beer, I have to let go my broom.

"I have to rinse," I say, pointing to the floors.

"Of course," he says. "Hey, dog."

Germs thumps his tail. I hang the broom on the wall beside the calendar with two naked girls advertising gaskets. I have been known to look at this calendar more than I probably should. Fuller is also known to have spied on us with binoculars, from across the street, to make sure we are not stealing, and also to make sure we are keeping our dicks inside our pants. Some guys will stick a radiator hose down their pants; they'll wait on a lady with a lot of kids and scratch their leg, just like an itch. Also, if you get in a car, and go up on the hoist, it's impossible for anyone to see you. I think, too, the beer must be a test, to see if I am loyal, a person of good behavior. I turn the water on as a truck pulls into the self-serve.

"We'll watch him," Bittner says, pulling on Germs's tail, a dangerous thing to do. "You rinse."

Bittner sets what remains of the six on the ledge of the brick flowerbed, and I whistle Germs in because I don't like him on the lot. Except for Elizabeth, whom I want Germs to protect, I don't like Germs hanging out with people who don't know how to work him. Now I light myself up a damp cigarette and hose off the soap while Germs returns to the office. Then I begin to squeegee the floors to keep the soap from staining. Fuller has promised me a ten-cent raise if I keep working out so well. Usually you have to be with the station for more than a year to get your first raise. Presently I am making two thirty-five an hour, plus seven percent on tires, three percent on hoses and belts. You have to mount the tires yourself, otherwise it doesn't count. What I have learned is there is order to a well-run station.

When Bittner returns, he asks for my key. We walk out to the center island, pop the drawer together, and I count him change for the cigarette machine—Standard Operating Procedure. When I close the drawer, it pinches my finger, as always. He wanders toward the cigarette machine, and now, picking out his flavor, Bittner says, "You gonna drink that beer or not? I brought it over special."

"Nope. It'll make me sleepy."

He looks at me, leaning up against the flowerbed, deciding if I am in fact a coward; he is, after all, the guy who trained me, and one thing I do not want to be is a disappointment. The air is full of engine grease and soap and the sweet scent of clean motor oil. He offers me a cigarette from his pack.

"In Europe," he says, "that's how it's done. It's rude, you know, to have a smoke and not offer one to everybody else. I saw it in a movie. Before you light, you have to share. Also you are supposed to make a toast. Before you drink."

I put fifty cents into the soda machine and pick root beer, but it's really cream soda, which still tastes a little like root beer if you don't think about the cream.

"You know, Mac, that time I beat you up, it wasn't personal. I mean, if I'd known you, it wouldn't have even happened. I mean, you're an okay guy."

I realize he's not really drunk, but drugged—he's sloppy and alert at the same time. One good thing about being around loaded people is knowing they can't tell if you are loaded, too. Still, I am not about to start drinking on the job, even if it is for only two thirty-five an hour plus, et cetera.

"I have school tomorrow," I say, meaning to be polite.

"School. Yeah, I suppose," he says, though he has long since graduated. "Had a close one down at the river bottom. You know. Danger."

"Oh," I say. "It's good you are okay."

"You have a sister, don't you?"

"Yeah. She's in college."

"I didn't know you had a sister. When I beat you up, I mean. I thought you were a single child."

"Child?"

"Kid. No family. Orphan. Like most of us."

"She lives in Massachusetts," I say.

"I didn't know that. She's a nice girl, I'll bet. Like Elizabeth. Nicest girl I've met. Little handicapped—that arm thing of hers. Still. And if a guy does something, like kicks the shit out of you before he knows you properly, it doesn't mean he'd go and do it again after he got to know you. Know what I mean? If a guy's an asshole that doesn't mean he's an asshole just because he made a mistake."

"Not unless he keeps on being an asshole," I say.

He crushes his beer can, which is aluminum, and not that big a deal. "You're tough, Mac. Want another?"

I hold up my cream soda and shake my head. "My sister, she's still upset about my dad. He died."

"Blew himself away."

I'm shocked, actually. I thought I had been keeping it a secret, like how much you have in your savings account, or the amount of time your sister has spent inside the Superstition Mountain Care Facility.

"Secret, huh," Bittner says. "Don't worry, I'm not telling. Though you should know the whole world—well, town, anyway, knows all about it. That's why Fuller hired you. Said he felt sorry, you coming around in your red Izod and blue corduroys every day. Said you needed some looking after. Said you'd be responsible."

"You told him?"

"Look, your old man does himself with a shotgun, even if it's in another state, word's going to get around. Your mom's gonna call the school principal, in case you get detention and start crying and whatnot. Then the principal goes and tells the vice one, and he tells your History teacher, and while she's doing it with Miss Fergusan the lesbian, after pizza and pop, nobody remembers anymore it's supposed to be a secret. Hell, after our little fracas, everybody stopped talking to me for a week. Said I was demented. Like you were cursed, Mac. Like you were dangerous to talk to. 'Course, personally, I don't go in for that curse shit. That's just fat girls looking to be talked to in the parking lot. Know what I mean?"

"Danger," I say. "Living on the edge."

"Absofuckinglutely."

I am surprised to learn that Miss Fergusan, my favorite teacher, is a lesbian: to the best of my knowledge, I have never met one, but each afternoon, at 1:38, she teaches me trigonometry. Meanwhile I step inside the bays. The floors are dry now; I've done a good job scrubbing. All that's left is to bring the cars up on the racks down to earth. Bittner steps over to the far hoist's lever, the one held together with part of a wire coat hanger, leveraging the seal.

"Hey," he says. "Let's race."

I grab my lever, pull, listen to the air from the compressor begin to leak. My car is lighter, though—a '73 Datsun wagon, in for a lube and flush. Bittner's hoist has a brand-new Pontiac Grand Am, which is silver, and looks just like the brand-new Buicks and the brand-new Oldsmobiles. Inside, under the hood, is the Iron Duke, a six-cylinder which is supposed to make Americans not feel too badly about the rising price of gas.

"No more V-8s," Bittner says, sadly.

"Yep."

"I need your help, Mac."

His car has almost reached the bottom, and even though I know that my car will not win the race, I don't latch the lever. Instead I stand there, hanging on, watching the cars descend. Except for my sister, I don't believe anybody has ever asked me before for help. It's a sign of friendship, I think. Of trust. My father couldn't trust anybody, which is why he blew his brains out. It's a new formulation for me, worth testing.

The hoists land, the cars settle on their springs. The station feels much more crowded now. To protect the wheels, we kick in beneath the cars the heavy metal stays; the metal, striking the cement, echoes throughout the garage. Then I follow Bittner out to his Camaro, where he opens the passenger door, and sits, his legs hanging out onto the pavement. He reaches beneath the seat and pulls out a pistol.

"It's loaded," he says, handing it to me.

I take the gun, which weighs about the same as a pocket dictionary. I make sure my hands don't go near the trigger.

"Thirty-eight," he says. "Take it everywhere. Not registered."

"Yeah," I say, nodding, oblivious.

He takes the gun back, opens the cylinder, spins it. "With a revolver, you don't get the speed. But you don't blow cartridges all over the place either. Automatic, you fire it, your empty rounds are ejected. You have to pick them up. With a revolver, they stay put, you empty them later and the cops don't get them."

I light a cigarette. The lights from the station make the parking lot especially blue. I realize he is discussing the nature of ballistics.

"Sometimes I run into danger," he says.

"In Tempe," I say. "The river bottom."

"These folks. They're fucking wild. They're crazy. I just want somebody . . . you know . . ."

"Somebody you can trust."

"Yeah. Somebody who's not a fuckup. Me, most of the guys I know, they're fuckups, same as me. But you. You're different. You're not even cursed. Believe me, I ought to know."

Drugs, I'm thinking, and of course I know that I am right. Bittner is the kind of guy who's going to want to make a deal. He's the kind of guy who's going to pull things off. Secretly, I am thrilled, and elated, and terrified all at once. Secretly I know that I am on the verge of becoming bad.

"Of course," I say, polishing off my cream soda. "Sure thing."

9

Having been used, her body feels good, as if it has a purpose. She has a fine bicycle, the wheels recently trued. After the first few miles, she always finds her stride; she can open up her mind and listen to the wind blow. Locomotion, she knows, is what causes energy and the possibility for the body to generate its own heat and speed and, when cold or otherwise necessary, wind resistance. What she likes most is going fast. The song goes, *Come on everybody* . . .

Her sweats are soaked; her calves, tight. Leaning her bike against the garage, she kicks off her sneakers and catches her breath. The air is still cool: late November, in Phoenix, with the sky hanging overhead, predictable as weather. In the backyard she rolls her bicycle up against the wall and turns on the switch to the Jacuzzi. Once inside she leans back into the heat, and steam, which is almost unbearable, but not quite, and she begins to pull off the wet layers of her clothes. First, the socks, which she peels off gratefully, a second skin, and then her sweatshirt. The clothes pile up beside her on the pool deck, and now she begins to stretch her thighs. She loves the feeling of a good stretch. Sometimes, late at night, she will hear her father out here, turning on the motor, taking a dip. Usually he is unbearably sad, or angry, depending.

She is not talking with her father again because he is angry with her; she did not remember to give him a message—Flip, at the

105

office—though she *did* remember, albeit only after being asked. Flip—her father's partner, a friend from college—used to be a lifeguard: another life, her father says. *We were young then.* Now Flip is overweight and looking to buy a home on Mummy Mountain. Before Carter came into office, Flip was an important person at Greyhound, which her father says is about to sell off its entire bus line—because of airplanes . . . *Who wants to spend a night in a bus terminal only to go fifty-five miles per hour?* Now Greyhound will strictly make soap—*Dial*—and hot dogs—*Armour*—and Flip has since changed careers and bought into her father's brokerage. Flip, her father explains, received a generous severance package, which is what people give you when you're fired on your forty-fifth birthday, to keep you from suing, during moments of scaling down, which Flip apparently could use a lot of. He really does eat a lot, and whenever she meets Flip, she pretends, in order to make things more bearable, that this will be the very last time. Mostly, and even with his wife standing nearby, sipping her wine, gazing at a wall, Elizabeth feels Flip's eyes wandering all over her. Lifeguards are used to gazing at the body, she thinks, especially one which at any moment might find itself in jeopardy. If you can catch a man's eye, she is learning, you can see most everything he wants to.

"Lizzie," her father said. "Did Flip call?"

She was in the den, putting away her flute; she had just been practicing, nothing special. Lately her playing felt terrible—manufactured and old hat, absolutely uninspired. To inspire is to breathe life into. Tonight she was supposed to have a date, a special night-before-Thanksgiving, because Patrick would be working through the weekend.

"Dad," she said from the den. "I forgot. He called this morning."

"He's been trying to reach me all day."

"Then he shouldn't have called you at home," she said.

"What's that supposed to mean? Just what's that supposed to mean?"

It was your ordinary kind of fight, the kind which ends up hurting people's feelings, especially those you love. She even said cruel things to him about her mother—his ex-wife—and he campused her, for sassing back, as if she were a farm girl.

"I don't sass," she screamed, slamming her bedroom door.

Actually she had hoped to break it—the door—she was that mad, mostly at herself. She was the one who had screwed up, even if Flip was a pervert. With a name like Flip, what else could he be? It made her sad, knowing that her father went to places . . . *drinks, the club?* . . . with a man named Flip. It was the kind of name rich people liked to call themselves, even if they had been fired, and were lecherous. If she were a bad girl, as in *evil*, she knew what she could do to him. At the next cocktail party in her living room . . . she could stroke him, just so, ever so slightly. She could whisper something to his wife. She could even say something to her father, who is angry with her, mostly for screwing up his messages.

"It's the kind of thing that ends up costing money," her father had said. "Sloppy communications."

Like alimony, she thought, which by design is meant to be expensive, as well as punitive for fucking up. Like Fernando and her mom, on top of the Mogollon Rim, holding hands and humming like a radio, which relies strictly on the atmosphere to carry all its messages. If her mother marries Fernando, which she won't, because she no longer believes in institutions, like marriage, or the Catholic Church . . . but if, just in case, if her mother marries a man named Fernando, then Elizabeth knows her father will be hurt. He is already lonely. That's why he goes with Flip to the club. The thought causes her to wince, as if she has been struck. In the Jacuzzi, days after their argument, her arms stretched out onto the deck, the thought of her father's loneliness causes her to wince mostly because she has a bicycle she could ride to France. She has a backyard, and plenty of school clothes, and perfect health. Because years ago her father fell in love with a girl who made his heart skip, and then he was left alone, all by himself, because somehow everything had changed, just like that. Because Elizabeth has, she understands, what her father has since lost, and it terrifies her now, quite suddenly, knowing just how it is done.

She has a new sweater, one she purchased with impunity, a gift from her father designed to improve communications. He gave her a hundred-dollar bill and told her to go shopping. "Buy yourself something nice," he said. "Something that will last. It's the biggest sale of the century!"

Quality, says her mother. "Quality always counts, Lizzie. Even if you can't afford it."

She went to the shopping plaza, downtown Scottsdale, by bus, where developers were building a huge indoor mall with air-conditioning. There were shops all along the parking lot. Shops for boots, and for purses, and shops for clothes that look casual but still make you look just like a fashion model. She went instead to the big department store named after the senator's family who wanted to bomb Vietnam with nuclear warheads. Of course that was a long time ago, and it's not as if he ever was elected president. On the bus she had sat by a man with one leg who explained all this to her. The man was on methadone, he explained. He had been a sergeant. He used to go into Cambodia, top secret, to re-educate people, and to kill them, and then he stepped onto a mine and his leg blew up. Instantly, said the man. For years the man had not been permitted to tell anybody where it happened, because it was a secret, the fact of his being in Cambodia. America should have never lost the war. He said we should have nuked Cambodia, too. "Hell," he said, pointing to her arm, "I got burns, too. Burns you could not imagine!" At her stop, she said good-bye to the sergeant, who smelled like urine, and shit, and stepped gratefully off the bus into the daylight.

"End of the line," he called from behind. "Eh?"

Inside the crowded department store, she felt lonely, and guilty, as if she should have been more polite: as if she should have never noticed. All he needed was a bath and a decent prosthesis; all he needed was a little love. She was looking at the sweaters, marked down, after having been previously marked up, like places on a map, when she saw the girl with red hair: Caroline McConnell. Caroline was wearing jeans torn at the seat and a green silk blouse. She was leaner than Elizabeth remembered. Then Caroline caught her eye, looking.

"I know you," she said to Elizabeth.

"Me?" said Elizabeth.

"I know you," she said again. "You're in love with my brother."

For a moment she felt relief; she hadn't been fully recognized. "You're home from school? You're Caroline?"

"For Thanksgiving," Caroline said, nodding. "Home for the holidays."

"Patrick said you were coming. He was really happy."

"He's working."

"I know."

She meant it to feel encouraging, for the sake of conversation. Elizabeth ran her hand through the fabric of a sweater, which was fine and light. A clerk stepped up to Caroline, breaking an unbearable pause. "Tomorrow," said the clerk, officially, "the price goes back up." Then the clerk turned to Elizabeth. "We're awfully busy today. May I help you?"

"No. Thank you," said Elizabeth, because she knew what she wanted.

Caroline looked at the clerk, waiting for her to leave. Elizabeth watched a married man nudge up against Caroline, looking for a bargain, his ring flashing in the bright light. Then Caroline reached across the counter and took her hand. Caroline looked at Elizabeth's hand, briefly, the thin bracelet on her wrist, and then Caroline said, pulling Elizabeth around to the side, behind some coats, "Don't tell him."

"What?"

"You can't tell him. What happened."

"I didn't think you'd remember," Elizabeth said.

"Of course I remember. I was cold."

"No," Elizabeth said. "I meant me. I didn't think you'd remember *me*. I called the police, that's all. I was just there."

Caroline let go of Elizabeth's hand. She watched it fall, brushing Elizabeth's hip. "It's not that simple," Caroline said. "That's why you can't tell him. About what happened. Promise me."

"Okay."

"No. Promise me you'll take it to the grave. Please?"

"I promise."

"It was my fault," Caroline said. "It was everybody's fault. I was stupid. You see I'm trying to forget."

"You were raped."

"No. Actually I was fucked out of my mind, which is a lot worse."

"I know them," Elizabeth said. "Some of them. Who were there—"

"I know you do. Look, it's over, I'm better. I just came home to say goodbye. Patrick loves you," Caroline said, smiling. "He keeps showing me your picture."

Loves me? Then what is the difference between a secret and a promise? She saw the man with the wedding ring, gazing longingly at Caroline's hair. Caroline's skin was Irish-pale, lit with freckles, a small crease by her mouth—pale, pale green eyes. Looking, Elizabeth thought about intent, and consequence, and the secrets she has kept from those she loves, especially Patrick: those things she has never told him—the cocaine, the sex, the strict nature of humiliation, often public. Once she went down on a boy she did not like in a movie theater. Afterward, there was popcorn in her hair, and she smelled like butter: was this something to be ashamed of? Was this something she was born later to regret? Standing there, looking at her boyfriend's sister, who most certainly also understood the nature of sin . . . *separation from God, a state not irrevocable* . . . she knew she was going to keep her promise.

Because she was in love with Patrick, she was almost certain, and at that very moment, shifting her balance, glancing at Caroline's wrist, she understood she was going to be in love with others, too. Because to be in love is to not cause any harm, or damage, even when it is no longer possible; because love means the damage is now at hand. Then she asked Caroline what time it was, and in the department store, walking away, Caroline stopped, turning on her heel, beaming with an afterthought. "You know," Caroline said, smiling. "You know you're very pretty."

"Thank you," Elizabeth said, which seemed to be an awful thing to say.

It's not as if she'd had anything to do with it. Hours later, at home, looking into the mirror, her new sweater smelling like a treasure, better than perfume, really, which tended to make her sneeze . . . her sweater smelled like a fresh ream of paper, like clean air near a lake . . . and now, hours later, Elizabeth poses into the mirror. First one way, then another. To her consternation, she still looks quite like a girl, not yet a woman. She is thin, not at all busty. Her long hair often requires ribbons, as well as hours each week worth of brushing. With the sleeves tapering down to her wrists, you can see the scars from her burn only across the top of her hand, which she has learned to disguise only when she wants to: one hand, across her body, holding onto the other. Or one hip cocked, her hand tucked into the seat of her jeans. Sometimes, when she's with Patrick, she watches the way her hand looks, brushing his hair, or stroking his body, and sometimes her own. She loves her body mostly because it is hers to do with as she pleases, and because most of all she likes to please. According to her mother, it's her nature . . . *You like to please, Lizzie* . . . and she loves the way she can make it feel: her body, as well as her mind. On her bicycle, in the Jacuzzi—so long as she works it hard, she loves to give it rest, and it amazes her, the fact of her body and her mind, joined so solemnly to the quick. *Thank you,* she had said to Caroline, as if she had a reason. *You are, too.*

•   •   •

The boy she used to date, the one who went to a community college, and later died—his name was Joel. He was several years older and smoked a lot of weed. Sometimes he'd ask her to steal for him: bills from her father's wallet; a jeans jacket from a clothing store; a candy bar from the Circle-K; once even a car. They were in a parking lot, walking by a station wagon, its engine running. Joel said, putting his arm around her, "Go ahead. She's all yours."

"No," she said. "You want it? You take it."

She had given him money, most of which had been blown on drugs. She had even stolen for him Hershey bars, as well as clothes he never wore. But that day, having made that particular formulation, she understood she was going to become a better person. *Take only what you want.* Of course, you'd also have to be responsible, at least to yourself, and she understood she had no reason whatsoever to be with this guy. He was not her heart's desire. He was just a prick. He was mean-spirited and vain. He didn't even like to bathe, and when he did, he smothered his body with cheap cologne—as if he were a gift, or some rare, exotic flower. Actually her father was right, he was just a punk, even she knew it, and so she asked Joel, nicely, to leave her alone. There were other fish in the sea . . . *okay? Honest, it's just not right* . . . and then, six months later, he died, while drunk, screwing around with a hot-wired Bobcat on a vacant lot. His mother called her, late the next day, to explain just what had happened; even with his neck snapped in half, he lingered for several days in intensive care. While he was there, Elizabeth sent a card, and then Elizabeth saw the notice for the funeral, to which she never went. She was sad he had died, of course, and she had prayed for his soul; and she had felt terribly for his family; but still she wasn't about to miss him. After all, with him she had done things which degraded and made her feel obscene—things she would be ashamed of until she died, or could forget, and Elizabeth did not want to forget anything. And so, after he died, she had wept, privately, and then she went to Mass.

Today, when her father comes home from work, she is reading in his study. Beside his bookshelf stands a new table, joining the edge of his desk, on which rests a dozen Neil Diamond albums and an Apple computer. Lately her father has begun teaching himself VisiCalc . . . *a spreadsheet, Elizabeth. It does all the math!* . . . which he believes is going to revolutionize the world. All those numbers, clear as day, lit up in view. "People will know more," her father says. "More things will count. Do you see? Count!" And then he'll make a demonstration, with her allowance, in order to illustrate the effects of compounding interest.

Just ten dollars at ten percent for, say, eighteen years . . . it all adds up. Sitting in his study, in the big chair, first she tried to read some poetry by Emily Dickinson, being in the mood. Then she saw a novel which had a lot of spies and mayhem in it and which turned out to be less interesting than the poetry. She also likes to read certain passages in a certain novel her father keeps tucked in the bottom drawer of his desk, beside the VisiCalc instruction manual—a fine, dark hair, marking her place. Reading, she has discovered, turning the pages, was simply meant to turn you on, like a switch.

"So," said her father, stepping inside the room. "Did you shop well?"

"Yes," she said, looking up from her book. "I'm sorry I messed up your message. I forgot, Dad."

"I know."

"I'll try to be better. I didn't mean those other things, either."

"Show me what you purchased, Lizzie."

"This," she said, pointing to her sweater. "This. It's *indigo*."

"Indeed. Very chick, dear. How was the bus?"

"Okay. I sat next to a Vietnam veteran who said we should have nuked the place."

"Indeed," says her father. He says, making a drink, "What kind of car do you think you should have?"

"Car?" she says, her heart quickening. "What do you mean?"

"You can't keep borrowing mine. Your mother thinks you should be able to come visit more easily. Her living on Mount Kilmanfujero and whatnot, that means you need some transportation. This isn't a particularly good decade for automobiles, though. So I was just wondering, off the top of your head, what kind of car do you think you should have?"

"You're going to buy me a car?"

"No," he said. "You want a soda?"

She shook her head yes. He popped a can, scooped some ice into a glass. He handed her the soda, and the glass, and then he dropped a slice of lemon into the glass, the way she liked it.

"Dad?"

"No, I am not going to buy you a car. I am going to buy myself a car. Then I'm going to let you use it. It will be mine. You will say, This is my Dad's car. He doesn't like to drive it very much."

"Why?"

"Because I like my car just fine."

"But why can't I call it *my* car, if you don't mind me asking?"

"Because you are too young to have a car. I mean what, are you going to pretend you bought it? I think not. And if you didn't buy it, that means somebody had to give it to you, and I'm not going to let you become some spoiled little girl who runs around with fancy presents just because you have guilty parents. You are not getting a car because we feel guilty. You are not getting a car because I want you to forgive me for something I have not done, like an affair, or something, because God knows I've never had an affair in all my life. Not even with your mother. Certainly not with somebody named Fernandina."

"How come?"

"Look—" he says, sitting at his desk, kicking up his feet. "You are getting a car because you need one in this day and age. We live ten miles from the nearest grocery store, for Christ's sake. But you will not be spoiled. I won't have it. And if you behave as if you are spoiled I will buy you a six-year-old brown Chrysler station wagon and give you license plates with your name on them."

"I won't be spoiled," she says. "I promise."

"No," he says, shaking his head, "you probably are. But it hasn't seemed to do you much damage. We should go shopping. It's the season, you know. End of the year inventories."

"I want a small car," she says. "One that's economical."

"There's the spirit."

"And a tape deck. Please?"

Her father says that locomotion—by which he means the iron horse, and not a song to dance to—tamed the Wild West. Personally, she prefers to dance, and that night, long after her father is asleep, alone, perhaps dreaming of an affair with an exotic woman, whom she hopes is warm, for his sake . . . that night Elizabeth sneaks out to the garage for her bicycle. Riding along Doubletree, and later 64th Street, she feels almost breathless. The night is spooky, not quite dark, full of ghosts. At one place, a truckful of boys hurls a bottle of beer, smashing right beside her, the glass spraying. Later another car slows to follow her, while she cuts through a one-way street, and then a vacant lot, disappearing into a parking lot on Scottsdale Road. Once she hits Shea, she's pushing hard, and she can make out the station lights, clear as day.

"Hey, honey," says a man, waiting for the light.

She rides in from the back entrance, resting her bike against a brick wall, beside the restrooms and drinking fountain. Patrick's truck is inside the station, where he has probably been working on it: for some reason, he changes the oil every two thousand miles. The paint is gleaming, glazed under the hard fluorescent light, and smells like fresh wax. Stretching, she waits to catch her breath, so as not to scare him, though still her heart is beating fast—refusing to settle down, as if on purpose. She takes a long drink of water.

Germs finds her, his tags jingling in the night, his tail wagging, and she feels instantly safe, if not a little silly. In the office, Patrick sits at the desk, tapping a pencil to his forehead, doing trig problems. Beside him rests a long, heavy wrench Patrick uses to protect himself. Eventually, he looks up, surprised.

"Hi," he says.

"Hi."

"I'm just doing homework."

"Guess what?"

"What?"

"My dad's going to buy me a car." This isn't what she meant to say, but she's hoping it will explain her breathlessness. "Rode my bike," she says, waving her hand. "There're some fucking assholes out there at night."

He stands, stepping over to her. "You okay?"

"Yeah," she says. "I mean, now I am."

He kisses her. Because his clothes are full of grease, she knows he will not put his arms around her.

"For college," she says, petting Germs. "When I go. He wants me to go out of state."

"Where?"

"I don't know. My mom says I should go to Pomona, like she did, and cut my hair."

"Where's Pomona?"

"In California. It's liberal."

"That's not far way. California. I can come visit."

"From college?"

"Maybe I won't go," he says. "It's not as if it's going to make me a better guitar player or anything. Maybe I'll go to law school, if I go. Later on. I don't know."

She takes her hand and undoes a button on his shirt. Then another. "Here," she says. "It's okay."

"What kind of car?"

"Dad says you should come help. He doesn't know anything about them."

"Yeah. Sure," he says, beaming. "I mean, okay."

Usually when he gets hard, he becomes embarrassed. She can feel him now, his body, pressed up against her own: his skin smells salty and dry, like the desert air just before a storm. The vein on his cock, once full of blood, is likely to explode: sometimes she can feel it, beating like a heart, right inside her. She takes his hand and pulls him toward his truck. "You're not very busy," she says. "Are you?"

"Well. I guess not."

She opens the door of his truck, steps inside, where it's cavernous. The gear shift is nearly two feet long.

"Wait," he says, shutting her inside.

He turns to the lever for the hoist and pulls it back. She hears a knocking begin—the compressor, a machine—and then she feels the truck begin to rise. She can see her boyfriend, standing by the lever, and then as the truck rises, and she is looking out the windshield, slowly he begins to disappear, bottom up. The hoist meanwhile is lifting her up into the air, and she is gazing out the windshield, out across the street, lit up by streetlights and the moon. The night is still empty, and she is waiting for her boyfriend, Patrick, to come and join her. First she knows he will wash his hands, in the station sink, in front of the naked pictures, and then his face. He will dry his hands with paper towels. Then he will climb up on a toolbox, eager, and step inside the cab. And by then she will be naked, still hungry, already warmed up.

"Before we get caught," she'll say, reaching for his sleeve. "Quick."

10

Three A.M., at the station, and it is raining, and cold. I'm wearing my long underwear, beneath my work clothes, standing on the center island. You can see the rain, falling in sheets across the street, and when the rain hits the tin roof, the beating drowns out even the radio inside the station. Still the air is clean, and this rain causes me to miss the Midwest, the places where I grew up. Also I am thinking about my father.

A guy in a van pulls into the station back lot—an old Ford, beat to hell. He stays there a while, idling, and I figure he is looking for the hose. His radiator is shot. Maybe he needs some air. I step inside the office, check on Germs. There is a long heavy wrench I carry sometimes when I am alone. Six months ago, a man was shot at a station across town. Every two hours, I make a drop in the safe, buried into the floor beneath the office desk. Once somebody walked in and stole a battery while I was helping a woman with three kids put air into her tires. The battery, a sealed Delco, came out of my paycheck—a matter of principal, Fuller explained. Also, the price of gas continues to rise, and there is growing concern we will have another shortage equal to that of 1973. There is trouble in Iran: hostages, and even the rumblings of a potential war in the Middle East. After I turned eighteen, last month, I drove myself to the post office and signed a document which would permit me to be drafted just in case.

A car pulls up to the full serve—a big one, gold like a Kruger-rand. I step out, leaving the wrench on the flowerbed full of butts, and inside the car sits a woman, dressed-up, wearing expensive clothes: possibly she is thirty-five. She has short, pale blonde hair—neatly trimmed; fine, like filament. When I go to the driver's side window, to see what she wants, I see that her hand is resting in her lap. I can see her legs are slightly parted, and her skirt has been gathered, possibly just to make her comfortable, but revealing nonetheless the tops of her thighs. Beside her on the passenger seat in a tangled pile you can see her nylons; her thighs are remarkably pale, and she is wearing her seatbelt, one which cuts directly across her chest, describing the shape of her breast. Smiling, she catches my eye, and I blush instantly. Then she asks, her voice southern, light-sounding, for ten dollars' worth. When she hands me her keys, holding the small key which will fit into her gas cap, our hands touch.

The current is electric. I hustle to the pump, set it going. I catch her eyes in the mirror, looking me over. She has out-of-state plates—a long way from home—and the license plate bracket which provides access to her gas tank is pinching the veins in my wrist. It's cold, too, and I am shivering. I slow the inflow of gas at nine ninety and then drive the pump quickly to an even ten dollars. When I come around, she says, not impolitely, "Aren't you going to wash my windshield?"

"Sure, ma'am," I say, handing her the keys to her car. "Usually when it's raining, we—"

"Please?" she says. Her legs are parted more dramatically now, one foot resting up against the rise of the car's transmission. "You're sweet," she says, dismissing me.

I take the squeegee, flick it properly, and begin to wash her windshield, wiping the squeegee on my sleeve, just so. Gradually I understand she has unfastened her seatbelt, and I am trying to avoid her eyes. Because her blouse has been loosened by two but-tons, I can see the edge of her bra. Her bra is black, made out of lace, and has a clip in the center, and I can feel my body leaning into the fender of her car, growing aggravated. It's disconcerting, and shameful, the way this happens: now the woman brings up her hand, which has polished nails, and a large diamond ring, and sets free the clip holding her bra together. Her breasts, once released, give way, though still they are partially concealed by the silk of her blouse. They are pale white and curve gracefully like a very fine glass—or a sail, recently filled. The wind is blowing hard now, cutting through my clothes, and when I finish washing her window, I step quickly, putting away the squeegee. She hands me a credit card, and I write the order up, and when I look up I see that she is looking at my waist, and the working of my imagination, which has continued to rise sharply beneath my belt in spite of the cold. Now I step closer to the car, to conceal her view, because I am feeling particularly naked and embarrassed and shamefully thrilled all at once. I remember instantly I need to run the credit card, set in a man's name, through the machine. *Right back,* I say, and at the island I clear the numbers, set the date. Then I'm back and she is smiling at me very gently.

"Here, ma'am," I say.

She signs the slip with loopy, pretty handwriting. Then she passes the clipboard back to me. "Thank you," she says.

I nod, and she says to me, tenderly, "You look cold."

"Not really."

"I know I would be," she says, starting up the engine. Now she turns her shoulder and smiles. "Tell me," she says. "Do you think I'm pretty?"

"Pardon?"

"Do you think I'm pretty?"

"Well. Yes. Yes, ma'am, I do. Very much."

"Do you have a girlfriend?" she says.

"Uh huh," I say, relieved to be safe. "I do."

"Then she's a very lucky girl," says the woman.

"She's really smart," I say. "I mean at school."

"I bet you are your daddy's son," she says.

"Yeah," I say, shrugging. "I guess."

"Step closer," she says, smiling. "I want you to close your eyes."

"Pardon?"

"Close your eyes. Lean down here. I won't hurt you," she says, holding up her hand, crossing her heart. "Promise."

With her hand in view, I can see the lines in her palm and the backs of her rings. Her blouse has parted more deeply, revealing a breast entirely. "To remember by," she says. "Twenty years from now."

"Okay."

"Closer," she says, moving a finger, smiling.

She blinks, and the corner of her mouth rises. I lean forward, close my eyes, and now I am breathing in the scent of her perfume. For a moment I can feel the tips of her fingers pressed up against my lips. Then she takes my face with two hands and kisses me gently on the mouth.

"Sealed with a kiss," she says, releasing me. "You take care."

My father used to tell me our lives were all mapped out in heaven. He'd say, pointing up at the sky, that all we had to do was wait for the perfect storm and everything would be made clear. Then he taught me to calculate the distance between the thunder and the lightning. He taught me to watch the sky for road maps.

And I know now that our lives become the sum of the various directions we take, that no choice is irrevocable, that all but the last lead us to the opportunity for another; I know that a person's character is not determined by any one decision but by the consequence of each. And sometimes I find myself wondering just what it was that woman in the car was running from. Or to. At the time she reminded me of the girl my father had seduced, in Illinois, the same who held me closely at his funeral and wept into my collar. She was also a reminder that we should pay attention to our ghosts, because of course we are not alone, which is also to say we share our lives with everyone—with those who came here first, and those who will come after.

It's a serious idea. A life, fraught with consequence.

In the late eighties, after the discovery of more efficient means of manufacturing cocaine, I stood across the street from a crack house in Chicago and saw a nine-year-old boy shot in the back of the head. He was with his father, who apparently had decided he didn't want to pay, or couldn't. This was not a bad neighborhood, just a changing one, but it was then, I think, standing on a sidewalk in Bucktown, that I realized the increasingly invidious nature of drugs and the people who control them. The middle class, that was going to be okay, at least for awhile; but the poor were going to be entirely eviscerated. Up until then, I had always thought about the issue as a matter involving individual rights, but of course that nine-year-old boy never even knew what hit him.

In 1978 we were no better than anybody else, but we were certainly a whole lot safer. Without consequence, one has no need to be responsible; I know this now. I know an argument based on individual rights works only when others are not destroyed by it. My father respected the rule of law, the fine blue line which allegedly keeps us safe, but my father also understood the laws of nature, which is why he taught me the duty of those with more was always to care for those with less, lest we come to bloodshed. If, as a result of this benevolence, one felt condescended to, so be it. This was his dominion.

He was a bit more equivocal on matters of fidelity, I think, which only proves he wasn't blameless. My father, he knew what he was doing, which is why he must have left open that gate to the stables. He knew that I would notice. He knew that I would wake up someday and find him.

I think my father knew exactly what he was doing, and during the chill winter of 1978, so did I. Of course, had I done things differently, I would have led another life entirely, but who could have told me then?

Who? And to what purpose?

Thus, one week later, after the rains . . . even then I understand I am not in this for the money. I am not in this because I want to break the law. I am in this because I believe in loyalty, and because I have been asked nicely by somebody I want to respect me, and, most importantly, because it seems like the right thing to do. If she knew, would Elizabeth be ashamed? Caroline would call me reckless. But reckless is a good thing to be, I think. It means you aren't afraid to die. Meanwhile, we are running, fast, Bittner and I, into the night over the hills of Papago Park.

The hills are built into boulders, built up along the Salt River bottom. In the distance, you can see the foothills, and the stadium, where an event is taking place—tractor pulls, I think: the air is full of the sounds of wild, racing engines, and clouds of dust are rising up from the stadium lights. Sometimes, you can hear the voice of the crowd, which sounds a little like an ocean, crashing into the cliffs. We have parked Bittner's Camaro behind the park, beside the tracks which go to Los Angeles; then we drove in my truck to a field, full of chaparral and palo verdes, where we left it parked beside a barbed wire fence. And now we are running the mile and a half to the meeting place on A Mountain. Bittner says you never want to make public your plan of escape, and you should always have two, anyway, which makes sense to me, though I realize the only way out now will be down the mountain we are climbing. Beside me, running, is Germs, who thinks we are going on a picnic.

"Mac," Bittner says, breathing hard. "Slow down."

I look over at him. The sky is bright enough to light up his street clothes, the gold chain he wears around his neck. I'm thinking he should have some camouflage, maybe, like the marines.

Tucked into the waistband of his jeans, beneath his shirt, rests his
.38 revolver. Five hundred yards out, we slow to a jog, and then a
walk as we approach the ridge, catching our breath. My heart is
beating like a railroad crossing, full of warnings and bells, I'm that
scared. In the distance, you can see the Rural Street bridge, which
crosses the dry river bottom. Only during flood rains does the
bottom ever fill. On the other side sit all the strip joints and mas-
sage parlors, places I have never been. Bittner says these guys are
nice, but still they're dealers. A thousand yards beneath us is a
parking lot for an enormous disco.

"Like us," I say.

"Hell yeah," Bittner says. He is slightly high, strutting now,
pregame warm-up, and as we approach into the shade of the boulders, we lose the lights from the night sky.

"Where we going?"

"There," Bittner says, pointing across an open space, toward
another ridge. "Other side."

"Maybe they're late," I say.

"It's twenty-four ounces," Bittner says. "They'll be here."

It sounds like a lot, twenty-four—dope, I presume, though I
have never even smoked a joint. I smelled it once and didn't like
it. I like sometimes red wine with a lot of 7-Up, but that's about it.
I am assuming, too, that *dope* means marijuana, though on certain television shows *dope* also means heroin, which is more dangerous. Skank. The White Tiger. I don't even know the name of
what it is I am here to fetch. I call Germs over to a boulder and
drop him to a down-stay. This way, he's almost out of sight, and I
know precisely where he is.

Bittner lights a cigarette. "You should smoke, Mac," he says.
"Calms your nerves."

Now, in the distance, we see two figures emerging slowly from
the darkness. Bittner calls out, "Hey, Gary."

"Bittner," says a voice, laughing.

They are our age, maybe older, but they are not Mexican—

they're Polynesian. Hawaiian guys with jeans and flowered shirts. Gary, the first, has a huge belly.

"Who's this?" says the other.

"My pal, Mac," says Bittner. "He's with me."

"Mac," says the other. "Hey Mac."

I nod, mostly because I'm afraid my voice will crack. Bittner steps forward and shakes hands—a complicated procedure, involving various maneuvers. Now I, too, am shaking hands—first this way, then that, a slide up to the elbow, somehow. It feels like a foreign language; I have no idea how anybody could possibly keep this procedure straight, and I feel like an idiot, but friendly, too. I am a friendly idiot. I like this guy, Gary. He's friendly and smiles real big, his teeth flashing in the night like a brand new Nikon.

Bittner takes out a wad of cash. He counts out several hundred dollars, and Gary tells the other, the skinny guy, to hand him a paper bag.

"It's good," Gary says. "Maui Wowie. Paca Lolo, Bittner." He says, turning to me, "Mac. You ain't no narc, are you Mac?"

I can hear Germs growing restless in the dark behind me. He has a growl in his throat. Then Gary bursts out laughing, as if he were contagious.

"What's that?" Gary says.

"My dog," I say. "Friendly."

I turn, and there is Germs, still in his down-stay, but ready to spring. Gary steps back and tucks his hand under his shirt. He keeps it there, resting, and I say, trying to lighten things up, "Lumbo Gold."

"I don't like fucking dogs," Gary says, smiling.

Bittner says, "He's cool, Gary. Leave the dog alone."

I realize, at that moment, Lumbo is what you call marijuana from Colombia, not Oahu. I feel myself tensing up and take a step back, toward Germs. "Easy," I say to Germs. "Easy."

The other, besides Gary, says, lifting up his hands, "Hey. We're fine."

Now Gary relaxes, and he smiles widely all over again. He says, "You want to go to the disco? Meet some girls?"

"Yeah," Bittner says. "Sure."

I don't have a false ID. I also don't want to go to prison. I don't know where I'd keep Germs. "I need to go," I say.

"Here," Bittner says, tossing me the bag of marijuana. "Here. I'll meet you. Tomorrow night."

"You sure?"

"Sure I'm sure."

"Okay," I say.

"Okay," he says.

Then I call Germs, and we head off, slowly, and I can hear them laughing, saying things. Now we pick up our pace into the dark: we take the other side of the mountain fast, skidding on loose rocks, hustling. I've never carried a brown paper sack before, not even for lunch. Groceries, maybe, to help my mother, but those are larger and weighed down with milk and juice and half-gallons of white wine. Once I hit the bottom, the flat desert, marked by cholla and mesquite, I really begin to run. I'm laughing, actually, and Germs is running right by my side. I am a drug dealer, I think. Like my father, I, too, am capable of breaking the law, and in the distance, you can see my truck, parked in the scrub. I am running to my truck and when I finally get close, running, I can feel Germs falling in behind and then I go—full speed ahead—straight into the barbed wire fence.

Disentangling yourself from a barbed wire fence at night can be a complicated procedure, especially if you are frightened. What's important to remember is that you do not have to insist you go right on through, regardless of cost. Meanwhile my body has flipped over the top wire, and I am up against the other side of fence: among other things, I have ripped my shirt and cut deeply my knee. My arms, having been bound up in the top tier of the fence, are dripping with blood. I can feel blood dripping down the side of my face, onto my neck, inside my open collar. Germs is standing there on the other side, barking, as if at a ghost.

I stand, shakily, and lift the bottom wire so he can scoot beneath. My truck is still there, gathering dust; I crawl beneath the bed to pin the drugs between the well of my spare tire and the bracket which holds it in place: on either side sit my large gas tanks, and I keep knocking my damaged knee against the rear axle. The wheel is large, twelve by sixteen with an off-road tire, and weighs over sixty pounds: it is also covered with dirt and mud. Later, Bittner will remove the drugs; he says he'll do it alone, when I'm not around, in order to protect me. I am simply to keep the truck parked in the front driveway of my house and to leave the porch lights off. Once the drugs are removed, he'll place a small patch of electrician's tape over the lock of my door: a signal, he explains; so there will be no need for conversation. And beneath the truck, holding the wheel with one arm, sweating, and bleeding, I'm spinning the bolt into place, securing the clamp. It's the kind of thing done a lot easier during the day in a well-lit garage, and while I am trying not to feel any real pain, I know I am. My shirt sticks to my back and I understand this is more than just a lot of bleeding.

Inside the truck, I'm not sure where to drive; I am also certain I am panicked. I don't want to go to the hospital, if only because maybe I won't need to. Obviously I can not go home. Instead I drive to the station, thinking I'll hose myself off under the bay lights, assess the damage, maybe raid the first aid equipment. Driving, I take the back roads, often with my lights off: it's fourteen miles, to be precise, and each car I see behind me I'm convinced belongs to a cop. For the first two or three miles, whenever I see any headlights, I pull into a driveway and cut the engine. It takes longer to get where you are going this way, driving in the dark. Following a sleepy road through half a dozen subdivisions, I imagine the sky to be full of helicopters, with searchlights, and that the main highways have now been entirely blocked off—our fine and overworked police, on the lookout for a boy with a dog and several identifying marks: namely, recent cuts to his body from a fence. *Lighten up*, I'm thinking. *Lighten up . . .* and in one neighborhood, I drive to the end of a cul-de-sac, then across a large field attendant to a grammar school, then through a vacant lot and onto the highway in front of me, hitting my lights. Germs, meanwhile, is sitting up, looking out the window. When I reach for the shift, he tries to lick the blood from my hand. Nearing the main highway, I feel close to fainting with God knows how many prison term sentences' worth of drugs beneath the floorboards of my truck.

I'm getting sloppy, driving: shock. Once in the station, I pull around back, and there is the owner, Fuller, talking with a black-haired woman—not his wife—sitting in a parked Corvette. The Corvette is green, of recent vintage, with a T-top. Fuller meanwhile is wearing his day clothes: a fancy velour sweater, harboring a vast array of horizontal stripes, and a pair of designer jeans. He's wearing a shiny watch, the type with all kinds of lights blinking here and there and an alarm. He gives me a big smile, which he is known for, his walleye drifting, and steps around back where I have parked. On his belt, tucked into a holster, rests his chrome der-ringer, and he says, scratching his belly, coming around the front of the truck, "Didn't know you were working tonight, Mac."

I am not working tonight. I have no reason whatsoever to be here. I am also suddenly embarrassed by my wounds.

"Air," I say, stepping out of my truck, aiming for the shadows. "Just needed some air for my tires."

Fuller steps up, lighting a cigarette, the bay lights glowing right behind him, and says, "Jesus. You get into a fight?"

"Not really."

"Hate to see the other guy."

"I didn't get into a fight, Fuller." Now I'm leaning against the truck, looking at the gash in my knee through my torn jeans. I look up at him and say, "I think I better sit down."

I'm on the curb, my head between my knees, and now Fuller is rinsing my knee with the station hose. He tells me to lift up my arms, which I do, barely, and he pulls my shirt over my head, not bothering to unbutton it. He's holding the hose up against my body, the water cold, and pouring it over my shoulders and arms, down my ribs. "Jesus," he says. "You go playing with a chain saw?"

"What happened?" says the black-haired woman, approaching. She has a pretty voice. I think Fuller must be having an affair, for which I am momentarily grateful. He's also been doing things he shouldn't.

"Here," he says, handing her the hose. He steps away, going for the first aid kit, on the shelf above the sink with all the naked pictures. When he returns, he is unrolling a wad of gauze, quickly, and then he says, "You should get to a hospital, Mac. You're going to need some stitches."

"No," I say. "Really. I don't want any."

"They hurt," Fuller says, nodding, "like a son of a bitch. Better that than bleeding to death."

"But . . ."

"I'll call your mom, take care of her: if we have to. Don't worry. But we're going to take your truck, okay? I just got my car detailed."

"Don't call my mom," I say. "Okay."

"Mac," he says, pointing to the woman. "By the way, this is Pam."

"Hi, Pam," I say.

Pam says, directing the flow of the hose over my knee, "Hi, Mac. How are you?"

Fuller has a scar on his cheek, about half an inch long. He drives me to an emergency clinic not far up the road. It's a new building, evidence of the city's continued expansion—encouraged by the progress of the Central Arizona Project, which intends to pump water off the Colorado River and send it hundreds of miles, by way of canals and dams, all the way to Phoenix. Just one year ago, Fuller's station was the last outpost of civilization, but already now the traffic has begun to pass him by.

The doctor who sews me up whistles through his teeth. He jams a local anesthetic into my knee and takes a long time. He puts another beneath my right arm. He doesn't bother for the stitches on my face. He also doesn't speak English very well; I think he must still be learning. Afterward he tells me I must be more careful and go to my doctor regularly for checkups.

When I step gingerly into the waiting room, woozy and sore, Fuller says, "You get any pain killers?"

"Tylenol with codeine," I say.

"Great."

"I have to pay," I say, realizing I have no idea how this is done.

"Took care of it. Piece of cake."

"What?"

"We have all kinds of insurance. Job accident, et cetera. Don't worry about it."

In the truck, on the way back, Pam is sitting between us while Fuller drives. She smells nice. I wonder if they are still going out on a date or if I've ruined it. I wonder if that's what married men do, date. Sometimes I wait on Fuller's wife, in her station wagon, all full of kids and toys; she always says, *Charge it.* Meanwhile Germs is sitting on my lap, which hurts when we go over the bumps, but it's a short drive.

At the station, Fuller steps out of my truck and says, "You see Bittner around tonight?"

I shrug.

"Can you drive?"

"Sure. I can drive. I'm fine."

"You drive yourself home. Go to bed. Rest."

"Okay."

"You want tomorrow off?"

"I'm okay. Really."

Now Fuller walks Pam to her Corvette. She waves to me while I watch him whisper to her ear. He reaches into his jeans and pulls out a roll of cash, flicks off some bills, as if counting, and then he says something else. He returns to me, tucking the roll into his jeans, the derringer winking in the light.

I start up the truck, pretending not to notice. "Mac," he says. "Bittner—"

"I don't know where he is," I say. "Honest. He could be anywhere."

"Be careful," Fuller says. "Bittner, he's a big guy, he can take care of himself. But he's not going anywhere."

I nod, because I understand his drift.

"You are," he says. "Don't get caught up in any of his shit. Be careful."

"I don't know what you mean."

"'Course you do. It's all right. Go find that sweet little girl of yours. She'll treat you right. Take her out to dinner, on me."

Now he slips me two twenties, each neatly folded in half. He says, "Pam, she's not related."

"I know."

"See no evil," Fuller says, sadly. "You stay away from Bittner."

"He's my friend," I say.

"No. Actually, he's not. Thing about guys like Bittner, and I ought to know, I've been around the block . . . thing about guys like that is they are always thinking with their dick. Not much room for brains there, inside your dick, most being only so long." He holds up his hands, to illustrate. "He's been working out fine here, but a guy who thinks with his dick, Mac, isn't a friend to anybody. You can't trust him, you see? You take care of your girlfriend. And don't you ever bring any of that shit back onto my lot again."

I'm too scared to say anything. Fuller lets out a sigh, lights a cigarette. He's a big man, too: once, he beat up a man on the lot who pulled a knife on him. The guy tried to steal a quart of oil, in broad daylight, and when Fuller went to stop him, he hit Fuller with a wrench across the face. Then Fuller put the man into a hospital, who later sued Fuller for assault and battery and fifty-thousand dollars. After that Fuller started carrying the derringer; next time, he'd just kill the son of a bitch, pop him in the back of the neck. Behind him now, lit up in the station bays, I can see the sign beneath the tires. *No fighting!*

"See," Fuller says, taking a drag, his eye drifting. "If you were Bittner, you'd deny it. You'd lie about it. That's why you have it now and he doesn't."

I look behind him and see Pam staring at us. She's pretty but much too old for me. And it dawns on me, right then, looking at Fuller's lover, the meaning of his rule: it means we are simply not supposed to fight each other, because we're like a family, or the United States, and a family is supposed to take care of its own. Now Pam turns to me and smiles, sweetly, wiggling her fingers into the air, and I say to Fuller, "Thanks. I mean, thanks a lot."

Fuller nods, turning, and says, "You're welcome a lot, Mac. You're welcome."

That night, after the woman with pale blonde hair kissed me, and drove away into the rain, I was standing there on the island, feeling cold and confused. Soon the sun would begin to rise, behind the station, in the east; sometimes I liked to climb up on the roof to watch. But that night it was raining, hard, and when I turned to step inside, I saw a guy with long hair stumbling toward me. He looked like a rock star down on his luck—heroin-thin, his clothes rags, his best instrument long-since pawned. He was carrying a beer and came up to me, stumbling, and said, "Want to get laid?"

"What?"

"Bitch in my car. You can fuck her. She'll do anything you want."

"No," I said. "Thanks."

I crossed the island, left him swaying there: I wanted to find my wrench, still sitting in the flowerbed. Germs came to the edge of the office, standing in the office door, and began to growl. Then the guy undid his fly and began to piss on a pump for unleaded. He stood there, pissing in the wind, and then I heard a woman, in the back, beside the beat-up van she had arrived in. She had a bruise over her eye, and her top was unbuttoned, exposing her breasts. There was a large tattoo on one—the shape of a wilting flower. She said, "Hi—"

"Head's back there," I said, pointing.

"That's okay," she said, walking toward me. She was stumbling badly, trying not to, and then the guy out front began to tuck his prick back inside his pants. Now he pulled out a knife—a large, folding knife with a long blade. The woman behind me was stepping closer, I could smell her, and he started toward me, the open knife in his hand. He said, "Just need some gas, buddy. Said you can fuck her if you want. I won't watch."

I said, not even scared, "Get the fuck out of here."

"Whoa," he said, laughing, raising the knife. "Whoa—"

Germs leapt and hit the man's wrist, twisting it in his mouth, blood pouring out of his sleeve. The knife fell to the ground. I turned to the woman, who had stopped, dead still, and then she let out a scream and ran out through the back of the station to her van. I pivoted, again, wrench in hand, and called Germs off. Germs returned, instantly, licking his chops. I raised the wrench, pointing to the man's chest, where I intended to strike, dead center. Then I said, "You can still leave."

He was too dazed to argue—bleeding, holding his wrist. I was shaking now, the adrenaline rushing through my body, and then he stumbled around back, and I followed him, and he climbed into his van. As they drove off, the woman was screaming at me out the window, calling me a faggot and an asshole. I gave Germs a bowl of water, to rinse his mouth, and when the police arrived, because the rule was to report incidents, the cop was a guy I knew. He was married and had two kids and told me if I ever needed him I should turn off the lights inside the bays; that way, he'd be sure to notice driving by. He explained he never gave a guy a ticket for doing something he did, too: if the cop ran a stop sign, the next guy he saw doing likewise would get a break. *But just this once,* he said, wagging his finger. It was his way of keeping order. Then he told me stories about chasing criminals at night, driving along the highways, his sirens lit like fireworks. I gave him a cup of coffee, thanked him for stopping by. Then I said it wasn't much, really—just some drunk guy, running out of gas.

"On his way to California," I said, shrugging. "Probably."

"By tomorrow," said the cop, "he's long gone."

Going nowhere, I realized, a week later, which wasn't all that difficult, and now it's eleven, maybe midnight, and I am on my way home my body swathed in bandages. The loss of blood has made me weak-kneed and sleepy, and when I drive into the circle which spans our front yard, the gravel crunching beneath the tires of my truck, I can just make out my mother, sitting on the front step in the dark. There's a yucca plant beside her, I know, as well as a new expensive barrel cactus. The light has burned out and she is waiting up.

"Where have you been, big guy?"

"Out."

Germs goes leaping through the truck door, though when he comes closer to her, he steps aside, his tail barely brushing her as he steps into the house. I know he's going to my room, where he's going to lie down on top of my bed, his head on the pillow. He'll be pretending he's a person, like me, not a care in the world. I can feel the codeine from the hospital making me light-headed, eager to be friendly, off to bed.

"I didn't know you were working tonight," she says.

"Went in for a couple hours. One of the guys was late. Fuller came in and sent me home." In this circumstance, lying, at least only partially, is better than not lying at all. It used to be I would never tell a lie, but now I am beginning to realize I have more reasons to, which frightens me. Meanwhile I'm trying not to limp, and I'm grateful for the darkness, concealing the blood on all my clothes.

My mother takes a drink from her wine; she's drunker than I thought. "I was hoping you'd go to the store for me."

"Sorry, Mom. Really. I didn't know you needed me to."

"I didn't *need* you to. Went myself. Through the drive-through!"

My mother's car—a long, blue station wagon—has several dents of recent vintage. Usually she scrapes the front bumper on her way out of the driveway at Blackwater's, where she knows all the people who work there, and calls them each by name, often the wrong one; because they know her, they also sell me supplies, understanding for whom they are intended. In the drive-through, you can see the blue paint, smeared into the stucco wall. Mr. Blackwater is preparing to run for office, and my mother claims to be a fan, though she is not certain if he is a Republican or Democrat. She says, as if reading my mind, which may be difficult, given the blurry state of her vision, "Jim isn't here. We've had a break in relations, I think. His wife may be getting better."

"I'm sorry," I say.

"Your father, you know, deep down: he was always a bleeding heart liberal."

I've never known what that means precisely. My mother usually says it in reference to the Great Society which does not appear to be prospering. My father, I do know, would never discuss politics at the dinner table.

"I'm tired," I say, faking a yawn.

"You were out with that girl. Elizabeth. You were out with her again, weren't you?"

"No," I say, grateful for an opportunity to the tell the truth. "No. Actually she has a test tomorrow. She's been studying. For Economics."

"Economics," says my mother. "That's an interesting subject. If you want to know about economics, you should find out how much a head of lettuce costs. Lettuce, when the price goes up, so does economics. Tell Caroline she should find out how much a head of lettuce costs."

"Elizabeth," I say.

"Yes, of course. You're not supposed to correct your elders, dear. You're late."

"I never thought of it that way," I say. "Lettuce, huh?"

"You and she blame me. I know that. I know she does."

"She does not blame you," I say.

"Your sister has abortions. Your sister sleeps with a married man. Your sister—"

"Mom, nobody blames you."

"I didn't tell him to load that thing. I thought it was for burglars. For ducks! I didn't tell him to have an affair with his God-damned secretary. Or Judy Langly, of all people!"

She's crying now, deeply. It's the efficient kind, usually fed on rage, that dries you out with a minimum of tears. She's sitting there, looking at her feet, which are bare, and now she says, looking up at me, "Your sister will betray you. She's just like him, you know. She believes only in herself."

"I have to go to sleep," I say.

"You have blood all over your hands, Patrick. You're guilty as sin."

"No," I say.

"Because you do not love your mother."

"No, Mom. Of course I love you."

"You love your girlfriend. Ask her where she was tonight. Ask her that!"

I'm angry now, if only because I know that I am right. My mother's anger has nothing to do with Elizabeth or my sister, or even with my father. My mother's anger has to do with me, and the fact of my late arrival, and Jim Walenka's departure from her life, and my as yet unspoken intention to leave home as soon as possible.

"Is she like Caroline?" she says. "Your Elizabeth? Does she—"

"You're drunk," I say to her for the first time in my life. "You're just drunk."

She stands now, barely. When she begins to fall, she reaches for the pillar which is holding up the roof above our heads. Now when she reaches to slap me, I duck. Her hand misses. So she tries again, and this time I let her. I let her slap me on the face, because I am angry, and bitter—capable of a hatred far greater than I have ever before imagined.

"There," she says, proudly. "That's more like it."

I step around her, ignoring the pain in my knee: if she knew I had a sack full of dope beneath the bed of my truck, would she call the police? My new friend who chases bad guys on the highways late at night? Just to teach me a well-earned lesson? My mother never made it through her first year of college, but still she is an expert on the cost of living. On Economics.

I go to the bathroom, start a shower. Across the hall, Germs is lying in my bed, dreaming: rabbits and squirrels, I hope—his legs twitching, as if he is running in his sleep, in chase. In the bathroom, I strip out of my clothes, and now I'm standing in the heat from the steam rushing into the air, fogging up the mirrors. In the mirrors, I am naked, and you can see the strip of hair which is descending from my navel—a newly paved route of which I am at times enormously proud, and you can see the shadows in my shoulders from the muscles I am growing, and my eyes, hooded from lack of sleep, and blue, and taking in the fog. Looking at myself, here, I understand I have become my father's son. And I understand I am desperately in need of discovering my own way out. I imagine my mother, and the things of which she has pretended to take notice—those things which I never did, but might have, had I not been too afraid to sin: to damn my soul to everlasting hell, which feels increasingly nearby, because I know that I have not yet begun in this life to commit my real share of sin, even though I am beginning now to want to. The heart, I realize, repairs what injuries it can, and then it simply hardens up like a muscle, or a stone. Like a four-inch scar you're going to carry always on your knee. Like all the imagined injuries for which your mother intends to hold you yet accountable, because she intends to hold you, regardless of cost, even if it kills you. Stepping into the shower, under the spray, the water pouring over my body, I can hear her now weeping in the distance. She is weeping in the distance and I am grateful, at least, for rules of common courtesy. At least I know for a while she will not come barging in so long as I am here, in the shower, trying to be clean. So long as the door behind me remains safely locked. And in the morning, I know, I will have to make amends, if only because I still have several months to go. I will have to make her coffee and pray she does not recall the things which she has said to me, because if she remembers, then she'll have to start up all over again just to prove herself. Assuming I get a jump start on the day, maybe do a quick trip to the florist, pick up a carnation or two, maybe then I will be able to cut it off. Add a couple aspirin. A fresh glass of water. It's amazing, I've learned, the way a false forgiveness, like a false spring, will bloom so eagerly despite the conditions of the soil. All in all, a pretty little flower, just waiting to be purchased.

"It's wrong," I say, wiping the soap from my eyes. "Something's got to give."

11

The brain may not feel any pain, but certainly the mind recalls it—at whim, but not always unexpectedly. Now into April, and the genuine rush of spring, Elizabeth has burn dreams. She is swimming in a lake of fire. Or she is falling, as if from an airplane, or satellite—her skin aflame as she descends straight through the atmosphere. Sometimes when she wakes she feels as if she is being consumed by fire, and then she realizes, afterward, after wiping the sleep from her eyes, and the attendant fear . . . afterward she understands this merely is the season—a breeze, following its course across the globe. She understands she has merely wakened into that particular time of year when her mother once spilled a pot of boiling water from the stove.

Mercifully the dreams do not linger throughout the day, though they do influence it. Today she finds herself nervous around the stove; she worries her hair will spill into the range. While heating water for her father's coffee, and her own cup of tea, she checks the handle often, making sure each time it is pointed toward the splash guard. The range is fed by gas, and she worries about catching a sleeve, or the back of her shirt, into the flame. Her father, sitting at the kitchen table in his Sunday clothes, reading the newspapers, asks her if she wants to go to the auto show.

"I've been stood up," he says. "Flip has obligations elsewhere. Besides, he doesn't need a car."

"The auto show?" Her father has not mentioned his intention to buy her a car for several weeks; she thought he had forgotten. She understands, too, that he intends it as a graduation present, to prepare her well for college. This summer her mother wants to take a trip to California to find her an apartment. When Elizabeth visits her mother, she takes her father's car, which is long and hard to drive in parking lots. She says to her father, checking the range, "I guess."

"Sure! Call up your Patrick McWinnihan. He's a boy. He likes cars, yeah? We'll make a picnic of it. Hot dogs? Pretzels?"

She calls up Patrick from the kitchen, checking the tea kettle, adjusting the flame. His mother answers and says, "Oh. It's you."

"I'm sorry—"

The phone falls to the ground, and after several minutes Patrick picks up another extension. He waits for his mother to hang up the other line. Then he says, "I was just practicing."

"What for?" she says, flirting.

"To be good," he says.

Weeks ago, when she snipped the stitches from his knee, and then his cheek, and then from under his arm, he hadn't said a word. He sat on her bed in his underwear while she took a pair of sewing scissors and clipped the threads. Then she pulled them out, one by one. The scar on his knee was healing up awkwardly. The one on his face was clean, though, and would hardly be noticeable in a couple years, unless you were up close enough to give a kiss. After she was finished, she kissed him, and they went swimming, and then they dressed in her bedroom, before her father returned home from work, and later they went out to the movies. They saw a movie with football players in it. In one place, somebody stuck a needle into a football player's knee: the scene reminded her of Bittner, actually. The way those men in the movie kept wandering around their locker room in jockstraps, scratching their bellies, yelling. After the movie, she was sullen while Patrick drove her home, and then he went to work. He was still working nights at the station; he slept usually after school, between three and nine. A date with her also meant for him a night without sleep.

At school he was always sleepy. Each month, once the weather warmed, their school gave permission for a student band to play during lunch and inspire community: that was the word, *community*, because the school counselors wanted to separate the idea of rock 'n' roll from sex and drugs. And in February, the week of Valentine's Day, and even though Patrick didn't play rock 'n' roll per se, the band teacher, Mr. Dyers, set up a special performance, complete with a new microphone and sound system on the outdoor stage, and then Patrick played for the entire lunch hour. He had two guitars—a twelve string and a six. One song was about a guy who worked at a gas station: it was funny, and rhymed the word *gas* with *ass* repeatedly: she knew he had written it, or as he would say, shrugging his shoulders, *Made it up*. He also sang a song about Sky Lab, which was presently falling, and another about a guy digging an endless ditch for the Central Arizona Project. All the rest he did were covers, because that's what people liked to hum: songs to which they already knew the melody. Between songs, he'd say something funny, once even about the principal, because on stage he was suddenly different. He was no longer shy. And sitting on the lawn, listening, along with a couple hundred other people, her arms crossed over her knees, rocking to the music, and even though he was now merely doing reruns of Cat Stevens and John Sebastian and Neil Young . . . sitting there she had a striking intuition, as if out of the sky, that he was handsome and going to make a living. He was going to be different. One song, by Jorma Kaukonen, always made her flesh goosepimple, and she felt jealous, sitting there, listening, especially afterward while watching dozens of people go forward to congratulate him. She knew he had risen, so to speak, that people no longer took him for a fool, or weakling. She knew people were not going to take him for a ride. If he wanted to, he might even become popular. For

weeks afterward she listened to people talk about him in the hallways, and that afternoon she understood, making her way up the
lawn, back to History, he simply no longer needed her.

Where there's hope, there must also be some misery: to need
requires mercy; to want, strictly an act of will. Maybe also some
opportunity? She wondered, too, if she needed him as much as, say,
she wanted to go to California and make him need her all over again.
Would he be lonely? For her? Having agreed to meet in the parking lot of the stadium, by the west gate, she catches sight of
Germs's tail. Patrick is standing by a lightpost in his sunglasses, hanging onto the special blind man lead for his dog. "Dogs like cars, too,"
Patrick says to her father, crossing to greet them, shaking his hand.

"Indeed," says her father.

"It's wrong, you know," says Patrick. "This blind-dog-only pol-
icy. I mean, Germs is an important part of my life. Without him,
I am emotionally handicapped." He says that again, drawing
emphasis . . . *emotionally handicapped* . . . and smiles broadly. "So
instead the system forces me to lie. I mean, I'm not really blind.
See what I mean? It's corrupt, I think."

At the ticket gate her father insists on paying, as always. The
ticket man looks at Patrick as if he were pathetic, and she reads the
sign on the gate—NO PETS OR ALCOHOLIC BEVERAGES, even
though there will be inside beer for sale. Then the man reaches
down to pet Germs.

"Please," Patrick says, bobbing his head, this way and that.
"My dog is working! Please do not distract him!"

Passing through the gate, Patrick goes straight to the woman
taking tickets. Then, as if remembering he is supposed to be
blind, he drives Germs through the doors but steers himself into
the wall. He makes a big show of hitting his head. The woman
drops her handful of tickets and Patrick turns, his hand to head,
beaming.

"He's just learning," Elizabeth says to the woman.

"Still new at this," says her father. "Terrible accident. Smoke for a thousand miles!"

Inside, her father says to her, "Corrupting, the entire system. Boy wants to be with his dog? Why shouldn't he? So long he doesn't go and take a dump."

She feels a rush of anger toward him—her father, and his taking sides with Patrick—as well as greedy about the prospect of picking out a new car. Ugly, she tells herself. *Don't be greedy.*

Air-conditioned, bright as day, as well as big—the auto show is inside the center of the stadium. Inside, where people usually play football, or basketball, sit parked hundreds of new cars and salesmen. She loses track in the general excitement, the lights and music; she's never walked before across an indoor football field. Her father is staring wistfully at a Cadillac Eldorado, bright green, while she wanders toward a section indicating Oldsmobiles. Amid the crowd are certain platforms, rotating, with new automobiles spinning, and sometimes you see women in pink and purple outfits, speaking into a microphone, describing the latest features. Elizabeth likes to watch the women especially, the way they seem to know precisely what they want to say about matters regarding suspension and fuel economy and acceleration. One woman is waxing enthusiastically about the nature of a particular kind of strut. The woman has long legs, her heels set in come-fuck-me pumps. When she catches Elizabeth's eye, the woman smiles, briefly, as if she were embarrassed, or about to take her clothes off, and then the woman turns her attention to a man. Mostly the stadium is full of men drinking from tall cups of beer, staring at the elevated women with pretty legs and perfectly made-up eyes, glittery as stardust.

"Where's McWinnihap?" her father says.

"Beats me."

"Want a pretzel?" he says, handing her one. "Let's go find some of those Nip imports everybody's talking about."

"They get good gas mileage," Elizabeth says. "You're not supposed to call them Nips."

"How quickly we forget," says her father, shaking his head. "Of course."

"It's not polite."

"Tell that to your grandfather."

Her grandfather, his father, died long before she was born. He was on an aircraft carrier, in the Pacific, the USS *Hornet*. The ship was famous for launching a raid on Japan shortly after Pearl Harbor, a squadron of B-25s, and then her grandfather was burned alive after a shell exploded in the battle of the Santa Cruz Islands. She's heard the stories, and she knows if it hadn't been for the war, then her father might have known him better, which possibly could have been a good thing. Her grandfather was a petty officer, she thinks, though she has no idea what that means. Her father was an officer too, a marine lieutenant. He went to Vietnam and came back alive. He drove a howitzer, which is a cannon on wheels . . . *Send you to the moon. And back.* In the pictures, he's missing a front tooth; he's thin as a rail, or fence post, and has all of his hair: sometimes he could be another person entirely. She says to her father, hopefully, "I like the Hondas."

"You gotta give 'em this. They know what we want. Detroit can't get 'em off the lot. Chrysler's got cars rusting, actually rusting, 'cause nobody will buy any. Now they got rebates: they actually pay you to buy a car, Jesus. You know they can sell steel cheaper than we can make it? The Japs? Can you call 'em that? Japs? You know what's happening in Pittsburgh? In Gary? Mills all shutting down. Subsidizing, Japanese government subsidizing . . . can't compete. Told Flip to dump his U.S. Steel years ago, but he's still hanging on like an idiot. No, what we make in the US of A is football players and movie stars and now Carter's dropped the B-1 Bomber. Gas over a buck a gallon. Iranians taking hostages while we make theme parks, that's what. Disney World. Great America. You ever listen to a Chrysler starter?"

"Not really." If she eats her pretzel, she thinks, she'll be fat, and never fit into a tight dress, especially one with sequins. She sets the pretzel on a table top with brochures for station wagons.

"Grind," says her father, shaking his head, because he disapproves of wastefulness. "They grind. Not like a good old Chevy. Your McWinnihoo will tell you," he says, wiping salt from his chin. He wads up the wrapper from his pretzel and tosses it in a wastebasket. "What people forget . . . youngsters, especially; people forget we've always had to go to war. It's a Goddamn fact. When you were born, Hitler hadn't been dead even twenty years. Most people think it was two, three centuries ago. 'Cause of black-and-white television, that's why. Everybody's used to color: see something in black and white, it's ancient history. 'Course it isn't," he says, reaching into his pocket. "You're younger than VE Day. You know that? Victory in Europe."

He directs her toward a counter selling sodas. "Tab? Sprite?"

"Tab," she says.

He lights a cigarette, coughs. "Your mother, she thinks we should all be holding hands, singing 'Kum Bah Yah,' drinking Coca-Cola."

"Is that why you got divorced? I mean, before . . ." She means before her mother's affair with his accountant became public, and her father threw her out of the house, and then let her back in to pack while he went out of town for several weeks. When he came home half of the furniture was gone, and for months her parents didn't even speak. This was before the divorce had become amicable. Initially, her father refused to fire his accountant; because he was his friend, he said. Loyalty still meant something, didn't it?

"No," he says, exhaling, collecting his change. He passes Elizabeth her Tab, reaches for his beer. "Who knows. She may be right. No, we got divorced because of me, not your mother. Because of me not being—"

"What?" she says, stepping out of line. She can't see Patrick anywhere.

"I don't know. The way she wanted me to be."

"How was that?" she says, turning. "How did she want you to be?"

"Elizabeth, I don't know. Germans are different from Italians. Some like pork, others like spaghetti. Nothing wrong with either unless you are a Nazi. It was my fault, not your mother's." He says, winking, "It's the imports that get good gas mileage, you know. I've been reading up on this stuff."

"How did she want you to be?"

He drinks from his beer, which leaves a little mustache. "She wanted me to agree with her. She wanted me to think she was right. I couldn't always do that. Because I didn't always think she was right. We argued once for over half an hour about the House."

"Cleaning," Elizabeth said, nodding.

"No no no. The House—Congress or Senate, or both. She was dead set that you should use the word *house* only if you meant to refer to both houses, because sometimes people might think you meant the Senate, and of course she was wrong; she wouldn't agree that *house* is common shorthand for House of Representatives, which is why people always say *the House and the Senate* to refer to a bill passed by both houses—Jesus," he says, his blood pressure rising. He takes a breath to calm himself, lest he explode all over again. "Anyway, she would not admit to it, because there was company listening, even after she realized she was dead wrong."

"Stubborn," Elizabeth says.

"That's when I knew we were through. When she was dead wrong, and knew it, and wouldn't admit it. That's when bitterness begins to lurk between two decent people. You see, so long as I wouldn't agree with her—politics, religion, whom to invite for supper—so long as we disagreed, she couldn't *like* me. In this life, either you're willing to disagree and still be friends or you're willing to be lonely. I didn't mind the disagreeing; it's normal, good for you, like jogging. No, what hurt me was afterward. The anger, the bitterness and spitefulness. The way she kept complaining about my listening skills and whatnot. My methods of conversation. I didn't respect her. I was rude. Blah blah blah. So after a while, I stopped trying."

"She shouldn't have left," Elizabeth says. "She always—"

"No," says her father, crossly. "Do not take sides."

She steps back, shocked, partially humiliated. In front of her stands a man, checking her out, his eyes lingering on her chest. Now her father takes her hand and squeezes it, turning to her, and says, "Your mother is a good woman, Lizzie. This is just my side, and so when I say it's my fault, I mean I could have been different. I could have changed. And I didn't want to."

"You get along now," Elizabeth says, almost bitterly.

"Well, we've always known each other best. And I miss her endlessly. Sometimes what you see in somebody else is yourself: the parts you want to change. Or the parts you can't. What's important is that it's okay to break up. In case you need to. Doesn't mean anybody's bad. That's all."

She thinks of Patrick, that which she would change about him. If she could, she'd make him need her the way he used to, when he was lonely, and new: she would make him need her so he would be more grateful to her for being just the way she is. He's changing, and she worries she is no longer keeping up, which is stupid. They've never even had a fight. About anything. They never even disagree . . . yet . . . and she can see Patrick, over by the Chevrolet display, and Germs. Now she turns her eyes back to the man in front of her, who feels himself being watched; the man shifts his balance, looking her over, smiling hopefully. She puts her arm around her father's waist and winks.

"This car idea," her father says, pressing by the man, entirely unaware. "You know it's her idea as much as mine."

"Okay," she says, breaking free. "I'll behave."

She takes her father's hand, leading him on to where Patrick is sitting inside an orange Corvette—convertible. Germs is in the passenger seat, beginning to drool, and Patrick is sitting in the driver's seat, his hands on the wheel, talking to a salesman.

"Where's the gear shift knob?" Patrick says, checking the rearview mirror.

"People steal 'em," says the salesman.

"Thieves!" Patrick says, nodding blindly.

"Four hundred sixty cubic inches," says the salesman. "Three hundred sixty horses."

Patrick lets off a low whistle. Then he says, "What's the speedometer go up to? Can you get one set in braille?"

A woman is laughing now, and a fat man in a brown suit with a plastic nametag is helping Patrick from the car. "I'm sorry," says the fat man in the suit, "but we don't sell cars to blind people."

Now a man is taking pictures, his flashbulbs popping. Patrick poses, his hand on the hood of the car, smiling. The salesman tries to grab Germs's lead, and Germs growls sharply. *Germs,* Patrick calls. *Heel!* . . . and Germs leaps over the car door, runs to Patrick, his lead flopping on his back, and sits by Patrick's side, perfectly. The people are amazed, watching; for a moment, Elizabeth is angry: this showing off. Patrick says to the photographer, raising his hands, "All I wanted was a Corvette. It's named after a ship, you know. A kind of ship. In French, you spell it with a *K.*"

Later, they wander toward the Hondas, Patrick and Germs in the middle. As Patrick sees it, the Hondas have it over the Toyotas. "They're smaller, more efficient. Fewer rattles. The Volkswagens are nice but always breaking down."

"The problem with a small car," says her father, "is people get killed inside of them."

Now Patrick takes Elizabeth by the arm, so she can lead him. She tries not to be cool, but still she's miffed and doesn't want to be, which makes it worse. She says, pointing to a woman on a stage for Mercedes, "Do you think she's pretty?"

"Who?" says Patrick, turning his head, this way and that, reaching out his hands.

"Stop it. You know who. Her," she says, pointing. The woman

is wearing a tight red dress, a slit up the side, sparkling. She has breasts the size of China.

"I do," says her father, laughing, nudging Patrick in the ribs.

Standing between them, Patrick kisses her cheek, quickly, so as not to be caught. He slides his hand over her arm, over the scars, which feel hot, conspicuously alive, especially today, and then he slides his hand across her ribs, glancing the side of her breast. "No," he says, "not especially."

She pushes his hand away. She says, at last the proper center of attention, and slightly ashamed for wanting to be so, "What kind should I get?"

Patrick says, turning to her father, "Truth is, Mr. Pinski, I don't know squat about cars. I mean, I can change the oil. Fix a flat. But a car's a car, so long as you're not hitting anything. Personally I'd rather have a truck."

"Not a truck," says Elizabeth. "Definitely."

"A bright color," says her father. "Yellow? Orange?"

"Yellow," says Elizabeth. "I'll drive safe."

In Driver's Ed, yellow is the color meant to instruct you to yield, especially to oncoming traffic. It's also the hottest part of a fire, and the color of the sun. She wonders if a new car will really change the way she feels. For Christmas, she bought her father a book by Henry Kissinger. She bought her mother a new scarf from Saks. But still it seems unfair, this distribution of income: what goes in toward her is decidedly more than what she sends out, which causes her to feel unequal and spoiled, as if she were on welfare. According to Patrick, a spoiled horse is one you can not trust; a horse becomes spoiled when you beat it—with a whip, or a board. You break its spirit. Her father, meanwhile, is smiling, patting Germs on the head, perhaps because he's been selling a lot of buildings lately. The boom, he says, just won't quit. The valley is hot. And everybody knows sexy is hot.

Once, when she was a little girl, after her accident, he had promised to buy her a dog. She was alone and in bed, crying, trying not to tug on her bandages, and he said, maybe, maybe someday they could get her a dog. One to keep her company. But because of the burns, and the risk of infection, the doctors had prohibited the idea for several months, and by then her mother had developed a history of allergies: mostly dog hair, and muddy footprints, which was another excuse meant to conceal the fact of the future skin grafts she would be going through. During the summer she spent six weeks at a burn clinic in Indianapolis: all around her, people were screaming, being dipped into tanks, dying slowly. It could take days, the dying, and she was lonely, and she wanted to feel loved, which is precisely what a dog brought you: the opportunity to feel loved, because this is what it had been bred to do, and for which in turn you agreed to love it back, if only because you had to. In exchange the dog protected you from men in bad suits and loneliness. Now, above her father in the distance, standing on a platform, Elizabeth sees a pretty woman selling car wax. The woman is looking in their direction. And Elizabeth knows the woman is waiting for her father's eye, because then the woman knows that she will catch it. It's what they are good at, some of them—like playing fetch, or retrieving.

"Yellow," says Mr. Pinski, looking up at the woman, smiling brightly. "Certainly it must come in bright yellow!"

A Honda Civic wagon, four-door, bright yellow with brown vinyl interior—the radio dial glows at night, along with the switches for the heat. The car is a stick shift and smells like new. She has spent a lot of time practicing, first in the driveway, but at least she hasn't been forced to learn entirely from scratch, because she remembers the instruction she received from Bittner, in his Camaro, which had a much firmer clutch, one which made her leg cramp, while they were still dating. Actually, he wasn't a bad teacher. She even recalls how to let up on the clutch on a hill, just so, in order to prevent yourself from stalling.

Or worse, rolling backward. Now she is driving up the highway to her mother's house in Jerome, where she is going to show off her improved driving skills, and her car, and spend the night. By the time she returns, she ought to have it just perfect, her system, and then she'll go to the station where Patrick is working and ask him if he'd like to go for a ride. *Hey there. . . . Want a ride? . . .* just like anybody else's girlfriend. At the auto show, her father wrote the man a check, right there, and afterward she and Patrick drove to her house separately—he in his truck; she following in her father's sedan. He took a lot of backroads and accelerated quickly, causing her to drive recklessly to keep up. At home, they were on the couch, fooling around, when her father drove into the driveway. She straightened her blouse and ran outside and Patrick, stepping out onto the backyard drive, asked her father questions about the number of cylinders inside. The engine was too weak, Mr. Pinski explained, to justify air-conditioning. Meanwhile her father has since delivered precise instructions regarding break-in procedures: she is not to drive over fifty miles per hour, and she is to accelerate slowly, and on the way to her mother's house, especially, she is to vary her speed frequently, between forty and fifty, which means now on the interstate a lot of people keep on passing her. After the first thousand miles, she'll be able to change the oil, and then, said her father, she'll be free to go just as fast as she possibly can.

"Not that fast," he said, smiling. "But that's why we got you one of these things to begin with. I mean, *me*. That's why we got *me* one of these things. Tell your mother she can borrow it, if she likes."

Now, pulling off onto Cherry Highway, just after Cordes Junction, and the hippie hangout, Arcosanti, she's driving down a deserted two-lane highway. On both sides are miles of vast tracts of land, not quite desert, fenced in. In the distance she can see a cowboy, a real one, riding his horse; he is checking the fence, and now he stops his horse, and dismounts, and by the time she passes him, he is still tending to it. Driving by, she waves, and he tips his hat. With the window down, and the radio up, she imagines this is just a taste of it—what's to come, with college, and then beyond. Eventually she makes another turn, and now she is climbing up through the mountains, over the Prescott National Forest, the roads twisting, turning into switchbacks. Some places she has to drive for a long time in second gear, slow going. As she finally ascends the top of the mountain, the sun has begun to set far behind her, lighting up the entire sky purple and orange, and she can feel the light in her hair. Driving faster, she's turning, hanging onto the wheel, and now she's pulling fast into the gravel driveway which belongs to her mother's homemade house.

Inside all is silent. She calls again for her mom, then Fernando. She sees a cat, reaches to pick it up, holds it to her cheek. The cat is purring, grateful for the touch. In the mountains, especially at this altitude, life is cooler and far removed. She wanders over the gravel floor, which has been covered with rugs—Indian rugs, picked up from trading shops all over the state, and New Mexico and Colorado. To wash them, you simply pour water on the top and let the excess drain into the earth. The walls are fortified with colored glass, created by old wine bottles which were set into the mortar and stone while being built, piece by piece, and set up against enormous windows. The sun is streaming in through the windows, and in the vast center room a fire is already blazing. Here, in this house, there are no doors, because each space is designed to permit access into the next, all leading into the *vortex*. In Fernando's study, a new large canvas—a portrait of her mother, nude, still in progress; her mother appears to be reading a letter. On another wall hang androgynous studies—faces, and necks, a pair of hands. As she wanders farther into the house, now heading toward the bedroom, she hears a shower, coming to a stop. A towel flutters, across the hall, and there is Fernando, stepping into the light.

" 'Lizabeth?"

He is tall, and tan, and fully naked—as in completely. She has never imagined a forty-year-old man could be so handsome, so complete, and then she thinks perhaps he is merely thirty-eight, which might explain it. Blinded by the light, and the sight of her mother's lover, age has become an elusive figure. She shields her eyes, squinting, and what's even more astonishing is his embarrassment. He steps quickly over to the bed, reaching for a heavy robe. Cinching it, he steps farther back, crossing his arms.

"We weren't expecting you."

"I called," she says. "Left a message." She is aware she has been blushing, and perhaps she is ashamed. What makes men different from boys is not that very much. Clearly her mother loves the very same things as she. Her mother loves this man, who speaks with a foreign accent, and gives her backrubs while they listen to Mozart, or Chopin, on the couch without ever having to be asked. Elizabeth has seen them.

"My fault," he says. "I haven't checked it yet."

"Where's Mom?"

"Your mother is in Gallup. She went on a reconnaissance mission. She is looking for a certain kind of ceramic tile, I believe." He says, brightening, "For the patio."

"Oh."

"You haven't eaten? We'll make dinner. Quesadillas, with green chilies and fresh salsa. And beer. Cold beer. But we will have to tell your mother," he says, wagging his finger.

"She won't mind."

"First I must change," he says, turning toward the bedroom, drawing a sheet across the doorway.

Even the bathrooms in this house do not have doors; just fabric, which one can fold down, depending. The body is a temple, says her mother. *What's left to be ashamed?* Not the body, certainly; rather, what one does with it. *To it?* Elizabeth turns for the kitchen, which is open, strewn with plants. From the kitchen window she can see her new car, and a huge ponderosa pine, swaying in the breeze.

Later, after he has returned, fully clothed—jeans, a loose cotton jersey—they make dinner, listening to music on the radio. They drink cold beer and sit on the big sofa eating, and Fernando wants to know all about her life—Patrick, and her father, and her music. "Music," he says, eagerly. "Music is what heals the soul."

"From what?"

"I do not know," he says, laughing. "Living, I suppose. But you must take care of your music. You must nurture it like a flame."

She says, pushing away her plate, wiping the back of her hand against her mouth, "Fernando, are you going to marry my mom?"

He laughs, politely, and then for a moment he is silent. He says, "Why would I want to do that?"

"To have a family? I don't know."

"We have a family. We have you, and we have our cats, and this big, drafty house."

"So you don't want to have a family?"

"Oh, I want to have it all. And with your mom, of course, I do. She is a wonderful woman."

"You don't want to have children?"

"I think in general we have enough. I am not opposed to it, I suppose. But I do suppose it would be difficult for them to get used to living with me. I like to travel. I do not like to work—not a good example. I might be in the way with them."

"Like me?"

He reaches across the sofa, takes her arm; there's paint on his hands, beneath the nails. "No. You must never say that. You are not in the way. You are the way. You are what brings us joy. Not Christmas, all those garish lights. But true, genuine joy. You are old enough to bring us that, now that you have grown."

"Eighteen," she says, loud and clear; it's the kind of message she'd like him to convey elsewhere.

He says, taking her hand, looking at the scars, "Do you mind them? Anymore?"

"Sometimes I feel them itching when they aren't. I want to scratch but don't have any reason too. Like the skin is moving."

"That's not the burn," he says, laughing. "Scar tissue is more sensitive. It feels everything!" He says, giving back her hand, beaming, "This just means you are alive!"

She rests her hand first on her lap, then on her shoulder: she is drawing the back of it down the side of her smooth face—as if polished, a still sea. What are you supposed to do with your hands during conversation? Suddenly each gesture has become fraught with complication. She says, pretending a yawn, bringing her hand to her mouth, "I used to think it was her fault."

"Yes," says Fernando, finishing his beer, nodding. "I suppose you did."

She means her parents divorce, not the burn on her arm, but she doesn't know this until it's spoken—what is meant by the fact of her visits here, to her mother's house, the woman who split her father's house apart. She meant to thank her mother, for the car, and the confidence it suggests, and she meant to welcome Fernando properly, at least into her own wing of the family, if only because her mother loves him. Of course her mother fell in love with a nice man. How could she not have? Tonight, Elizabeth will sleep in the library, and tomorrow, after her mother returns, they'll all go on a picnic. And she knows, too, that if she looks Fernando in the eye, if she opens up her mind, and catches it, his eye . . . she knows that she will become entirely out of bounds. As a daughter, it's not her place to approve of her mother's life, just to visit. She says, rising to her feet, preparing to say good night, "My mom—"

"Yes?"

"I wish she had been here. That's all."

She's been thinking lately, over the past couple months, about the Kyrie, Bach's Mass in B Minor, the one she knows so well and has often played: the opening measures: following the initial introductory chord, the pattern of insistence, building, leading eventually to the tenors, and then the sopranos: it's a pattern which seeks always to be resolved, and which builds up a greater and greater complication: one long, celebratory tease, leading however far removed to its final, surrendering chord. Afterward, applause, or maybe an audition at Juilliard, assuming you haven't screwed up too significantly along the way. And what matters most, she knows, is what one feels along that very way: the ascending thirds, the complications of melody and rhythm, their endlessly flirtatious tangling, all seeking to conceal the general strain necessarily required to glorify God—and those very voices. When Patrick sings, often when he believes nobody is listening, it is possible to fall in love with him all over again. It's as if his voice were plucking some reed deep in the center of her body, though certainly she is in no possession of any specific reed. As for the flute, this is a hollow instrument, through which blows the breath of life, of God, and through which she is capable of realizing the nature of melody and song. Just once, just once she wants to come when he does, and not afterward, all alone, as if servicing a debt. This, in spite of the slow circles she is generating inside her body, this rising and falling, this endless pitch. Sunday mornings, lying in her bed, the sun outside inquisitive and alert, generously warm. And when she does come, her voice breathless, a little frightening, she'll cover her mouth with Patrick's shoulder, or with her pillow, or the edge of his blanket. But alone, lying on her belly, her hips rocking on her palms . . . alone it is difficult, she is realizing, for a woman to make a sound when she is in fact all by herself.

Today they are riding along a ridge north of the city, and beneath them lies the Valley of the Sun. There are birds, singing, and wildflowers. Spring. Patrick, meanwhile, has promised horseback riding. She likes to ride a big, slow horse named Strawberry. The wrangler is nice, and often flirts with her; he gives Patrick a strong, frisky horse and praises Patrick's seat—the way he gathers his reins, the way he cocks his heels, just so. He says he likes the way Patrick collects his horse. Germs is chasing hummingbirds.

Patrick rides beside her, wearing his gas station pants, and cowboy boots, which are pointed, he has explained, in order to permit the foot to slip easily in and out of stirrups, lest the foot be trapped. Before Patrick taught her to ride a horse, her experience with stirrups lay strictly with doctors and fashion designers. She has a pair of tights with stirrups, though she rarely wears them. Patrick, meanwhile, practices tight turns with his horse. He says his horse is sloppy, that it spends too much time carrying around people who don't know what they are doing. His horse sometimes rears, the muscles in its neck convulsing, while Patrick lets it lift him into the air. He never startles, either. He is confident, the way he was up on stage, playing his plump twelve-string, entirely secure. He says, while patting its neck, firmly, that this is a very good horse. He holds out his arm, slackening the reins, to preserve the horse's mouth, which Patrick says is soft . . . *a soft mouth* . . . and his arm is tan and full of muscles, something she hasn't recognized before, at least not in this light. His arm is full of veins—leading to his wrist, to the back of his hand.

He says, entirely out of the blue, "Elizabeth, would you still like me if I were poor?"

They've never really talked about money. Her father, she knows, intends to send her to college. She's had several applications already accepted, and she has spoken to people on the phone, admissions counselors, exclaiming about all her extracurricular activities . . . *so many clubs!* . . . as if a club, that which was often used to bruise, had anything to do with the quality of an independent mind. Glorified salesmen, her father says, who is a salesman. He also tells her not to be so cocky.

"What do you mean, poor? You aren't poor. Of course I would. I mean," she says, laughing, "I don't care."

"I mean if we had to move. If I didn't have any money."

"You don't have any money?"

"I was supposed to. I mean, not supposed. My dad, before he died . . . he made sure there would be money for us later. Me and Caroline."

"So you're not poor."

Patrick says, cautiously, "I think I'm going to sell my truck. Before it gets too old. Then it won't be worth very much."

"You're going to sell your truck?"

"Well, you know, work isn't very far away. And I can always use my mom's car, and I won't need it when I go to college, anyway. Most people live on campus."

When she goes to college, Elizabeth is uncertain where she'll live, though definitely she intends to take her car. She says, "California isn't very far away. You can take the bus. To come visit me?"

"Yeah. Sure. Thing is, I'm not certain I want to go to school here. I don't know. Maybe I'll go to New York City, play in clubs. You can't have a truck in New York City, either. There's no parking."

He rides his horse close up to hers, leans his body, and kisses her. He says, "I'm kind of tired."

"You worked all night."

"That's why I'm tired, I guess. I'm cold, too."

She says, "When the body gets tired, it chills easily. I read that in Science."

Now he pulls away. He cues his horse into a lope, and Germs barks, following. Her horse follows, naturally, and she spends a lot of time making sure she is hanging on properly. Patrick scolds her when she uses the saddle horn. She is following, and she can feel the grit kicked up by Patrick's horse in front of her, stinging her face. She is riding, almost going fast, the wind in her hair, her breasts bobbing painfully; she can feel the heat and sweat from her horse soaking through part of her jeans, and her socks. After a few hundred yards, Patrick slows to a trot, which is even worse: all that bouncing, each direction possible. She pulls on her horse, to stop it, though it won't. Then she pulls again, and now she cries out, "Stop!"

Patrick stops, turns, trots back. "What's wrong?"

She attempts to get off and now her horse flutters beneath her, causing her to lose her balance. She falls precisely on her seat. She scrambles up and punches the horse in the hip, which twitters, as if struck by a fly. A small fly, she thinks, dusting the seat of her jeans. The horse steps away, snorting, aiming for the barn, still several miles off, and Patrick, leaning down from his own saddle, scoops up her reins. He ties the reins to a palo verde, and then he dismounts, and approaches, the reins to his own horse still in his hand. Overhead a large cliff shadows them, the wind gaining speed.

"Hey," he says. "What's wrong? You okay?"

"He's bigger than me," she says, still dusting herself off.

"He's supposed to be."

She says, looking up, "If I told you a secret, would you be mad at me? Would you hate me, for telling you?"

"Like what? You can tell me anything."

"Anything?"

"Anything. I mean, of course you can."

He's wrong, of course. There are things she could never tell him. His naiveté, she thinks; it's a wonder. But at least he didn't laugh at her. At least he wants to believe she can tell him anything. She says, hitching her breath, "You should stop hanging around with Bittner."

He smiles now, as if he understands. Sometimes he seems just like her father—like a man, the way a man smiles at you, not when you're sexy, but when you're being a girl and they think they have invented the meaning of the world. When they think you don't understand: things about cars, and cylinders. Just because you're not interested in cars, and they are; just because you're not particularly graceful on a horse. They get that stupid smile on their faces and want to pat your arm. Like a dog, needing affection.

"I'm serious, Patrick. He's not a nice person. I know."

"Because he broke up with you?"

"Is that what he told you? That he broke up with me?"

He shrugs his shoulders, smiles, looking at the ground. He says, shivering, because they are standing in the shade, "He just said he burned you pretty bad. Do you want to go home?"

"My God. You think he broke up with me?" She steps forward, rising on her toes. She studies for a moment the point of her toes. She says, rising, falling, and rising again on her toes, "Do you know why people keep secrets?"

"Nope."

"Because they are always true, Patrick. Because they are true and because you don't want people to find out."

He looks away now. He rubs his eye with his fist. "Okay," he says. "I just figured it was none of my business." He says, shrugging, "I don't care, I mean."

Hours later, standing alone in the den, skimming the books on the shelves . . . hours later she realized, belatedly, what it was he thought. He thought she was preparing to break up with him. She was trying to break it to him gently, and he shivered again, and turned away, leading his horse toward her own, standing beneath the palo verde. And then she was following him all over again, and she hated this, following, as if she simply were expected to—as if he were an insult, and she the rushed apology. Still she followed him, and then his horse, into the wind. And she thought, I could break up with him. *Right now. Right at this very moment.*

"Hey," she said, running up to him, taking his arm.

"Hey," he said, turning away.

She could tell he felt bad already. He had spent the entire night at the gas station, and his clothes were damp from cleaning the floors, and he was cold. He had taken her horseback riding, because he was nice, and because she knew he loved her, if only because Caroline had said so, and because he felt he had to. She felt suddenly ashamed, and tired, terribly sad. She knew that she could tell him secrets—some of them her own—and it made her feel lonely and cold, because she also knew she never would.

She kissed him, making up her mind, which could go either way. She said, for the very first time in her life, "I love you, Patrick."

And then he smiled, quietly . . . a slight raise in the corner of his mouth. He looked away toward Mesa. Then he led her to her horse. He held him steady while she climbed aboard, and then he handed her the reins, checking her cinch. Now he swung up on his own horse, without even using a stirrup, showing off, and he began to ride away from her at a trot. He was riding into the sun, just like the movies, and she was following all over again.

"Wait up," she called, not wanting to be angry.

Because he had not said he loved her back, which thrilled her to the quick. It meant she could be surprised, as well as misunderstood. It meant he was still very dangerous to her heart. He could make it bleed, even, especially when he didn't want to. She felt her horse pulling her into the direction of the sun, which was still rising, and dead ahead, and she closed her eyes, briefly, in order to let it all sink in. And she took it in—all of it, by way of a long, deeply felt breath. *Let it go*, her father had said, often, especially when she was young. Years ago, when he had promised her one day to buy her a dog. Instead he had given her a car. Lying in bed, years ago, after one of her surgeries—skin grafts, especially those from the hip—she would be lying in bed. She wanted a puppy, something to feed and sleep with at night, when she was lonely and couldn't sleep, when time simply refused to budge, the bandages swelling all around her body, and late at night, crying, she often woke her father. If she waited long enough, sometimes for eternity, her father would eventually slip into her room. He'd be sleepy, and fall onto his knees, and she'd listen to him praying, actually praying, the Lord's Prayer, over and over again, as if it had become a psalm, or a hymn, and then he'd take her hand. The good hand, not the bad, and then he would whisper to her stories about a little girl with ponies and dogs, a cabin in the mountains . . . a cool stream flowing, always flowing from the mountains. Run off, from the melting show . . . and the pain in her body, simply too exquisite to extinguish, too fine to give up yet without a struggle, or regret, because it was hers, after all . . . because she had claimed this for her very own, after all . . . and then she would listen for her father's voice, inside and out, whispering softly as possible, *Let it go, Elizabeth. Just let it go.*

Where, she would say. *Where?*

And he would say, releasing her good hand, pointing to the moon, or possibly a rising star, *There, Lizzie. There.*

12

Inside of his room he is sitting on his bed, facing the window, looking out. He is holding his guitar, fingering chords: one here, one there. He instructs his fingers to strike the frets discretely—an exercise, designed to instill precision.

A chord, he knows, is worth far more than the sum of its separate notes. The value of a major seventh, his favorite, is that it always presents the need for resolution—like a good book, or adventure. The major chord, always polite, welcomes you like a handshake from your guidance counselor, but with not much else to say, afterward. The seventh leans toward complaint; the minor, a Dylan tick, tends to whine, to close itself off from possibility. What is needed is a sense of arrangement, or harmony, and bitter, always, is the enemy. The minor and the seventh will work only when struck precisely. Perhaps someday he will teach himself to work with open tuning? He wants to teach himself to use a slide. Meanwhile it's this particular idea of the major seventh—allowing itself to remain open, independent as Orion, or Aries—which tonight he wants to remember, to carry with, similar to the shape of the moon traveling across his window—the angle of incidence clearly lit up, as if by a beam.

"Bottom line—" said Big Jim Walenka, last month, standing in their living room. "Bottom line, things don't look so good."

It was the first he'd been to their house in several weeks, but the news of Jefferson Thrift, and its sudden declaration of bankruptcy, had been well-documented by the media: the kind of story which hit closely to several thousand homes. Each of the investors, most of whom had entrusted their modest savings to the local thrift, was completely wiped out. At school Patrick's teachers talked about the failure as another fine example of middle-class greed gone awry, especially his Economics teacher, who knew well of such things. Even Fuller was talking about it, having lost several thousand he had intended to put up against a summer house in the mountains, as well as a new car for his wife, lest she begin threatening to leave him. Meanwhile all that remained of Patrick and Caroline's trusts were several lingering legal fees.

"Meaning?" Patrick said to Jim. "Meaning?"

"If I could take it all back, Big Pat, I would. But this looked good. Things were bad everywhere, as you may recall. This was a good thing. Solid management."

"So what happened?"

"Margin bets, too heavy. Combined with heavy losses in copper. The president flying off to Acapulco. Bad management, you see. Derivatives. It's complicated."

Patrick's mother sat quietly on the sofa, sipping a glass of wine. She waved her hand and said, "Pshaw."

"Pardon me?" said Patrick.

"I've been broke before. Long before I met your father. I grew up in the dust bowl—"

"But *you're* not broke," said Patrick.

"Not completely," said Jim. He adjusted his tie, hiked up his slacks to sit on the sofa. "You've taken some big hits," he said to Mrs. McConnell. "That mine in Heber wasn't a particularly good idea." She had loaned Jim close to a hundred thousand dollars in venture capital, not to mention her own stake. Risky, he had explained. *Tremendous potential!* Meanwhile work on the house, the addition behind the garage—all that would have to stop, simply because they no longer had any cash. Patrick would sell his truck . . . *her truck* . . . which would help to cover legal fees. She would need to borrow for the time being on his and Caroline's insurance policies. *Time being,* his mother liked to say, as if it were alive . . . and she would need to tap Patrick's savings from his work at the Shell station, approximately two and a half thousand dollars. She said to Jim, who was fidgeting with his vest, "If we don't finish work on the house, we won't be able to sell it. I'll just have to get to work!"

Now that Jim had returned to her living room, her mood had lightened considerably, becoming almost buoyant. The future, she indicated, broadly, by waving her hands, had turned wide-open. They could move to California, be closer to the action. Jim was moving there next month, just as soon as he placed his dying wife into an institution, to work at a securities firm in Orange County.

"Best to hold onto the house," Jim said, heading her off. "If you can, that is. Capital gains. Plus interest rates hitting thirteen percent. Not a good time to sell. Wait till things settle down. Couple years. At least till we get Carter out of office."

"I'll be all alone," Mrs. McConnell said. "Then what?"

"Then you'll be free," Patrick said, bitterly. "Scot-free."

"Watch your tone, young man."

"My tone?" he said. "My tone? Mom, this did not have to happen. You know this did not have to happen."

"Know how you feel," said Jim. "Know exactly how you feel, Big Pat. The world's a jungle out there."

"Do not call me that," Patrick said. "Do not ever call me that again."

In his Economics class at school, which was required by the state for graduation, and where one received instruction on the proper way to balance a checkbook, Patrick had come to understand copper was not quite as valuable as gold, which was good; or silver, less so: for this he received school credit. During one project, the class had been instructed to use Monopoly money to invest in the stock market, to show how easily riches could be made, though Patrick doubted his Economics teacher had ever paid much attention. According to the rules, you could pick only one stock, and Patrick had bought Uniroyal, the manufacturer of the tires on his truck, at 2.34 a share, and over the course of the semester he had lost a total of one hundred fifteen dollars, Monopoly. His teacher gave him a D, not because he'd lost so much, but rather because Patrick's graph utilized only three colors. In addition, each day a student was expected to provide a presentation, one which would last the entire class period, which meant of course the teacher never taught anything. And because Patrick's film—a movie on the depression, in black and white, ran short—and because Patrick then had to explain things . . . it was bad, made worse by people buying on the margins . . . which he even explained, quite clearly, and having now some personal experience, which he did not explain, because nobody likes a know-it-all, unless you are paying him for bad advice . . . because Patrick's presentation nonetheless was not as interesting as the girl who brought in her uncle, an ex-convict, who instructed the class on new-improved methods of committing forgery; or the boy whose quadriplegic neighbor once worked for the telephone company, and talked very fast, explaining from his wheelchair various ways to repair phone lines in a thunderstorm . . . and also because Patrick just didn't like his teacher very much, his teacher who took attendance twice a day, in order to hold them each hostage, and because Patrick chose never to speak in class unless called upon, thereby diminishing the alleged value of his class-participation grade, he was to receive a C- in Economics.

Now he was supposed to go to college in the Midwest. His mother thought it was a fine school; somebody she once knew went to a basketball game there . . . a fine reputation, another said briskly, in the guidance office, *very conservative*. His admissions counselor at the college, after cold-calling him in March, had stressed on the phone the school's independence—the fact that it would accept no federal money, as well as the fact of its endowment. He liked the sound of it, *independence,* so he said he'd go, just like that. Meanwhile there was talk on the television and local newspapers calling for an indictment of Mr. Jim Walenka, talk which further explained why Jim had left the state entirely. He had become a television personality, in absentia.

This afternoon, arriving home from school, his mother was sitting in the television room—formerly a garage, meaning there were no windows. All the lights but one were off, and she sat on a new reclining chair she had bought several days ago to add to the decor. She was watching the news with the sound turned off.

"We've been robbed," she said to him.

"You're telling me," he said.

"No. Seriously. I mean we've been robbed. I was out back, watering the plants. I'd left two rings on the television, to have them appraised. When I came back the rings were gone!"

"What rings?"

"Diamonds," she said, nodding. "Belonged to your father's great-aunt. The stones were for you and Caroline. For your weddings. Hah!"

"Stolen?"

"Priceless. Old cut. I mean, not worth much to sell. But irreplaceable, you see." She was crying now, dramatically. She lit a cigarette, exhaled nervously. "I called the police. They were here. In plain clothes. Said he must have come in through that door. The burglar. Right there," she said, pointing behind him. "Asked if anybody else had access to the house."

He was tired and needed to sleep. In five hours, he and Bittner were expected to make a drug buy. Caroline was in town, though they had kept the fact secret from their mother, and now the family jewels had disappeared. Also he had to work tonight. Three months, he told himself, maybe less, then he could leave. He said, "What else did the police say?"

"Said to call the insurance company. They'll pay the appraised value," she said, wiping her eyes. "Isn't that nice of them?"

"Was the door locked?" he said. "Was it?"

"No," she said, weeping. "The gardener? The pool man? I don't know, Patrick. I just don't know anymore. Oh Patrick, why couldn't you have just locked the damn door?"

Midnight, May fifth—Caroline arrives as planned. She knocks gently on the glass of his window. Tugging on his jeans, a T-shirt, he steps gently outside of his room. In the dark hallway, Germs leads the way. He can hear his mother snoring, just down the hall, loud enough to wake the dead.

Were his father buried more closely, who knows? The front door to the house is split at the frame, after having been slammed during a particularly violent argument. His mother was drunk, though he understands her drunkenness to be no excuse for his rage. That night she had called Elizabeth a SOTE . . . *Scum of the Earth* . . . her most bitter epithet, because he refused to invite her for dinner graduation night. She had her own family, he said. And then his mother called the Pinskis snobs . . . *white-trash utter snobs!* . . . and he left the house, slamming the door. Afterward his mother stepped outside and threatened, loudly, to kill herself. She promised to swallow up all her Valium, she screamed, and when he came inside, later, after smoking half a pack of cigarettes, and after gluing the door frame back together—an act of contrition, securing the frame with wood clamps from his father's toolbox, now his, because of matters of inheritance . . . when he returned to the house he went into the kitchen, rummaging through the cabinets, where he found her medication, beside the cooking spices, long neglected. He thought about setting the medication in plain view, perhaps leaving a note of encouragement; he knew the neighbors, once she began screaming, could hear each bit, loud and clear. And given her previously failed attempts, the threat was false, he knew that . . . *No such luck* . . . but this new impulse of his toward sarcasm made him feel sick. *Sarcasm is cheap,* his father would say, *and cowardly. It means only to belittle and hurt* . . . so he placed the medication inside the refrigerator, behind the milk, where she would never find it. The refrigerator felt like a safe, the way it sealed in the cold, and kept air out, lock-tight.

Outside Caroline is sitting on a large rock, one of many which cost several hundred dollars, apiece, each placed artistically beside the mailbox. The mailbox has been stuccoed into a pillar, decorated with ceramic tile—the southwestern touch. It's the place where all his mail ends up, mostly letters addressed to his name, demanding payment in full, and occasional notices from the college in Wisconsin: hints regarding study habits, and lists of restaurants, free passes for miniature golf. Nearby the school lives his Uncle Punch, whom he hasn't seen in years, and to whom his mother apparently owes several thousand dollars. Uncle Punch, says Caroline, warned their father never to marry their mother; consequently, Uncle Punch never comes to visit. "He's almost family," their mother said once, terrified. "He knows our secrets!"

Caroline lights a cigarette. At the sight of Germs, she smiles widely, sets the cigarette on a rock, and hugs the dog. Then she stands and puts her arms around Patrick and holds him tightly.

"Where's Duane," Patrick says, breaking free.

"In the car. He wanted this to be private."

In the street, behind a palo verde, sits a small, foreign car with out-of-state plates. The car is dusty from having been driven hard across the desert. "Private," Patrick says, lighting a cigarette, nodding. "There's nothing left."

"I told Uncle Punch. He says there's nothing he can do. Since it's already gone, that is. You know she made Dad keep him out of the estate. He was supposed to administer it, but she was afraid of him."

"Mom says I have to sell the truck."

"Are you going to?"

"It's her truck. I don't need it. I mean, I won't, when I go away to college. I can work at the gas station through summer. Then I'll go."

"I can't pay my tuition," Caroline says. "And I owe fifteen thousand from this past year. And Mom won't fill out the financial aid forms. The school says I have to declare myself an independent and that will take months. Maybe a year."

Financial aid is what they were supposed to be without. They are silent for a moment. Patrick kicks a stone and says, shrugging, "It wasn't ours to begin with."

"Mom's okay," Caroline says. "Isn't she?"

"She can't work," Patrick says. "Nobody would hire her. Now that Walenka's left the state, she's stopped writing screenplays. She keeps buying raffle tickets."

"What about her friend the senator?"

He laughs. "I think it's a bit one-sided, that friendship. His secretary won't even call her back."

Still, their mother is set for life, so long as she doesn't tamper any longer, and so long as she sells the house before the balloon payment comes due, and so long as she stops pretending to be rich. Patrick knows something his Economics teacher does not: he knows that what distinguishes the rich from the middle class is their ability to lose a shit load, and those who stay rich do not lose it often. Meantime, there still exist back taxes, and their mother won't be able to buy a new car next year. But it's not as if she will have to find a job; most of the money she put up at risk, and lost, was his and Caroline's. The nature of a trust, Patrick thinks, is that it is placed in confidence.

Caroline takes a small notebook from her back pocket, then a pen. She begins to write a name and address. When she tears off the sheet of paper, it skims along the top of her finger, and she cries out, sharply.

She looks up at him, her thumb tipped by a crimson cycle. "Paper cut," she says, laughing. "Stings."

"Suck it."

When she lifts her hand to her mouth, he can see the healed line of a cut beneath her wrist. She catches him looking, her thumb in her mouth, and raises her free hand to hold her wrist, the piece of note paper held loosely between two fingers. On her wrists she wears silver bracelets . . . *bangles* . . . she bought last summer on an Indian reservation. Sometimes, with their tinkling, you can hear her coming. "Here," she says, biting her thumb.

He takes the address, looks. "St. Louis?" he says, stuffing the address into his jeans.

"Duane's sister. Do not tell mom. Duane and I might get married. After he divorces his wife. We're going to L.A. now to tell her. And to pack."

"What's she doing in—"

"Long story," she says, impatiently. "Dull."

"Elizabeth is going to California," Patrick says. "I want to go there. Someday. She's going to college there."

"It's lonely there, too, Patty Mick. Trust me."

Caroline shifts her weight, restlessly, because she's eager to leave. When she leaves, this time, maybe she really won't come back. She says, "I'm sorry I won't be at graduation."

"Ahh. Big deal."

"That's what I thought. Big deal. You can visit me, and Duane, next year. Uncle Punch says he can't wait to see you. And Germs. I've told him all about Germs!"

"Can I come to your wedding? I mean, if you get married?"

"It will be a small one. Duane's embarrassed. On account of my being a student—you know. His family won't approve. We're only doing it so I can get tuition. Also, if we're married, the school won't fire him."

"Do you want to get married?"

" 'Course not. It's practical, though—"

"Then you shouldn't get married like that," he says, shifting his weight. "Not that I should tell you what to do. You're the older sister. But it's not right. I mean, don't get mad. Can't you come back here?"

"The rules, Patty Mick. They don't exist anymore. You know? There's no system that works. It's just you. I can't come back. You see that?"

"Yes."

"Besides, I love him. I really love him."

"She's getting dangerous," he says.

"I know."

"No, you don't. I mean it's worse. Worse than before. She's getting really dangerous and she makes me feel like it's my fault."

"Oh," says Caroline, suddenly. She puts her arms around him, and holds him, the way she used to. He can smell the soap in her hair; her breasts are pressed up against his chest. She has freckles on her breasts, he knows this, and scars on her wrists. As she holds him, rocking, she says, "Patty Mick, you are the strongest man I know."

"She's completely out of hand!"

"You are so strong," she says. "Shhh."

"I don't feel like it."

"Swear to God," she says, patting his back. "Swear to God and hope to die."

He steps back, squinting. "Don't say that," he says. "It's not fair."

"I love you."

He takes a breath. He knows she loves him—not the way she loves Duane, but more. She loves him because she does not have to. There is no act to justify, or explain: no fucking to get in the way, which explains why they have seen each other naked, with neither shame nor gratitude: because she is his sister, who understands the nature of the universe, as well as the fact of his prick, occasionally rising despite his fierce convictions. If she saw it, his prick, lifting against his jeans, then she'd simply ask him how it felt. Stands to reason, she'd say. The fact of two bodies.

"Okay," he says, nodding.

"No," she says. "Say it back. Say *I love you, Caroline.*"

It's why we have to speak; he knows this now. Because nature does not listen; and because you have to be absolutely clear when it matters most. "Okay," he says. "Okay, I love you."

She turns on her heel, smiling, and now she's walking away, her feet crunching the gravel. She is walking away to a car which will take her to California, at least for a while. Across the street, beneath the light of the moon, she steps up on her toes to wave, and then she slides into the passenger seat, and the car starts up, properly, and the lights come on, which surprises him. Inside sits her new lover, just waiting to take her places, and then the car drives away. Standing, watching it drive away, Patrick listens as the car finds its gears—first; then second. Then all the way up.

Graduation, at night, because it's already hot. His mother has forced him to attend, despite his sincere intention to avoid it, this pomp and circumstance . . . high school graduation, which seems designed strictly to provide his mother with an opportunity to gloat, which is sad, because it's not as if she has a lot to gloat about. It's not as if he's brilliant, or magna cum laude, or even honors. Elizabeth has honors, as well as an academic scholarship to Pomona. Sometimes he thinks maybe he'll run a kennel and train dogs for a living. Sometimes Mr. Windham stops in at the station while Patrick's working and offers him a job: mostly room and board, in a place up by the New Mexico border, near Gallup, where Mr. Windham trains dogs and quarter horses—a summer place to escape the heat. According to Mr. Windham, you can't buy experience. He could use a hand.

But he's also supposed to go to college. At the graduation, dressed in his red and orange outfit, according to school colors, Patrick stands in line. Then he sits in a chair. Then he is in line again, and eventually he is handed a diploma with a nice little message signed personally by the principal, who is of course a very nice and very busy man. The message is thoughtful and encourages him, in proper Hallmark fashion, to find wind beneath his wings, to reach for the stars, to shoot for the moon. Then somebody gives a speech, declaring not for the first time this evening to be in fact *our day. Because we've earned it!* After a lot of hand-clapping, the person then uses the word *myriad* often. Afterward a local Dairy Queen owner gives a speech full of interesting stories about people who also became successful: Charles Lindbergh, for example; and Sylvester Stallone, the movie star. Captain Cook, who sailed around the world and discovered Hawaii. Even Helen Keller.

She was blind of course. He knows lots of Helen Keller jokes. In Illinois, he and Caroline used to stay up late, in her room, telling Helen Keller and Dead Baby and Polack jokes. Elizabeth is Polish, but she tells Polack jokes sometimes, too. Sometimes, telling jokes, Caroline would laugh so hard she'd begin to pee, in her pajamas, making her laugh even harder, and then their father would step inside the room, grumpy, sleep in his eyes, and scold them properly. His father, he understands, was always proper: then he was often out of town. He was a quiet, polite man with a violent temper who blew his brains out with a pump shotgun, and then he had left his children a tremendous amount of money . . . *in trust* . . . which now had also vanished. Meanwhile it was time for speeches, and after the ceremony, tonight, Elizabeth would not have a curfew: now they could watch the sun rise legally. Patrick's mother intended to sell his truck before the end of the month.

If he thought about it long enough, it made him angry, then sad, for feeling angry, and ultimately embarrassed for caring about something with a lot of miles on it. It was just a truck, after all. It made him ashamed and eager to leave the state. If he went to college, he could become a lawyer, or an astronomer. In the advertisements, the buildings of the college in Wisconsin were pretty and had a lot of windows and sometimes, at night, he could imagine himself there, in the library, becoming an intellectual, or maybe just a better musician. Unlike everybody else speaking up at the podium, he has no idea what he is going to do with his life.

His mother, of course, thinks the college in Wisconsin to be a fine idea, because it is private, and because that will be worth talking about to her neighbors, should they sometime soon engage in conversation. Let's face it, she said to him, standing by the kitchen sink. *You're not Einstein.* Sometimes his mother was so lonely it made him feel entirely at fault.

After the class of 1979 tosses up its caps into the hot air, Elizabeth runs across the field to him. She kisses him, her breath hot and sweet, like a Lifesaver, and then they are running through all the people to the stands. There her father shakes his hand, smiling, and her mother kisses him, on the mouth, and Fernando gives him a big hug—macho style, with a lot of clapping on the back. It's odd, but he feels suddenly beloved by these people he's hardly been related to. Then his mother, standing by herself, dressed up for the first time in months, as if this were a date, calls to them, waving them over.

"Patrick!" she exclaims. "Your shoes are all dusty!"

"Sorry," he says. He polishes them on the back of his slacks, a pair he's never worn before, paid for by his wages at the station, because this is supposed to be a special occasion.

"What a fine speech," she says. "You should have given one." She says to Elizabeth's mother, "He gives wonderful speeches. He's going to college in Wisconsin, you know. Did you know?"

"Maybe," he says.

"Of course you are," she says. "And I'll be left all alone with Elizabeth."

Mr. Pinski smiles politely. He places his arm around his ex-wife and says, "Well—no, actually. But we'll be here, of course. And Fernando."

"Of course his sister couldn't be here. Far too busy," Mrs. McConnell says, biting her lip.

Elizabeth takes Patrick's hand, gently, and now her mother says something to his mother, and Fernando leans back on his heels, eager to leave. His mother is nervous, he understands, which accounts for all her silly talk. Sometimes it is simply impossible for her to shut her mouth, and he understands she means no harm, per se, which makes it worse: this constant source of embarrassment.

Elizabeth's father says they certainly did have nice weather. He says, turning, growing impatient, "You kids are going out, I presume?"

"Yes," says Patrick, gratefully.

"If you get drunk," says Mr. Pinski, "then call somebody. Everybody hear that? If you get drunk, call somebody up. Do not break the law publicly."

"Patrick doesn't drink, Dad."

"Of course he doesn't," says Mr. Pinski.

"No, really. He doesn't drink."

"I tried it a couple times," Patrick says. "Makes me sick."

"Oh yes," says Mrs. McConnell. "Patrick is a model of sobriety. It's a shame, though, he couldn't have cleaned his shoes properly." Now she reaches out to him affectionately, because she has meant to tease, but this is not the way it has been received, her criticism, and she recognizes this. His face burns hot, and he brushes her hand away, because he *did* polish his shoes . . . *twice* . . . and now he can see the shame building up behind her eyes.

"If you didn't want me to come," she says to him, in front of Elizabeth, and her parents, "then you should not have invited me!"

"Mom—"

She turns away now, without even saying good-bye, and begins walking home across the lawn: with her heels in the grass, she will have to find her footing carefully. Her house is still a few blocks away, and he wants to do something to make her not feel so badly; he wants her to stop criticizing his shoes, or his hair, or the way he fixes her dinner. Mostly he wants to leave on terms which will permit return, someday later, after she is better. After she has found a way to save herself. Watching her walk across the lawn, he says to Elizabeth's mother, because she might understand, being a mother, "She's been real tired lately. My mom. She's mad at me, too."

"Of course," Lydia says, wrapping her arm around his shoulder, hugging him. "Happens to everybody."

"And sad," he says, nodding.

"Isn't there a prom or something?" says Mr. Pinski.

"That was last month, Dad. Tonight's the night we all go skinny dipping in the river."

"Everybody?" Lydia says. "What fun!"

"Of course," says Mr. Pinski. "Skinny dipping. If you drown, call somebody. Promise me."

Elizabeth kisses him. "I promise, Daddy."

"Well, run along. Be safe."

And now they are sailing across the field, hands held, their robes unfurled, gathering in the breeze.

His father loved to sail. He taught himself to sail long before he met Patrick's mother, and while she was pregnant with Patrick, his father began to build a boat to sail on Lake Michigan. He built a Thistle, a small sloop with a jib and mainsail, and because he was particularly thrifty, and equally concerned about the future, he built the boat in his garage—piece by piece, accordingly, and as he could afford it. The project took well over two years, and as Patrick's second birthday came into view, his father still hadn't been able to afford either the sails or the rigging. There were lingering debts from Patrick's delivery, and his father wanted special lines and brass cleats: he wanted to do this properly. And wanting to please her husband, because they were still happily married then, Patrick's mother began a savings fund, into which she delivered all of her loose change from the groceries, and the milk man, and the tollways. She filled the jar with change, day after day, setting it aside when full and beginning another, and finally, when there was at last enough to make the final purchase—the sails, the perfect rigging—she constructed a pretty little card in the shape of a sailboat. Inside the card was a picture of Patrick, lying on his back, stubborn, and beneath the picture his mother had taped two shiny pennies, beside which she had written, in the voice of Patrick, *I wanted to put in my two cents worth.* Over the years it had become one of the happy stories, and she would tell it often, to show how proud she was of him: actually, it was one of the stories which made Patrick proud of *her.* At the time, of course, Patrick did not know he would someday want to grow up and please his father, and unlike so many of the other stories, to the best of his knowledge, Patrick understood this one to be true—all of it, even the part about the card, which had been tucked inside his baby book. Missing only were the two coins, having been spent. Then after they moved into the big house, being landlocked, his father sold the boat to a man named Mr. McCloud, and Patrick remembers that he was sad, his father, and that he did not want to lose it. Eventually, too, his father stopped pointing out the night sky—the constellations, or Venus. His father never sailed again.

Actually, Elizabeth has fibbed: *everybody* is really at a party in the desert—a boondocker, fortified with kegs of beer. But Patrick and Elizabeth go to the river, forty-five miles into the hills—the one true source of water. Driving, up through the dark hills, she asks, "What are you thinking about?"

"Everything," he says, looking out the window. "I guess."

Once there, with the hot moon skimming across the water, Elizabeth slips off her new dress, beneath the trees, and hangs it on a limb. She unbuttons Patrick's shirt, while he slides out of his slacks, and then they are stepping into the water. The water is cold, rushing about their ankles, and he can feel the muscles in her hand, guiding him. Mostly he is grateful for the light on her skin. Inside the water, cold as ice, he feels his breath escape.

A cool breeze. When a woman's nipples become hard, the way they do each week on "Charlie's Angels," it usually means the woman is either cold or a well-paid actress: sometimes it might mean something else. Sometimes, when he has to take a leak, his cock grows hard as walnut. Shame, he is beginning to understand, belongs outside the fact of his body. Shame is becoming a drug dealer when you do not want to be a drug dealer. Thus decided, he will have to make his position clear. He is going to have to stop, because it is wrong, if only because he doesn't want to do it.

"Careful," she says, letting go his hand. "You can't step in the same place twice."

"I guess not."

She says, stepping forward, "Do you feel any different?"

"No," he says, tossing his arms, warming them up. "But I'm waiting to."

"I've decided," she says. "I don't believe in coincidence. Not anymore."

They dive into the water, catching the current, because here there are no locks. For a while they are drifting freely. Eventually she reaches for him, pressing his body up against the river bank. He sputters for air, and he can feel her using him, warming herself up, preparing the way, something she's never done before, not like this, and now she is sliding her body onto him: the heat inside of her descending over him like a flame—the sun, when you're outside, without your shirt, and it begins to bake into your skin. If you look too closely, you'll never see again, and above him her eyes are gazing into his own. Watching her, her pale breasts, her hair wild and brushing his cheek, damp on his chest, he knows she's found her rhythm. And now she closes her eyes, because she has brought him home, here, inside her body, where he knows he wants to stay just as long as possible.

"No," he says, reaching for her hips, slowing her.

"What?" she says, opening her eyes.

"I don't want it to end."

"Me, too," she says, wiping her hair from her eyes. "I don't want it to end, either."

He lifts his head to kiss the tip of her breast. Then he lets his head fall, behind him, into the riverbank. A breeze skims across the water, chilling them partially, because they are still in reach.

Beneath them the current is alive, and she's looking into his eyes, and somewhere overhead the constellations appear to be traveling fast. Astrology, he knows, is like a secret; it's a key the ancients made to unlock the meaning of the universe. It's what you look for when you want direction, like what job to take, or whom to marry. But all he wants right now is this. All he wants is to lie very still, with Elizabeth, inside the very heart of sky.

"Like this," he says, brushing her hair from her eyes. "Stay like this."

13

At breakfast, in a hotel in California, drinking fresh-squeezed orange juice, and coffee with two creams, her mother says a man may be assertive, but a woman behaving likewise will always be a bitch.

"Why's that?" says Elizabeth.

"Because it's a man's world," says her mother, smiling. "And because he knows a woman can take it away from him, whenever she wants, just so." Her mother lights a cigarette, blows the smoke toward the ceiling fan, to be polite. "In college, you learn how to read," says her mother. "You train yourself to think. But to live, properly, really properly . . . first you have to get there."

Elizabeth says, digging into her grapefruit, "It's expensive. College."

"Lot more expensive without." Lydia reaches for the ashtray, knocks at the ash. "It's fear, you see, fear on the part of all the men in the world that makes a woman seem a bitch . . . fear, combined with a longing to be held by her."

"Uh huh."

"Men, you see, feel constantly betrayed, because most of the time they are."

Elizabeth feels herself blush, hotly, as if she might begin to steam. The orange juice, despite being fresh-squeezed, mingles with the toothpaste she has used to brush her teeth. She has clean teeth, pink gums. Her mother she understands can see right

183

through her. One thing she is certain of is her desire to betray nobody; at the same time, what distinguishes night from day is the location of the sun, or moon, in relation to yourself—just which side of the world you happen to be on. She says, considering, "Why are they betrayed?"

"To begin with, we want more than they can offer. And we can also get by without. Them, you see. It hurts their feelings." Now her mother crushes out her cigarette, in the spirit of trying to quit, and says, "A woman, if you do her wrong—a woman will forget. We'll let it go. We like to get along. That's why women always make up. But a man, you see—a man remembers everything you do to him. Every single thing—"

"Okay."

"And if you don't forget," says her mother, reaching for her coffee, "then how can you possibly ever forgive?"

"I don't know."

"This makes a man dangerous," her mother says, exhaling. "It also makes him capable of enormous tenderness, because when he does forgive, when he does it truly, you know he still remembers. Just go ask your father."

Elizabeth says, eager to change the subject, "Should I be taking notes?"

Her mother laughs, instantly. "No," she says. "Did you call Josie?"

Josie is Lydia's hair stylist; she also costs a fortune: for extra, you can be picked up in a limo. "Yes," Elizabeth says, nodding.

"Good. She's very, very good."

"Okay."

"Elizabeth," says her mother, "you are going to hurt people, like it or not. And men are going to hurt you, too. They'll betray you simply because you do not understand them. Because men and women hurt each other. It's a fact, you see. They hurt each other because they are not the same. It's what makes love possible to begin with."

"I know," says Elizabeth. "The hurting."

"Yes, the hurting. But also the danger. It's the danger—the very promise—that brings you close. The very thrill of it."

When Elizabeth saw Fernando, naked, standing right in front of her, his body was still dripping with water. She feels, sitting here in a dining room full of seascapes and pastel drapes, absolutely naked and misunderstood and immature. If possible, she would slip inside a pool of water; she'd begin to drift away from view. She'd begin teaching herself to behave properly.

"Getting naked," says her mother, waving her hand, "heavy petting? Fucking around. That's not the half of it, you know. And I'm not talking about ax murderers or syphilis or herpes. Sex is dangerous, no doubt about it. But the real danger is being honest. Absolutely honest. All-the-time honest. No secrets. No lies. You get that in a relationship—with a lover, Elizabeth—then you've got the thrill of a lifetime. I promise you."

Elizabeth sips her coffee, still hot, and bitter: a taste she's getting used to. She glances at her watch, a graduation present, then the window. If she is not careful, she will start to cry.

"Not to worry," says her mother, taking her hand, smiling. "You're growing up, is all."

"I'm not," she says. "Worrying, I mean."

Her mother says, turning Elizabeth's wrist, looking at her new watch, "I know." Then she says, releasing her, "Hey. We have a plane to catch!"

He rises early, lets Germs out to pee. In the kitchen he puts away the empty wine bottles and pours a glass of juice, fixes himself a bowl of cereal. He sets out Germs's food—three scoops, plus a vitamin—and laces up his work boots. It's summer now, June, and he is entirely on foot. The man who bought his truck was a born-again Christian and talked a lot about fishing. Patrick has never been fishing, and it seems a particularly difficult thing to do in a state which is mostly arid. Christ, said the man, was a fisherman.

He was also of course the Son of God; in this light, it is helpful to view the world through Ray•Bans. He calls Germs and follows a series of trails through vacant lots, soon to be developed, by people in the know, and which will lead him to the highway. His mother has been advised by various flyers tucked into her mailbox to oppose the development, because of fear of renters, and their inherent risk to property values. As for the sun, it is already beginning to burn off the morning breeze, and now Patrick is cutting across a span of private property. Everywhere there are signs: and a bird, sitting on a barbed wire fence; a backhoe, preparing to lay in a new foundation. Crossing the private property, soon to exchange hands, he waves to a work crew preparing for a good day's work: men, in boots just like his, greeting each other in the morning light. Because today everybody knows it's going to be a hot one for at least another three months. Simply he cannot wait to leave for someplace where it snows. What he misses most about living in the Midwest, beside the snow, in February, or March, is the church he used to go to, and the early Sunday services his father always drove them to, and the sweet comfort of the liturgy therein: sitting there, dressed in his choir robe, tucked into the cool balcony behind the organ, he had taught himself to pray. *Forgive us our trespasses . . .* because only then, by asking, was it possible to have a reason to forgive—to be kind, and to let things slide, and to prevent yourself from bitterness . . . *as we forgive those . . .* and by the time he hits the intersection where the gas station sits, the last outpost of civilization, at least for another month, because things are booming, everyday, especially on Shea Boulevard . . . by the time he hits the intersection he is jogging fast with his dog beside him. On the lot sit pickup trucks full of teenagers and girls with inner tubes, tying up, and boys, scratching at their bellies, inflating tires and checking under the hood, loading up coolers full of ice. The tubers are going to the river, and it is important, Patrick knows, to get an early start, because the river belongs to anybody who can get there. At some places, girls take off their tops. He's never been to the river during the daytime, but Patrick intends to go down at least once before he leaves for good. It's a promise he's made himself: to go.

Flying home, she is riding on a plane, in a window seat, gazing out the window. The airplane is climbing up through the valley which surrounds Los Angeles, where there is also a lot of smog and turbulence. Her mother, sitting beside her, says flying is natural, like light.

Her mother says the flight will not take long despite the altitude. In California she and her mother spent most of their time in Claremont, at Pomona, wandering around the campus. One library is constructed precisely like a church. Her father, speaking to her on the phone, while she sat on the bed in a hotel room sipping a glass of wine, wanted to hear all the news. Mostly her father agrees with her mother. You get precisely what you pay for. Price is not an issue. You snooze, you lose.

Across the aisle from her a man is snoozing. Her mom, she knows, despite her best intentions, is as elitist as they come: the Nicaraguan outfits are more an apology than a ruse. Meanwhile what Elizabeth wants most is a school without a serious music program: this way, she will not feel compelled to pursue that which has merely brought her comfort. According to Aristotle, making metal breed is unnatural, as in banking, but her father says that if you want to understand the culture, by which he means his own, as well as hers, then you must also understand that which moves it. Money is the grease which makes the wheel go 'round; the wheel is driven by Lady Fortune, and not Pat Sajak: Boethius, in prison, had come across a lot of bad luck. And if fortune is a wheel, then what goes 'round comes 'round, like the globe, or the sun, blazing outside her airplane window, and she imagines herself someday becoming a banker, and sending her own kids to school, if she ever has any; she imagines cutting her hair short and proving Aristotle wrong . . . *if you prick me do I not bleed?* Unnatural or not, even Shylock had a pound or two of flesh. It's not as if he was an alien, which it had now become illegal to be, especially in California. Maybe she'll also be an English major, or a biochemist. Maybe she will be an airline pilot.

One thing is for certain: she is going to go to school in California, where there is an ocean, and a beach. She is going to move away and lie out in the sun, sometimes without her top, and she is going to live in her own apartment because in California, people are liberal, and progressive, and because it's time she started making her own way. Her mother, glancing through a magazine, flipping pages, looking at expensive items—massagers the size of elephant schlongs, and face masks you store inside the freezer . . . her mother looks up at her, smiling. Eventually the turbulence dies down, and a woman offers her a soda with complimentary peanuts, meaning they are free.

"Wine," Elizabeth says. "Do you have some white wine?"

"Of course," says the stewardess. "But that you have to pay for."

"For two," says Elizabeth's mother. "Chablis. We'll share a little bottle."

Later, a bit higher up in the clouds, her mother asks, "What are you going to do first? When you get back? First?"

"I don't know."

"Patrick will be sad," her mother says. "We all will be. We'll miss you terribly."

"He's going to Wisconsin, anyway."

"Trust me," her mother says, brushing a lock of hair from Elizabeth's eyes. "He's going to be sad."

The wine tastes metallic and sweet, like gasoline. Sometimes Patrick smells like gasoline; she knows he will be sad, despite his best intentions to conceal it. But first thing, after telling her father, and asking him to send a check, to confirm her acceptance . . . first thing next she is going to cut her hair. Short, just to see precisely how it feels.

"Fernando," says her mother, sleepily, taking her hand. "Fernando wants you to pose for him. If you're interested, that is."

Fuller sees him coming and calls out from the center island. Because there is a gas shortage, in full bloom, by noon Fuller will be out of unleaded. Behind the station you can see cars lining up to get in, idling in the heat. Meantime a new self-service station is going in down the block, which will undercut Fuller's prices by three percent. Nothing, Patrick understands, nothing is ever free.

"Hey Mac," says Fuller, brightly, winking his bad eye. "Hey there, Germs."

"Hi," Patrick says, jogging up the lot.

"I didn't know you were working today."

"I'm not. I came to see you."

"Bittner's taking over the evening shift," Fuller says. "Going to make him manager." This will mean a salary for Bittner, not just a raise; this also means Fuller wants Patrick to go to college, and not come back: otherwise, and because he is responsible, and because the married ladies think he's sweet, Fuller would have offered the position to Patrick.

"Uh huh," Patrick says. Tonight he and Bittner are going to make a drug buy, his very last. He has decided, among other things, he does not like being thought of as a mule, or expendable; he does not want to go to prison; most importantly, he does not ever want to have to do it, and now that he actually needs money, it scares him, this immediate and easy access. He says, "I need more hours, Fuller. I need to make more money."

"You're already doing forty," says Fuller.

"I could work days. I've got three months left, before I go. You could bring me up to sixty. If I worked days then I could sell more, too. Nobody buys tires at night. Batteries. I sell a battery, I make ten bucks right there."

"Days then," says Fuller.

"Is that all right?"

"When you leaving?"

"August, I guess."

"What about that little honey of yours?"

Patrick shrugs, looks at the toes of his boots. "I don't know."

"If you go to days," Fuller says, sneezing, like a farmer, one finger pinched over his nostril, snorting snot all over the lot, "then I won't have anybody I can trust for the graveyard."

"If I don't go to days I won't make enough money. I need two more thousand by September fifteenth, plus plane fare, plus a typewriter. You can't go to college without a typewriter."

Fuller brings him inside the station. The mechanic, Butch, is cursing beneath a GM station wagon. Butch is wearing boots, cowboy boots, and he's been here only for a month or so: one finger, where his wedding ring used to be, is just a purple stump, the color of a penis, because Butch got the ring caught in a metal lathe. Then he got divorced. On his hip Butch carries a small automatic pistol, because once he was shot by a guy breaking into his house; also, Butch was a marine in Vietnam. Sometimes he tells stories. Over his tool box he has placed a sign which instructs people not to ask to borrow, lest they risk extreme peril.

"Hey Butch," Patrick says.

"Hey there, Mac. Sure is going to be a hot one!" Then Butch says, reaching for a wrench, "Lost your wheels, eh?"

"Yeah."

"Get a lot?"

"About four thousand," Patrick says. "Waxed it up real nice."

After the man delivered a cashier's check, Patrick went to the bank and deposited it into his mother's account, to pay for legal fees and a set of tires. The car Butch is working on, the one up on the rack, is of the same vintage Patrick's mother drives: she goes through a set of tires once a year, because of the way she accelerates over curbs, always wrecking her alignment. Lately she says she misses her analyst . . . *my analyst* . . . meaning Jim Walenka, who even Patrick understands has ripped her off entirely.

"Too bad he's not a very good one," he said, once, and then she exploded and threatened to make him get rid of his dog.

"He's always shedding," she said. "Why can't you ever say anything nice?"

"He's a dog, Mom. I'll brush him."

Then she disappeared. She disappeared this time for nearly an entire week, during which Patrick felt mostly glad, which in turn made him feel guilty, and later worse. Fuller says to him now, pouring a cup of coffee, looking him over, "You can have days, Mac. You can have any of the days you want."

It hurts, almost, this kindness; it makes him feel small and needy. "Seven," he says, "if it's okay. I'd like seven."

"Overtime under the table, of course."

Now Butch, who's been looking out the window, and eavesdropping, gives off a whistle. A new truckload of tubers has pulled up. Somebody's looking at the tubes, inflated and badly patched, now marked up to fifteen bucks a pop, because it's summer. Because it's what the market will bear.

"I could ask twenty," Fuller says, nodding, looking out the window. "But that would be plain robbery."

"Oughta give 'em away," says Butch, laughing. "Love ya for life."

A boy in cutoffs with greasy hair steps inside the station to ask about prices, and Fuller nods. He calls out to the new kid on the island who's taking numbers. When you take the numbers, you register how many gallons are still beneath the ground in tanks: premium, regular, unleaded. Fuller is considering letting Butch go, on account of his chattiness, and now that unleaded has become so scarce, Fuller is also considering getting diesel. After the new kid takes the numbers, he will have to dip the tanks, which are made out of fiberglass. Meanwhile the kid is scrambling, because Fuller's watching him, and then Fuller says something about the kid, sniffing . . . *sniffing fur* . . . which means looking at the girls in bikini tops and cutoffs . . . *May I wash your window, ma'am?* . . . and Patrick is lighting up a cigarette, petting his dog, Germs, and leaning into the door frame, looking like a pro, he's been here that long. He's leaning into the door frame, shooting the breeze with his boss, and now this fine particular girl in front of him is getting on her knees, looking over a tube, inspecting a patch. She is leaning over a patch, and then her T-shirt, stylishly ripped in several places, falls loose, revealing a bare breast. Truth is, it doesn't even faze him.

"Tuesday," Fuller says, behind him. "Start on Tuesday."

The air feels heavy, like eucalyptus and wildflowers, if you could carry as much as you want. Outside the airport, Sky Harbor, they walk by a flowerbed, freshly planted in anticipation for the new terminal, which will be indoors, like a real airport. Above them the sky is full of airplanes, and Elizabeth can not remember where she parked her car.

"Aisle three?" her mother asks.

"Beats me."

"Three is a good number. Let's try three," her mother says. "Aisle three, blue."

They wander among rows of parked automobiles, though Elizabeth's car does not appear to be among them. Her luggage, a new carry-on bag, purchased specifically for this trip, is digging into her shoulder blade; the bag also has her initials embossed on it—a gesture which causes Elizabeth embarrassment, given her inclination toward anonymity: also, and far worse than bragging, embossed initials imply your parents are still afraid you will become entirely lost. It's a device, like branding, to remind you who you are. Her mother stops, setting down her own bag, and rests her hands on her hips. Now with one hand shielding her eyes, her mother is scanning the parking lot, looking precisely the way she used to look for her daughter at the park, when Elizabeth was young, and fragile. Lydia would stand on top of a park bench in Michigan, or on a picnic table, and scan the horizon for evidence of her daughter playing in the distance. Frankly, Elizabeth can't imagine ever doing that: having a child, and loving it, and then hoping she grows up safely. Hoping you don't spill a pot of boiling water on her arm, or leg, or face. Things could have been worse. She could have even died.

Once, when she was little, she slammed the car door on her mother's foot . . . *by accident* . . . and her mother had screamed for several minutes. Her mother had been wearing sandals, and three of her toes had bled profusely; one even had to be sewn back on. At the time Elizabeth had been angry with her mother, a quarrel regarding a new outfit, with stripes, for school. But it had been an accident, she was sure of it. An accident, of course, meant it hadn't been done on purpose. An accident was the same as a stubbed toe, or a midair collision. It was the kind of harm nobody could ever possibly mean to commit.

Always before she thought she was mad at her mom because she left her dad. But that's not it, precisely, because sometimes people just have to go away; they have to take a trip, or build their own house, or go away to school. "Mom," she says, because she is figuring things out. "Mom?"

"I don't see your car, dear. Imagine that?"

She lets the moment go, this opportunity for apology, because she loves her mother, and because she knows her mother will want to talk about it for a very long time, which will be almost humiliating, humiliating as brand-new towels to take away to school with your name sewed into them . . . *Elizabeth* . . . in loopy script, or a new hot water pot, already packed up in the garage, just waiting to be sent to you through the mail. Bonding is important, her mother will say. Like a free market, or a woman's independence. Like bodies of water, and rain.

•　　　•　　　•

It has not rained for several months: not since the February floods, when the city was set awash with dirty water from the streets, rising, and the traffic sat stalled at intersections for hours. Once water hit your distributor cap, you had to wait for it to dry; even the bridges, all but the Mill Avenue bridge, the city's oldest, had been flooded out. At home, hot and tired and dusty from the walk back through all the vacant lots, soon to be developed, Patrick steps through the sliding glass doors. In the kitchen, sitting in the dark, behind the blinds, he catches his mother's profile.

"The problem with your father," she says, loudly, and to nobody in particular, "is that he was always long-winded."

"Hi, Mom."

She turns, sharply, absolutely startled. "Where were you?"

"At work. Wanted to check my schedule. Fuller's going to let me go to days." He lifts his dog's water bowl, reaches into the fridge for a bottle of cold water, and pours Germs a drink. He sets down the bowl and then begins to fix himself a Coke. He supplies the Coke himself, with his own money, after picking up all the other groceries and wine and scotch. Usually his mother says it's bad for him, all that sugar. He says, looking up over the ice tray, "May I fix you something?"

She points to her water glass, which is full of Chablis. "Long-winded," she says. "Sometimes he just couldn't stop."

It's dangerous, he knows. He can sense combustion: the quiet which precedes a spark, a match just waiting to be struck. Actually, he can't remember his father ever talking enough. Sometimes, he can't even remember the sound of his voice. He says, carefully, "Well, eventually he did. Stop, that is."

"Yes he did. He most certainly did." She says, pulling a dark object from the pocket of her robe, which he recognizes instantly, "What is this?"

"That?"

"In your desk. I found this in your desk!"

The desk is also where he keeps all his letters: from Elizabeth;

from his sister, Caroline. He has a picture of his father in his desk, wearing a tie, his coat off, sitting at a desk. In his desk he keeps his pencils and loose change and his social security card and Germs's pedigree. He says, sitting down at the table, lifting his Coke, "It's a knife, Mom."

"It is not a knife. It is a switchblade!"

"A switchblade?"

"I know what a switchblade looks like. And what I want to know is why do you have a switchblade inside your desk? Do you carry it with you?"

Years ago, while bored, he read a book which rests on a shelf in the living room, *The Cross and the Switchblade.* The premise seemed to be that if you believed in Jesus, you had no need to carry a knife or shoot heroin. Eventually somebody made the book into a movie, possibly starring Pat Boone, or Johnny Cash, which meant, or course, it was a plot no longer available to his mother. Pat Boone, he thinks. Definitely.

"Mom," he says, hopeful to avoid escalation. "You know, I've never seen a switchblade, except in movies. But I do believe that isn't one. It's a folding knife, with a lock, which I found at the station. Rosewood handles, look. Some guy left it by a pump."

"It is a switchblade," she says, rising, "and I will not have my son carrying it around."

"That's why it was inside my desk."

"This is my house, Patrick. And I have every right to go anywhere I want so long as you are living in it. Do you understand? I was looking for your financial aid forms."

"They're on your desk, where I put them. Last month."

He's trapped her now, which is of course a mistake: once cornered by a lie of her own making, she will become vicious. It's the pattern. She says, looking at the knife in her hand, "You are grounded."

"What?"

"You are grounded, young man. You may not leave the house. And if I have to I will ask Jim Walenka to fly out and teach you some proper manners. He says it's about time you felt a man's hand."

"What are you saying?"

"You need a lesson. You carry knives. You're probably doing drugs. You may not do that in my household and Jim Walenka—"

"Jim Walenka should be in jail, Mom. He's a fucking thief."

"You may not speak like that—"

"I will not be grounded. I have to work. I have only ten more weeks and then I will be gone and you can ground me all you fucking like."

"That is what you think. I do not have to fill out those forms. I saw those scars, you know. You said it was a fence!"

The deadline for the financial aid forms was long past due, anyway; he was going to have to borrow thousands from a special program for independents and orphans. "It was," he says, laughing. "I ran into a fence. Barbed wire. I do not know how to knife fight, Mom. Nowadays people shoot people, anyway. Knives just aren't as popular."

"I told you, I will not argue. And I do not have to fill out those forms. I will call that college and tell them what you really are!"

"Which is?"

"A perverted little thief. I saw you. I saw you two, out at the pool. You think I didn't see that. Your father, too . . . did you think you really were the first?"

"You are a liar."

"Oh God, Patrick. Look at those scars on her wrists. They weren't even deep!"

She is weeping bitterly, and he has lost his center, no longer certain. He takes a breath, recalls the silver bracelets Caroline wears on her wrists. He says, trying to be calm, "Mom, I will not hate people just because you are afraid of them. You cannot make me hate them. Jesus," he says, his voice rising, "what are you so afraid of!"

She throws the knife at him—like a rock, or stone. Patrick

ducks, and then steps across the kitchen floor, reaching for it. There he unfolds it, properly, the way his father once taught him: but she is correct, it is a dangerous blade. He takes the knife, holds it up to the phone cord, dangling from the wall, intending to test its edge. But once started, he knows, there's no going back. He cuts the line.

"Ha!" she screams. "Big man. Big man with a knife. You going to stab your mother? You going to stab your mother because she grounded you? Huh, little man?"

It's a gesture, he knows, like John Wayne—riding into the sun; like your old man, leaving the sticker price on the stock of his shotgun. Did he really mean to forget? He takes the knife, folds home the blade, and tucks it into the back pocket of his jeans. He says, "I am not grounded. If you like, then call Jim Walenka. Use the other phone, Mom. But go call him. Tell Big Jim to come give me a proper thrashing. A man's hand? You go right ahead."

"Where are you going?"

"Out."

"You are grounded!"

"I need to borrow your car."

"You may not. Not my car. I do not give you permission to borrow my car!"

"Mom, I'm not asking."

"Honor thy mother and father," she says. "Because God knows, Patrick McConnell. God knows! Everything," she says, "everything I do is just for you. For you alone. But no, you think that little slut—"

"Which one, Mom?"

"You think I don't know a slut when I see one? You, coming home with your shirt buttoned all wrong . . . you think I was born yesterday? She has turned you against me, her entire family, and I will not have it!"

Now, on his way out, he calls to Germs. And he can feel the knife, wearing away the fabric in the seat of his jeans like a wallet full of cash. He has a set of keys in hand and close to twenty bucks and a job to do. Three years ago, when he found his father, dead in the stable, his brains smeared into the hay, and tack, the walls all covered with blood, he had no idea what he should do next. He didn't even know his father had been sad. What do you do when you discover a dead body, especially one which happens to belong to the man who taught you not to lie? To polish your shoes and scrub behind your ears? When he and Caroline were little, in the old house, on Wilmington Street, they would take showers with his father: the shower was in the basement, a pipe sticking out of the wall, beside the furnace, and they'd all be in the shower, careful not to slip on the painted floor, which was slippery, the paint peeling off the cement in sheets . . . and then their father would tell them to scrub themselves good, the private places, too, and when they were done their father would wash himself, lifting his big arms, and then his hand reaching into the complicated nest between his own thighs, all that hair and mass, briskly, as if it were a chore, or duty, and then their father would wash their hair, his big hands scrubbing at your head: if you complained, he'd scrub even harder, until you laughed, and then he'd say, *Enough. Enough before you drown . . .* and then he'd help dry you off, with towels the size of blankets, thick as cream, the kind he'd pour on your cereal, half-and-half, to start your day off special with raspberries. Then, before leaving for the train, he'd check your socks, and make sure you'd brushed your teeth, and walk you to the bus, holding your hand, yours and Caroline's: sometimes you could feel the ring on his big hand, cutting into your own: he loved Caroline; he loved you; and then he blew himself to oblivion—the barrel tucked into his mouth, opened wide. Sometimes, late at night, Patrick would hear them, his father and his mother, yelling in the bedroom. Once he and Caroline heard them fucking, his father silent, his mother wailing to the moon, or God, and Caroline explained this was the way grown-ups made up, after all the screaming, to show they hadn't meant it, and then she said when their mom and dad became divorced they'd get to go with their dad, because he was responsible, and hadn't ever been institutionalized . . . because he wasn't *alcoholic*. In the stable, looking at his father's dead body, Patrick had hid the shotgun by sliding it beneath a bale of hay. Then he let out the horses, into the paddock, so he could grain them properly. You could see the steam from their breath, rising up into the sky. Afterward, he forgot about the horses entirely, and then he sat down on a bale of hay and didn't speak for days.

"Where are you?"

"At the station. I have to run an errand tonight."

"Tonight? I just got back."

"It won't take long. My mom, she kind of went off her rocker."

She knows him well enough, even from this particular distance, measured by the telephone line, and a sufficient lack of privacy, to take his meaning. Standing in the kitchen, beside the refrigerator, she shifts her bare feet on the cool tile floor; the refrigerator, meanwhile, is covered with notes and telephone numbers—including Patrick's, which she wrote down in pencil well over a year ago. By now, of course, his number has long since been committed to her memory—the way a song will make itself felt, even if you've only heard it once. What matters is the way you cannot let it go. And her life, she understands, is becoming full of oddly scrambled connections—telephone calls, music on the radio, acts she has committed with her body, especially one to another. The way she used to blow Bittner in the seat of his Camaro, the gear shift digging into her ribs, and the way that made her feel, afterward, as if she had been deserted on a distant planet, high above the moon. After Patrick comes, he always holds her tightly. Her father says lonely people, meaning Patrick's mother, become dangerous when they don't let go, like a disease, which insists on lingering within the body. The body could be heavenly, like a planet, or else it could be poisoned, inclined toward lunacy. Lately her father has been worried about cancer, which explains the metaphor, since his partner, Flip, has it in his liver.

"With Bittner?" she says, into the phone, feeling anxious.

"He just wants some company."

"Don't get into any fights."

"I always lose, anyway."

"Patrick," she says, dangling the cord through her fingers, "you okay?"

"I miss you. That's all."

"Tonight," she says. "I'll have a surprise!"

Her father, sitting in the den with her mother, is having a hushed conversation. Allegedly they are discussing the future costs of sending their daughter to college in California. There has been talk of liquidation, though she does not know what exactly—something about municipal bonds which her parents have been saving, jointly, for a rainy day. In Arizona. She's never understood exactly how a bond is supposed to work, but she does know it involves a lot of debt, as well as the hope for accumulated interest. The rate of inflation plus unemployment, her father has explained, is called The Misery Index.

She whispers into the phone, "I'm going!"

"Great," he says. "That's really great."

They agree to meet later tonight, at his house, in the driveway. In the background of the telephone, she can hear an engine revving, and a man's voice, yelling. She hangs up and enters the den with her parents, who both look up surprised, as if caught. They're even holding hands.

"Dad," she says, "I'm going out for a while."

"Ask your mother."

"Really?"

"No," he says. "I was just feeling sentimental."

"You can still ask me," her mother says. In her loose clothes, all billowy and light, her mother looks almost like a girl. Lydia says, "At least when I'm here."

"Okay," Elizabeth says. She understands, belatedly, that her mother has been crying. "I'm going out?"

"You're going to get your hair cut?"

"Uh huh," she says, beaming. "Short. I'll be home late."

"Just be safe," her father says, looking up. "We do not intend to let eighteen years of wear and tear go for naught because of one reckless moment of abandon."

"What?"

Her mother says, "Just wear your seat belt, Lizzie. Tightly."

What is the value of rage, improperly placed? Driving, a bit recklessly, his mother's large station wagon, losing several ounces of gasoline each time he accelerates, sharply, he is following Bittner down Scottsdale Road: weaving in and out of traffic, passing everyone. Bittner is driving his Camaro, shiny blue, patched together with Bondo and racing stripes. Still it is a fast car—a Hurst shifter, four on the floor; Bittner wants to buy a set of headers next. Driving, following a car much faster than his own, Patrick understands that he is angry, that his hatred is becoming increasingly sharp, and it frightens him: this fear of becoming what he hates most. Pissed-off, and dangerous. Just plain mean.

"She's sick," he is telling himself. "It's not her fault."

Eventually Bittner pulls into a shallow ravine. He leaves his keys under the mat, as planned, and jogs over, opens the passenger door to Patrick's car, stepping inside. "Go," Bittner says, pointing. "Go."

Germs slides over, almost resentfully, into the middle of the wide seat, and Patrick guns the station wagon, spitting dust and gravel. Then he remembers Bittner's car and worries he may have caused the gravel to fly into the Camaro's new paint. Bittner, though, doesn't seem to care. Now that Fuller has promoted him at the station to evening manager, Bittner is going to buy another car. A Firebird, or maybe even a used Corvette. He wants to be a collector.

"Wish you weren't leaving," Bittner says. "We make a good team."

"Not really," Patrick says. "I just hang around."

"You're afraid of risk, is all. Risk it all, I say."

"Actually I'm just afraid of doing the wrong thing."

"What? Breaking the law?"

"Fuck the law. It's being wrong, that's what I don't want."

"Too complex for me," Bittner says. "I say in general fuck 'em. I need a new exhaust. Mine is shot."

"I may move out," Patrick says, deciding. He knows he can live elsewhere, maybe with Mr. Windham, training dogs and horses. Of course then he'd have to borrow more: he might be in debt for the rest of his life, moving out. And if he moves to Gallup, then he'll in effect be breaking up with Elizabeth even sooner. He wishes his father were nearby; he wants some advice from somebody who also went to college. Mr. Pinski, he thinks, could help, but he knows Mr. Pinski has other interests: namely, those belonging specifically to his daughter, whom he intends to send to college out of state. Still, it's not as if Patrick wants to get married. Fernando thinks Patrick should go to Mexico and travel first. Wander down to Central America—Nicaragua, El Salvador, Costa Rica, and Peru. "See the world, Patrick," he said. "Take your handsome dog with."

It's dusk now: not dark, not bright, the dirt blending with the sky, streaks of violet filling overhead. Sometimes it almost looks as if it might rain. Patrick parks the station wagon in an empty lot off the Salt River bottom: in the back, there is a lot of pipe, stacked up in skids. Behind the lot is a trail people use to traverse the river bottom, leading beneath the Scottsdale Road bridge, then into Papago Park and A Mountain. It's a two-mile jog, and with Germs beside them, in the cooling evening, though still it's over a hundred degrees, he and Bittner take up a loose pace with Germs now leading the way. When Germs trots, you can hear his dog tags, tinkling, and the soft pads of his feet. After this trip, Patrick will have helped Bittner make some twelve thousand dollars transporting drugs into Paradise Valley, though Patrick refuses to take a cent. The air is full of mesquite and Bittner is explaining he has dealers all over the city, selling—mostly high school kids who want to use cheaply. Someday Bittner figures he won't have to work at all.

"It's like Amway," Bittner says, jogging.

"Amway?"

"You know—the pyramid scheme. The more you have beneath you, the higher you rise to the top."

"Uh huh."

"Parents used to sell Amway," he says "Doesn't work as well with laundry soap. You gotta have a product people really need."

Now Bittner shifts his jeans, and the pistol inside his waistband, which makes running for him awkward. A stupid thing, running with a gun tucked into your pants. On television, Starsky and Hutch each use a shoulder holster and drive a red Torino; Jim Rockford, who drives a Firebird, keeps his gun in a cookie jar, because he's not supposed to have one, on account of being an ex-con. Now they are passing beneath the Scottsdale Road bridge, recently rebuilt, and here they are surrounded by vast cement pillars. The next Stonehenge, maybe, the way they rise up from the dirt of the desiccated river bottom, entirely indestructible, and Patrick feels his heart rate rising. He's hit his stride, and he imagines himself living someplace else, training dogs, saving as much as he can on expenses, maybe in Central America. Meanwhile the sky is emerging overhead, from beneath the bridge as they pass, and the wind is picking up.

The salon smells like a holiday, certainly the beginning of an adventure: perfume, and shampoo, and the steady *snip snip* of shears. Elizabeth, for her very first time, changes into a loose blouse which ties up at the waist. When the light is right, you can see right through.

Josie, her stylist, is almost twenty-six and asks questions about her mother and Fernando. Josie explains that *her* lover is also a painter; she has a show right now in a gallery downtown. They met while skydiving. Sometimes, Josie makes exhibitions of her own photographs. As a hair stylist, Josie has a waiting list, she's that good; also the salon will give you a cup of coffee or a glass of wine if you like. Thrilled, Elizabeth is beginning to realize the ambiguities of that particular term . . . *lover* . . . as well as its spectacular precision: what matters, simply, is that one loves, or fucks. As Josie shampoos her hair, she wipes a drop of water off Elizabeth's cheek. Josie has gorgeous hair—yellow, rich as cream—falling in waves over the back of her neck. Once Elizabeth reaches out to touch it, briefly, despite the risk.

"Yes?" Josie says.

"It's so fine," Elizabeth says. "So rich."

"You are going to be beautiful," Josie says. "You have a beautiful face. No more hiding."

"I've never had short hair before. I'm going to go to college soon. In California."

"Tight," Josie says. "We'll cut it really tightly. You'll fit right in!"

Later, sitting in a chair, looking at the mirror, Elizabeth gazes at a portrait of a woman—her knee to her face, her leg framing her pose—tucked into the edge of the mirror. The woman's hair is tied up, though evidently long once released; the woman has a long, narrow spine. Posing, Elizabeth thinks. She could be like that. Meanwhile Josie turns the chair once, then again; she pumps the chair so that Elizabeth rises into view, her wet hair limp, hanging down her back—bedraggled as a dog, caught in a storm. With Elizabeth's face framed into the center of the mirror, Josie smiles, kindly, and lifts up a lock.

"Relax," Josie says, gently. "Take a breath."

"Okay," Elizabeth says, taking a breath.

"What conceals," Josie says, "also must reveal. It's like free-falling. Sometimes it gets scary."

"Yes."

"Breathing is key," Josie says, stepping back. "We can go slow. Do six inches; get used to it. You can come back for more?"

"No," Elizabeth says, tossing her head. "One fell swoop."

They stand on the side of the mountain, overlooking the stadium, and the city of Tempe: on the other side, the flour factory rumbles in the distance, its white towers full of grain. The sun has burnt off the last of the day, slipping beneath the horizon, lighting up the sky for a last few moments of self-congratulation. Look at what it can do, the sun. Look at what it can make.

Dark, descending fully. Germs is sitting on a ledge, behind Patrick. Bittner shifts his weight and begins to pace. The waiting is disagreeable, and also it is hot. Later Patrick will have to shower, before he meets Elizabeth, who has a surprise. A T-shirt, he thinks. *From California.* He lights up his third cigarette; he'll also have to brush his teeth. He's never even smoked in front of Elizabeth, though certainly she must know he does. He doesn't smoke in front of Elizabeth because he doesn't want her to think he's bad, a drug dealer or a punk. Now, tossing away the match, he wonders if he should quit smoking, too. Change himself completely, become another person? He takes a drag and, eventually, they hear two voices, chattering, climbing up the trail. One of the voices calls out, as if out of breath, "We late?"

"No," Bittner says, pissed. "All the time in the fucking world."

"Really?"

Miko and Gary are both out of shape; and Gary is still fat; and it's a long climb up the mountain, even at night. Now they all shake hands, friendly, drug dealerlike, loop de loop.

"So where's the dog?" Miko says.

"There," Patrick says.

"Germs, bro. Germs the dog! Like Rin Fucking Tin, eh?"

"Fucking dog," says Gary.

"You guys want some money?" Bittner says. He has removed a

wad of cash from his pocket—set in hundred-dollar bills. Miko, meanwhile, has slid off a day pack, the kind which are becoming popular on college campuses, for books and calculators and a change of underwear, and from inside he takes out a paper sack which weighs about the same as a couple grapefruit. Now Bittner is looking inside the sack, giving off a whistle.

"Okeedokee," he says.

Germs leaps off the rock, turns a circle, then another: he's sniffing wildly at the air. Something, Patrick realizes. There's something in the air. He says to Gary, "You have a cat or something?"

Germs is working faster, running circles, searching. They can hear it now, the dull thudding rotor of a helicopter, its blades thumping in the distance. Now out of the sky a light: a huge, enormous beam, wandering across the valley below the mountain top. Bittner turns, gazes at Gary, taking the pistol from his jeans. Bittner has it aimed right at him.

"Hey, Bittner," Miko says. "What the fuck?"

"Hiker," Patrick says, signaling to his dog. "Somebody stuck?"

"Cops," Bittner says, panicking. "They're cops."

"Wait," Patrick says. "What?"

The helicopter has wandered south, still searching. Bittner says to Miko, cocking the gun, "I want my money back."

"What?" says Miko. "What? Don't you—" and now Miko explodes. "Don't you know who the fuck I am? Bittner, I'll stuff your mother's throat with poi. I'll slit your fucking prick to threads. And if not me, somebody else. You think—"

"We're fucked," Bittner says. "Look, just give me my money back." He tosses Miko the paper sack. "It's all yours. I don't want it."

Below them, in the stadium parking lot, cop cars are lining up, their lights ablaze. The helicopter is sweeping away from them, having passed overhead, missing them for all the boulders—the shadows they cast.

"He's a narc," Miko says to Gary. "Not me. Not you. Him," he says, pointing to Bittner. "He's a Goddamned cop!"

Patrick turns, struck. Germs is on point now, growling, ready to break. Patrick says, "Could we please just get out of here?"

Bittner takes the cash, jams it into his jeans. He says, waving the gun at Patrick, "Jesus Christ—"

"You piece of shit," Gary says, pulling out his own gun, an automatic, pointing it—at Bittner, now Patrick. "You piece—"

Germs leaps, aiming for Gary, who sees him coming and fires twice. Hit midair, Germs cries out, and drops. Now Bittner is firing and the Hawaiians are running, scrambling down the hill. It's clear Bittner is not aiming. He's firing his gun into the air—one shot, then another. Now he turns to Patrick, uncocking the pistol, and says, "Whatever you do, stay off the trails. You'll be all right."

Bittner tucks the gun into his jeans, steps back into the shadows, then disappears. Suddenly overhead there is a voice, descending from the sky, and Patrick realizes the helicopter is following the Hawaiians, giving chase. The voice above is far away, distant, instructing people not to move, and Patrick is kneeling on the ground, holding his dog. He lifts, staggers at first, and begins down the other side of the mountain. He knows the way down: twice he falls onto his seat, to slide, the rocks tearing at his jeans while he cradles his dog, sliding down. Because it is dark, he cannot see just where it is he is going: behind him the light from the helicopter has stopped to focus in one place, as if resting, and there's that same voice, looming overhead, giving instructions. At one place, Patrick finds a huge crevice, and he steps inside it to rest. He lays Germs down, who is whimpering. Twice Germs tries to stand, then falls. He gazes at Patrick, and then begins to lick his hand. Only then does Patrick realize he is covered with blood. When he lifts Germs again, his dog cries out, and he can feel the wound beneath his dog's chest, hot and slippery. Carrying his dog, it takes another twenty minutes to make it to the bottom, to skirt the side of the stadium, by way of an irrigation ditch. When he comes to the highway, the long, wide bridge overhead, Patrick leans against a pillar of the bridge to rest. He steps farther beneath the bridge, laying Germs down on the embankment, and now he's putting his fingers into the wound, to stop the blood, which is still pumping, and suddenly Germs's whimpering changes pitch—he sounds lost, the way he did when just a pup, years ago, or when he's dreaming. He's whimpering, frantically, and now, after suddenly choking, he stops breathing.

"No," Patrick says. "No!"

Overhead, traffic is passing by. He turns his dog, opens its mouth. He opens his dog's mouth and begins to breathe. He can feel the dog's teeth, scraping against his cheek as he breathes: first once, then again. He takes a breath and tries again. He's breathing hard, listening to the bubbling from the wound. His breath, he understands, is passing right through his dog, and he can feel his breath on his fingers, holding the wound, deep enough to fit most of his hand. His breath feels cold and wet.

There's no need to rush. He waits several hours, sitting there, his dog on his lap. And when he decides, as if by accident, he does so quickly: one rock, then another, the very heaviest he can lift. The river bottom is full of rock. And it takes him another hour to make a perfect space, deep enough to protect his dog from raccoons and strays, from crows. Eventually, after weeping bitterly, he lays Germs into the grave, and overhead the traffic, passing, is finally slowing down. He kisses his dog one last time: a kiss, deep in the center of his forehead, so neither will forget. Then he removes the collar.

Now the rocks—to conceal the body, to protect it from the elements. To properly lay his dog to rest.

"There," Josie says. "You look beautiful."

"Really?"

"Truly. Truly you do."

"It feels lighter," Elizabeth says, tossing her head. She feels no longer any resistance, and this particular gesture causes her to feel transparent. She can feel the ceiling fan, up above her, blowing cool air across the back of her neck. "Lighter than I'm used to."

"The shortest distance been two points," Josie says, putting away her scissors, "is always going to be a curve."

"A curve?"

"According to Mae West. It's the nature of the body, to curve."

Elizabeth changes. Then she pays her bill, and leaves a proper tip, the way her mother has instructed. In the parking lot, she can feel the heat lingering in the night air. Once in her car, she checks herself repeatedly in the mirror: one profile, then another. She can see things in her face she's never seen before.

And she feels lighter than before, like air. She drives with the windows down, shifting gears through the intersections, taking Mockingbird up past Mummy Mountain, toward 68th Street, the way Patrick would, because tonight they've got a date. Entering Patrick's neighborhood through the wide streets, which also curve, she feels herself giddy with delight. Tomorrow she'll have to be careful in the sun, to keep the nape of her neck from burning while swimming in the pool. Now she pulls into the circular drive in front of Patrick's house, the same place where Patrick used to park his truck—the gravel still worn and torn up from his parking there. Stepping up to the front door, she knocks.

She knocks again, but still no answer. Patrick must be at the station. Maybe he's left a message for her at home? She returns to her car, standing beside it, her arms resting on the warm roof, deciding, when she sees another car entering the street, driving fast. It skids right past the driveway entrance, goes into reverse, and now she recognizes her father's car. He pulls into the drive and skids once again on top of the loose gravel—a tearing sound, like fabric.

"Lizzie?" he calls.

"Yes. Hi, Dad. What are you doing?"

"Get in your car. Go home."

"What?"

Her mother is with him, stepping out onto the drive. "Honey," she says. "Why don't you wait in the car."

"What's going on?"

"The paramedics are coming, honey."

"What paramedics? Nobody's home!"

Her father stands at the front door now, knocking hard. He waits, very briefly, then knocks again. Elizabeth's mother is standing beside her now; she puts her arm around her shoulder. "Honey," she says, "Mrs. McConnell is sick."

"I know."

"You know?"

"I mean she's kind of whacko . . ."

"No, honey. She called. Looking for you. She said Patrick stole her car. She was very upset."

"I'm coming in!" her father yells, and now he's shoving his weight into the door. Clearly he is trying to break it down. He is hurling himself at the door and Elizabeth calls, beginning to panic, "Dad, it's probably just open!"

She steps up, turns the door handle, while he shoves into the door once again, this time breaking the jamb. The wood tears, a sickening sound, and now her father is inside the foyer, searching for a switch, because it's pitch dark.

"There," she says, pointing.

"Go out to the car," he says. "Go out to your car and wait!"

"What?"

"She said she'd taken pills," he says. "She was blasted out of her fucking mind."

She can hear a siren now, wailing, though still in the distance. The porch light flicks on, lighting up the bougainvillea, all the yuccas and barrel cactus, and she turns to lead her father through the halls of the house. Doing so, she understands she's been in Patrick's bedroom only once, where he keeps a picture of her, with long hair, on his bookshelf. He has a small stereo and a saddle and a wall full of paperbacks and three guitars. Also, there is a picture of his dog, framed, leaping through the air.

"Pills?" she says.

Mrs. McConnell is lying in the hallway, just before her bed-room, the phone in her hand—beside her, a pool of vomit, and an open bottle of Cutty Sark. Her bathrobe has fallen open, revealing blotchy skin and a sagging, yellow breast, as if it were full of poison. The sirens are unbearably loud now, and close up, and men in uniform are marching into the house, giving orders. There's a cop, and then another: there are people carrying cases full of items to stop a heart attack. Somebody is speaking to Mrs. McConnell now, covering her up, trying to revive her.

Elizabeth's mother says to her from behind, "Living room. Go to the living room."

She goes, and there she sits on the couch, her hands in her lap Patrick says this couch has been in his family for over a hundred years, though it has twice been re-covered. His mother, she knows, is not going to die. And after a while she can hear Mrs. McConnell, screaming. She is screaming at her son, Patrick, for betraying her. The men in uniform are trying to calm her, being patient, and eventually they wheel her into the foyer. Her father, meanwhile, is speaking to a cop. Mrs. McConnell rests on a metal bed with wheels; she has an IV in her arm, descending from a plastic bottle—a viscous, clear fluid. You can see drops going down, and Elizabeth, gazing down, meets her eye.

"You," says Mrs. McConnell, her hand outstretched. "You cut your hair?"

"Yes," Elizabeth says, rising. She steps closer, reaching for her hand. "Are you all right?"

Mrs. McConnell pulls back her hand. "You," she whispers, her eyes slitting. "You cunt."

Elizabeth turns, stunned. Her father puts his arm around her and guides her back into the living room. Behind her, Mrs. McConnell is screaming, all over again. The paramedics hurry Mrs. McConnell outside, into the van, where she continues to scream, and where it is a little darker. Now a door, heavier than that belonging to a mere car, thumps shut, like a vault.

Her mother says, holding her, "She's distraught, Lizzie. She's upset."

"But why is she so mean?"

"Look," says her mother, taking her by the shoulder. "This is not about you. Okay? This is not about you at all."

A paramedic steps back inside the house, and says to her father, "She's going to be okay. We'll pump her stomach. We're going to take her to Scottsdale Memorial."

"Okay," her father says, though she can tell he's angry. It's an anger different than she's used to: mostly because it's directed outward—away from her, and her mother. He's picking splinters off the broken doorjamb.

"This has happened before," the paramedic says. "After this one she'll probably be sent to detox. Somebody will have to tell her son."

Now her father signs some papers, on a clipboard, to claim he is not liable. And Elizabeth, sitting on the couch, her knees curled up to her chin, her head between her hands. She's closing her eyes and her mother, sitting beside her, takes her by the arms.

"Lizzie?"

"What?" she says, looking up, blinking. "What?"

"Patrick," her mother says, gently. "Do you know where he is?"

At night the station is always lit up, because the station is always open, here to serve. A new guy is standing out at the far island, watching people at the self-serve, in case somebody tries running off. Bittner is inside the far bay, beneath his blue Camaro, flat on his back, banging at his exhaust. Patrick recognizes his sneakers.

Bittner calls out from beneath the car, "What took you so long, Mac?"

"Nothing."

"Nothing? You got away. You're not going to prison."

"Had to bury my dog."

There is an awkward silence, and then the compressor kicks on. The Camaro is resting on a floor jack, lifted ass-end.

Bittner says, "Sorry about that. Could've been worse, you know. Those guys will blow up your house if they feel like it."

"Worse?"

"They were set up. Been in the works for months. "

"You're a cop? You really are a cop?"

"What do you think?"

"But all that dealing?"

"Dime bags, Mac. Cops said if I didn't behave, they'd send me to prison. It's not a real choice, you know." He says, peeking out from the side, pointing, "Hand me that nine-sixteenths."

"You could have told me," Patrick says, kicking the wrench across the floor.

"Told you what? That I'm a narc? I'm your best friend. I tell you, then the bad guys have to kill you, too."

"You're not my best friend," he says, stepping behind the Camaro, resting his hands on the trunk.

" 'Course I was. I'm your only friend. So Officer Fucking Friendly, he tells me to mingle. Mingle or go to prison. He wants the bad guys. He's going to make our schools safe—ta da, ta da."

"Why me?"

" 'Cause I could trust you. 'Cause you didn't have a clue. 'Cause with you we were just a couple fuckups."

Patrick smells the blood on his clothes, not unlike metal, or iron, just before it rusts. The floor jack operates on a hydraulic seal. The handle, sticking out, is well within reach. Bittner's chest lies directly beneath the rear axle. Now Patrick rests his hand on the handle: to set the jack free, all you have to do is twist, then turn away.

"Need a new tailpipe," Bittner says.

"I'm leaving," Patrick says.

"Of course you're leaving."

"To college."

"You betcha," Bittner says.

"Okay," Patrick says, letting go of the jack, stepping back.

Bittner, oblivious, crawls out from under the car. He wipes himself off, standing. There's grease on his shoulder. Now he fishes out a pack of cigarettes, offering one to Patrick. "Like in Europe," Bittner says, smiling.

They light up. Patrick says, "Fuller know?"

"Yep. Had to explain why the cops kept hassling him. Almost fired me. Then he told the cops he'd make me evening manager. So I could be honest."

"Anybody else?"

"You mean like your girlfriend?"

"Elizabeth."

"No. Only you. It's not the kind of thing you brag about. Technically, you were never supposed to go to jail—they promised me that. But by tomorrow you'll have to go to Tucson to buy a joint. Cops say it oughta last a week. Colombians will fill in the gap. Ship it up right through Nogales. But they got the Hawaiians. Got 'em all. They send it over in pineapple crates."

Patrick steps over to the sink, takes off his shirt. Above him there's a picture of a woman straddling an inflated wrench. He rests his cigarette on a ledge and begins to wash his face.

Bittner says, "Just so you know, I'm sorry. I'm sorry about your dog, Mac."

He's washing his face, now his arms. He still has blood on his face.

"Some cop came by," Bittner says. "Apparently your mother reported her car stolen. Get that?"

"Stolen?"

"She mad at you about something? They have no idea who you are, if that's what you're thinking. No connection. You should go home, though. I told them you didn't steal that car."

"Thanks."

"Look, you're still afraid, aren't you? Still afraid of getting caught?"

"No," Patrick says. "Not hardly."

"Being bad, then?"

"No."

"Look," Bittner says, smiling. "There are two kinds, you know? You—you're the good kind. You passed the test. See what I mean?"

"Clear as day," Patrick says. Now he shakes his head, his hair, and begins to dry himself off. He wads up a pile of paper towels, tosses them in a can. Long ago, he used to be a choir boy, but nothing changes where you come from. Nothing changes how you feel . . . empty, too tired to even say it. He puts on his shirt, which once belonged to his father, leaving it unbuttoned.

"Far as they're concerned," Bittner says, "you do not even exist. Never even told 'em your name. You are anonymous. An anonymous source, officially. A ghost."

Patrick turns, heading for the garage door, which is wide open. Certainly he is not a coward, he knows this now. He knows he is not afraid, because he is beyond that now. Overhead he can hear the distant streetlights buzzing with electricity. Mercy, he thinks, smiling bitterly . . . mercy belongs to those most seriously in need. Otherwise, what have you?

Bittner calls out, "Still there?"

In the shadowed lot, keys in his hand, Patrick wipes a thread of soap from his eyes. Then he turns, briefly, to call his dog. It's a mistake he realizes instantly. He can feel a breeze now, picking up, pushing him along, and he knows sooner or later he is going to have to go home. For a little while, at least. For at least a few long hours to explain precisely what he's learned: that mercy is a place you go when everything else is fucked. Because he knows he's going to have to stay another night: it's the place where he's been raised, after all. And having been decided, there is no need to rush, because this is also the place where he has come to. And maybe, maybe if he's lucky, Elizabeth will be waiting for him. Maybe he'll be able to hold her in his arms, the same way she has taught him to. First, of course, you have to know you love her.

Then you call out her name. And when she turns to you, her eyes lit up like a promise, then you have to say her name.

Elizabeth, you might say, because you've been taught to say it, long after it's too late. *Elizabeth.*

14

I never grew my hair long again. It's frightening, I think, the things you remember. The things you can't forget. The things you do.

I remember Patrick believed in ghosts. Not cartoons, like Casper, but the very real spirits: the people who disappear on you without a trace. He said that's why his mother drank, because she was afraid. She was afraid of the dark, and she was afraid to be left alone. And then what?

Throughout our senior year in high school, Patrick worked the graveyard shift. Nights, he would do his homework or practice his guitar; sometimes he'd climb up on the roof to watch the sun rise. One night, while he was hosing down the front lot, preparing it to be scrubbed, a Jeep came tearing down the street, out of control. Patrick recognized the Jeep, driven by a guy who stopped in often, usually loaded, trying to make his way home from the bars, and that night the intersection was full of water from the station, pouring into the street. Patrick stood there, watching the Jeep approach the corner, the road suddenly slick, and then the tires screaming. The Jeep rolled completely over—smashing its CB antenna, bouncing off a lightpost and, miraculously, landing back on its wheels. And I imagine Patrick, letting go the hose, calling to his dog, Germs, and running for the street. Most likely, he feels responsible, for causing the road to be unexpectedly slick, and by the time he arrives at the curb, he catches the driver's eye—a pale, drunk man with a beard, lit entirely out of his mind. Then the man waves, silently, starting up his engine, and drives away.

The man drives away from the intersection, leaving a case of beer spread all over the pavement: beer cans, here and there, have exploded, hissing like so many tiny rockets. Then Patrick hears a voice, laughing. Entering the street, he finds a man, sitting spread-eagled beside a woman, popping open a beer. The woman is laughing, half out of her mind, as well as her dress. The man tosses Patrick a beer and says, "Hey. Have a cold one."

To which Patrick must have replied, "Thanks. I don't drink."

He helped them up and brought them into the station. The man and woman sat in the office for a while, beside the heater, drinking their beer. Maybe the man tried to pour a little into Germs's water dish. The man had a broken nose, and the woman—a girl, actually—had scraped her elbow. They had been hitchhiking, and the man in the Jeep had picked them up. They were going to go to his house and party on to oblivion. In the meantime, they had no way of getting home, and that morning, after his shift had ended, Patrick drove the couple all the way to Buckeye. He said the woman was pretty well far gone, by which I think he must have meant crazy. Emotionally disturbed? This was, after all, the seventies, and things were pretty crazy then. The Me Generation, all that.

What I mean is Patrick was always rescuing people. He pulled a drunk man from his car after it rolled through that same intersection two months later. Once at the station an attendant lit himself on fire, after spilling gas on his sleeve, and Patrick put the fire out with his own shirt. Telling me these stories, he said he was always afraid, not of becoming hurt, but of not knowing what to do next. If a man breaks his neck in a car accident, do you move him, and risk further spinal injury? Or do you wait for the paramedics and hope the car doesn't explode while you stand by, holding onto his hand? This is what he didn't understand, he explained. How you were supposed to know.

I never told him about Caroline, and what happened to her that night. I thought he wouldn't understand why I was there in that house to begin with; I didn't want him to use that fact as an excuse not to trust me. And I was grateful, actually, for having promised Caroline I would never let him know. Looking back, I understand now the danger of a secret, the way it causes you to feel invisible, and transparent. Once started, too, a secret, it's hard to take it back. Why didn't you say anything to start with? What did you have to hide?

Patrick never liked to have his picture taken. For school pictures, he simply never showed up. The only photograph I have of him is from a newspaper: he is standing in front of an obscene sports car with his dog, Germs, pretending to be blind. The paper has since yellowed, increasingly fragile. My guess is eventually it will turn to dust.

And then where will he be?

When I think about the seventies, I think of velour, and blue eye shadow, Steely Dan and Fleetwood Mac. Blondie. I think of puka shells and patronizing sitcoms and hairdos parted in the center. Lip gloss and the sexual revolution. I think of my boyfriend, Patrick McConnell—the boy with a dog.

That night Patrick's mother attempted suicide, after calling up my parents, and thereby ensuring she would be unsuccessful, Mrs. McConnell claimed I was in fact responsible. At the time I was young enough to believe I was. At the time she was also chronically alcoholic, which is a disease, like it or not. Certainly no one had ever called me a cunt before, at least not to my face, and the truth is I was afraid of her. I was afraid of what she might do next. I was afraid of what she might do to Patrick.

After sending me to my house, my parents waited in the driveway for Patrick to come home. My parents, later that night, said he was very pale and kept apologizing. He asked if he could fix them a Coke. My father gave him the phone number of the hospital and asked him if he needed any cash. At the door, seeing my parents out, Patrick shook both their hands.

That night, after my parents returned home, my mom sleeping in the guest room, I waited for them to fall asleep. Then I put on a pair of shorts, beneath my nightshirt, and let myself out through the back. I remember I was barefoot. Because my car was blocked in the drive, I took my father's, and then I drove to Patrick's house, using my big toe to hold down the accelerator. He didn't answer the door, of course. It was late, nearly four, but Patrick was used to staying up. I climbed over the wall leading to his backyard, scraping my knee, and there he was, sitting on the diving board, looking at the pool. The moon had finally come out, and you could see it, the light, glowing on the surface.

"Patrick?"

He wasn't even startled. He was sitting in his underwear, shivering, holding himself with his arms. I remember putting my arms around him, to warm him up, to hold him, but he turned his head away from me as if he couldn't breathe. I remember, when he did that, I could feel my heart lurch—as if it had skipped a beat, or run up against a wall.

"Patrick," I said, sitting beside him. "Are you okay?"

He nodded, looking at the pool. "Yeah," he said. "I'm okay."

"Your mom's going to be all right," I said.

"I know."

"No, really."

He looked into my eyes, and then turned away, and shivered. He dipped his foot into the pool. A slight ripple traveled along the surface, away from us. "It was the wrong one," he said, watching the water. "My dad. It shouldn't have been my dad."

I knew instantly what he meant, even though he'd never told me his father had committed suicide. I knew he had. I also knew Patrick had found the body and that his mother had sent him away for months in order to pretend otherwise. I moved, to sit closer, and then I started crying, which even then I knew was the wrong thing to do. After a while he put his arm around me and said, "Shhh."

"I'm sorry," I said, feeling stupid, wiping my eyes. I could feel his hand, which felt cold, on the back of my neck. "It's just she was so full of hate!"

"She was afraid of you," he said, nodding. "Because I love you."

"I should have been nicer to her," I said, frightened. "More polite."

"No," he said, shaking his head. He withdrew his arm.

"I want it to be my fault," I said. "Because if it's mine, then it can't be yours. Don't you see?"

"She just needs some rest. She's just tired."

I said, taking his hand, "Do you want me to stay? Tonight?"

"No," he said. "Your parents will worry. They were real nice to my mom."

"Just for a while," I said. "Before you fall to sleep."

He was gazing at the water in the pool, the light on the surface. He said, "My sister and me, we used to come swimming. Out here. Late at night."

"Caroline," I said.

He said, pointing to the light on the water, "Thing about the moon—when you're on the water, it doesn't matter what direction you're going. You could be going anywhere, but the moonlight is always going to be right in front of you."

"I didn't—"

"It's like a path," he said. "My dad. He taught me that."

Then he stood, and took my hand, and led me across the yard. He was barefoot, of course, leading me across the granite. At the gate he undid the latch and kissed me. He kissed me on the mouth, as if he had something more to say, and then he let me go.

•   •   •

I didn't see Patrick for several days. I kept calling, but he wouldn't answer, and my mother said I shouldn't press him: he was going through enough as it was. Years later I understood that my mother had brought him groceries; I understood she had advised Patrick to go away, if he could, in order to give Mrs. McConnell time to recover: at all costs, my mother and father privately agreed, Patrick had to escape from that house. They also knew that if I were gone, he could leave more easily. It was all so carefully orchestrated, designed to keep everybody safe.

My mother wanted me to live with her and Fernando; my father wanted me to accept a summer internship in Tucson. After several arguments, we compromised, reasonably, sitting in the den, my parents on the couch, and decided I would move to California and go to summer school. We spent the next week packing sweaters and jeans and three new dresses, a miniature encyclopedia: my parents wanted me to be well-prepared; they wanted to keep me busy. My mother, I remember, prepared a care package for Mrs. McConnell—fruits, and flowers—and she visited Mrs. McConnell in rehab often, because my mother knew then what I still did not. She knew that what the tired body longs for most is rest, and escape, and the possibility of forgiveness, even if you're never brave enough to ask for it. At least it still might just be possible.

Eventually Patrick called me up and asked for a ride to the police station, where his mother's car had been impounded. Somebody, he explained, had reported it stolen, mistakenly, to the police. Standing alone in his driveway, waiting for me, his eyes were hollow, and he was pale, and thin, as if he hadn't eaten for a week. I remember, too, it was late afternoon, and a storm was coming from the west—a monsoon, the sky dark and pressing. The sky would later fill with lightning, the kind that rips the sky to shreds. I drove him to the Scottsdale Police station, and we were sitting there in my car—the lawns manicured, the sprinklers ticking, the cruisers all arranged neatly in a row—when Patrick said, "I'm sorry. I'm really, really sorry."

"So am I," I said.

"She'll get better," he said. "I've talked to her doctors. They say she's had a crisis, but she's going to be okay."

"Patrick," I said. "I'm going to California. Next week."

"Uh huh."

"I don't know," I said. "Things change, I guess."

"We said it wouldn't," he said. He turned his face, gazing out the window. He rubbed his eye with the back of his fist and said, "We said it wouldn't happen. Not like this."

"When you visit your mom," I said. "You can take Germs. To cheer her up?"

"Yeah," he said, crossing his arms, nodding. After several moments, he opened the door and stepped outside the car. He was standing on the sidewalk, and then he leaned in through the open window, and took my hand. "No matter what," he said, "it's not your fault. Honest."

"Will you write to me? Come visit?"

"Okay," he said, letting go. "Sure."

A cop walked behind him, adjusting his belt. I remember I was wearing a dress because I wanted to go to Mass. And maybe, maybe if I hadn't left that night, then maybe things would have been different. If I'd made myself stay. But the truth is I was glad he let me go. I was afraid, and I think he must have known it, because when he kissed me, that night by the gate, I knew then if I wanted to I could have stayed. I could have put my arms around him and never let him go. Instead I went out to my father's car, and started it, and drove myself home. By the time I pulled into the drive, the sun was rising, and my mother was in the kitchen making orange juice. It's the nature of faith, I guess. Of knowing precisely what you believe because you want to. My mom said we all—meaning Mrs. McConnell, and Patrick, and myself—just needed a little time. Life is long, my mother said. Things work out.

"I like your hair," Patrick said, brushing my cheek. "It looks nice that way."

And then he turned and walked away. I watched him walk up the steps into the police station. He was wearing shorts, and a shirt with a collar and long sleeves, two sizes too large, and his big, brown shoes. Once he reached the top of the steps, he didn't turn and wave.

Two months later, I sent him a birthday card, which he never answered. I remember, while writing the note, that I was torn over how to sign it.

Sincerely? Love?

I settled finally on using just my name, *Elizabeth*.

I never spoke with him again. Sometimes, when I was home visiting from college, my mom would bring me up to date. He went to college in Wisconsin. His dog had died, hit by a car. Mrs. McConnell, having dried out, was in recovery. My first Christmas holiday, late at night, I drove by the station and saw him, out front, standing on the island. He was taller, stronger, and he had let his hair grow wild. That night I drove straight to my father's house and called the station, waiting for him to answer, just to hear his voice. I called him seven times that night, though I never said a word. I kept thinking he must know it's me. Who else calls you up in the middle of the night?

Once, in law school, I saw a boy sitting on a lawn. Behind him stood a tall bank, the kind constructed out of mirrors. I was walking by on the sidewalk, my arms full of books, the sun on my neck. The boy was wearing a red sweater, and looking at him, sitting there on the lawn, I could see my reflection in the building behind him. I could see myself, standing there, my books to my chest.

That night I called Patrick. He was living on the East Coast, and it must have been two or three there. On the fifth ring he answered, I am sure of it, though of course I didn't know what to say.

I wanted to say, Are you okay? Are you safe?

•   •   •

I do not know what keeps us safe. I know only that we are blessed—my husband, and our two children. A boy and a girl.

My father, after a string of lonely romances, never married again, and claims a bit too loudly that he doesn't miss it. Flip, his partner, died of cancer, and after the real estate market bottomed out in Phoenix, my father began looking for something else to do. In 1987, after the October crash, he sold his business and moved to Philadelphia, where he launched a mutual fund company with his former commanding officer in Vietnam, a retired army colonel. It has since grown to several hundred-million dollars in size, and he specializes in what's called a balanced fund, providing a mix of bonds and large cap stocks, and where he limits his expenses to one percent while keeping safe the retirement funds of thousands—myself included.

A year after my father moved to Philadelphia, my mother finally married Fernando, on top of Mingus Mountain. There were birds, everywhere, chirping, and the air was full of the scent of pine. There were nine or ten of Fernando's cousins, as well as his brothers and sisters, all speaking Spanish, and my father, not realizing the wedding would be held outside, showed up in his banker's suit with a woman wearing a red knit dress, tight as a nylon, slit up the side. She was polite, though, and held onto my father's arm, and she laughed often, which we took to be a very good sign. At least she had a mind.

In college I passed up a career in music thinking I might instead save the world. I'd become one of the good people. Then I met a few too many of those people and decided that we'd all be better off if I stayed closer to what I knew. As my father likes to say, the fruit doesn't fall far from the tree, and so I became, of all things, a tax attorney. If the power to tax, as the adage goes, is also the power to kill, then in this light I might also have become a kind of doctor, constantly at work trying to heal the sick. All endings, of course, are sad, if only because they end. Meanwhile, my husband and I both sing in a fine local choir, and I spend most of my working hours discovering ways which will permit my clients to pass on what is rightfully theirs to children and cousins and various nonprofit institutions. It's not glamorous, but if you know, say, what an inheritance tax really means, what it really looks like, then you call me up for help.

My thinking is we come to each other like gifts, entirely unexpected, dropped from the sky.

Sometimes I dream about him. We are in my father's house, standing in the kitchen, having a conversation: all around us, a party is taking place, a party celebrating something to do with me—a baby shower, or promotion. My flute is packed in its case, the lid open, beside a blooming amaryllis and the good silver. And standing there, the guests I do not know milling all about, Patrick and I are tender with each other. We have a lot of catching up to do. My father moved to Philadelphia, I explain. *These are pictures of my children. Look, we finally got a dog.*

Sometimes I dream I hear him—an instrument of God, perfectly voiced. He is singing a song, and in the dream I know the words, and I am singing with him, though we are separated by a great distance, at least a half-dozen states, and when I wake the music vanishes. I have no clear understanding of where I've been or what I have been doing; I'm uncertain even of the language; but I can feel his presence—as if he has become the very song I can feel inside my life.

When I was a little girl, my mother used to say we live forever, and I know now what she meant. She meant that when you give away a piece of your heart, it merely grows inside another. It's how we become immortal, like a god. It's how we rescue our lives from oblivion.

What do I know? I know that nothing disappears without a trace. I know there always is a trace, like an echo. And I know that I am afraid of heartache, and that it will come again, sooner than I expect, and that when I was a little girl, I used to believe the world was absolutely mine. That if I closed my eyes tightly enough then I could make it go away. That each night, after saying my prayers, if I were not to wake, then the sun, too, might never rise again. And I know that soon after I moved to California, I was standing on a beach, thinking of him, and the person that I once was. A thousand miles away, across the Pacific, lay Hawaii: paradise, according to all we have been led to believe. But in California, the sea was still dark, like the sky ahead of me, which it very well might have been. I remember I was barefoot, and the sea was washing up against my toes, and the sun was rising far behind me. I could feel the light on my arms, the back of my hands, which felt luminous—as if it were of my own making, which of course it no longer was. Standing there, I was thinking about a boy I knew who changed the way I saw the world, because even then I was beginning to understand that this world did not belong to me alone. When you draw a line in the sand, or the initials of a boy who once loved you, it's just a matter of time before the wind erases it. If you're lucky then maybe you'll get to feel the breeze. And I understood that this world belonged to those who loved it. That night, after Patrick walked away from me, without ever waving good-bye, I went to Mass and took Communion and prayed to God to forgive me for my sins—all of them, each and every one. I was sitting in the back row, and I knew my life had changed. I remember I was sitting in the back row all alone, and I could hear the storm, overhead, rolling across the sky. Outside, the sky would be full of lightning, the fierce kind which always leaves a shadow, and I was sitting alone watching a woman and her two little girls enter the cathedral. I watched them cross beneath the high ceilings to pray and light a candle. Somebody, somewhere, was lost, and I knew that my heart simply ached, and I remember thinking *So, this is it. This is what it means.*

15

What Patrick remembers first is his father, leaning over his bed, tucking him in for his nap. His father is explaining Patrick will have to go to sleep now, just for a little while. It is early afternoon, a Saturday, the light pouring through the open windows, and in the distance he can hear the trains. *Go to sleep,* his father is saying, leaning over his bed. *It's just the train.*

For years his father took that train to work. Then their fortunes changed, and they moved far away. Asleep, dreaming, Patrick understands that morning comes because it has to. Lying in his bed, before the open window, a wool blanket tucked to his chin, Patrick can feel all around him the day beginning to stir. Just a few miles off, the Santa Fe freights go running by, heading east, or west, depending on the cargo. Opening his eyes, he knows he hasn't missed it yet—the sun, rising, and the morning train. He can just make out the frayed edge of the sun, peeking above the plateau some hundreds of miles off. Here in New Mexico, at the very top of the world, the sun rises differently than elsewhere.

His mother asked him what he was going to do in New Mexico. In the rehab unit at the Superstition Mountain Care Facility, his mother had slipped on a crack in the sidewalk, breaking her arm at the elbow. She explained, sitting on the outdoor furniture, cradling her cast, that she intended to sue. Given the nature of the break, she ought to make a bundle.

229

"I'm going to change your oil," Patrick said, "before I go. I'll balance your tires, too. One last time."

"But what are you going to do there?"

"Train dogs. It will be nice. Mr. Windham says he really needs a hand just now and he has some new quarter horses, too."

A guard came by, in tennis clothes, making sure Patrick wasn't violent. His mother introduced him. The guard, it turned out, knew a lot about motorcycles. He was a born-again Christian and a recovering cocaine addict. He shook hands with Patrick and said, "Any time, brother. You wanna talk. Any time."

"Thanks," Patrick said, embarrassed. "Okay."

When the guard left, his mother asked if Patrick had brought the insurance papers with him. He had. Beneath them, in her desk, he had also found two diamond rings, tucked into an envelope, along with a pendant which had belonged to his father's grandmother. Before his mother met his father, she'd never had any jewelry whatsoever. She said to him, almost tenderly, "Are you getting enough to eat?"

"Yeah. Sure. I went shopping."

"Mrs. Pinski brought me some nice fruit. She's been very supportive. You know, she's been here, too, Patrick. Three years ago. Emotional exhaustion."

"Uh huh."

"Sometimes, people get wore out. Mrs. Pinski understands. You would, too. You could come to our psychodrama class."

"She's a nice lady."

"How's Elizabeth? Have you been going out on any dates?"

"No. We broke up."

His mother lit a cigarette, exhaled. She said, waving her hand, "You're young. You're free. You're going to go to college. I think that girl just wanted a ring, if you ask me. At graduation. She wanted a ring."

"Mom," he said. "Before I go, I'll make sure your car's in good shape."

He stood, preparing to leave.

"It's not that simple," she said, looking at the lemon trees. "Is it?"

"What?"

"Hating your husband. Your parents. You can't just hate them. It's the law. Otherwise it just eats you up. Ask me, I ought to know. You have to forgive."

"First you have to ask."

She bit her lip and turned away.

"I'm glad you're better," he said, hugging her. "And by the time you're all better, then I'll be gone, and you'll be able to take good care of yourself."

He turned and began walking across the lawn, looking for the gate out.

He tugs on his jeans, a T-shirt, his old maroon sweater. Through the thin walls of the cabin, he can hear Mr. Windham, puttering in the kitchen, stubbing his toe in the dark, muttering, starting up the coffee. As a rule, they don't wear boots inside the house, which has only four rooms. The outhouse is in the back, by the dog runs. On the side of the cabin Mr. Windham has recently installed an outdoor shower—a treat, given the scarcity of water. Mr. Windham built the cabin years ago with his son.

They know each other well enough not to have to speak. It's going to be a fine day. They ought to get a lot of work done. Going through the screen door, stepping around the half-dozen goldens, and Mork, the black Lab, Patrick hugs himself in the chill air. He sits on the steps, reaching for his boots. He is facing the runs, a dozen, each with a fine gravel floor, and today after chores they will begin this week's project—cleaning and repairing and repainting each of the dog houses. Because Mr. Windham is getting older, his health beginning to fail, he intends to use Patrick for all he's worth. Also, he says, it's nice, having someone he can talk to, should either feel so inclined.

He calls out now through the screen, opening the door, and passing Patrick a mug of coffee. "Pancakes? Or waffles?"

"Waffles."

"Me, too," says Mr. Windham. "Waffles."

Truth is, they never have pancakes, on account of the new waffle iron Mr. Windham picked up secondhand last month in Flagstaff. But it's nice, Mr. Windham explains, knowing you can always change your mind. When he makes mashed potatoes, on Thursdays, he makes them from scratch, with real potatoes. For lunch, during "Donahue," he always makes Patrick a milkshake. On Saturday they are going to go typewriter shopping.

"Ready when you get back," Mr. Windham says.

He means Patrick's ride—on Zoe, Mr. Windham's new mare. Mostly Mr. Windham prefers to work with Morgans, but Zoe is special—all muscle and blood and fire. Rising, taking his coffee, Patrick heads first for the outhouse, to take a leak, and then to follow the path behind the dog runs, leading toward the corral. He's still sleepy, knuckling the sleep from his eyes, and the sun is now coming into its own, lighting up the roof of the sky. In the corral he scoops a handful of grain, to sweeten the moment of his arrival, wandering through the loose horses toward Zoe. She's a sorrel mare, fifteen hands, with three white socks—still a touch leggy, like a girl in junior high. When she sees Patrick coming, she nickers gently, high-stepping to greet him, her mouth muzzling the grain from his palm. He grabs with one hand a fistful of her mane, squeezes her nose gently with the other, and leads her to the lean-to where he keeps his saddle.

His father bought him the saddle, a working saddle, at an auction years ago—a firm tree, a high cantle. They replaced the fenders and etched his initials with a soldering iron on the underside. The stirrups are freshly wrapped, and Patrick knew when he first slid the saddle over Zoe's withers they were going to make a good fit. It's a fine sign of disposition, Mr. Windham says, when your saddle fits your horse. Turning, Patrick remembers the hay, and he reaches into his jeans, pulling out his knife, unfolding it. Now he bucks half a dozen bales into the manger, simultaneously cutting the strings, the hay spreading out like a fan.

He slides on Zoe's hackamore and leads her out of the corral, where he mounts easily, swinging up the way his father taught him to. It's still cool, and he can feel she's eager to run, but he keeps her to a walk, her fine, muscled gait pushing her further onto the plateau. Eventually he turns her toward the reservation, miles and miles of empty sky.

Easy, he says to her, patting her neck. *Easy there.*

They are waiting for the train, which always arrives, as if on schedule. The train, a Santa Fe freight, with over a hundred cars, is headed east toward Amarillo. Now, when he sees it coming around the bend, he cues his horse—a gentle nudge with his heels, a slight click with his teeth.

And she's off: because she's fast, because she's been bred to run. He gives Zoe her head, letting her find her stride, taking her lead, not checking her, and now he's aiming for the first locomotive, racing along the tracks: the wheels on the rails, grinding, cutting a straight line off into the horizon. A half-mile away, the train will take a slight incline, leading to a bridge. The bridge spans an arroyo, a dried-out streambed, and it is there, racing his horse, that Patrick intends to meet the train, passing right beneath the first locomotive—their two paths converging, at just this particular moment, in the middle of nowhere. It's a sign of luck, he believes. Of good fortune, and now he's urging on his horse, racing into the wind. He can feel the wind in his hair, and his eyes, blinding him, and for a moment, headed just this way, he knows he's going to make it. He's going to beat the train. He's set his jaw, he's leaning into his horse, riding for all he's worth into the very break of day.

Acknowledgments

This novel was written with the support of a fellowship provided by the National Endowment for the Arts.

I also want to thank especially Jane Rosenman, my editor, and my advisors, Charles East, C. M. Mayo, and Eric Pankey.

To Maxine Groffsky and J. D. McClatchy, my deepest gratitude.